MIDNIGHT
IN VEGAS

by
Rebecca Randolph Buckley

Published by Rjbpublishing.com

© 2019 by Rebecca Buckley

First Printing 2019

For information about special discounts for bulk purchases, please contact: rjbpublishing@aol.com.

ISBN: 978-0-578-50832-0

"Born on the Seventh of September, I share my birthday with Queen Elizabeth the First,' Rebecca Buckley says with a mischievous grin. Her contemporary romantic suspense novels are mostly set in England and reflect her love for the country and its people.

Although American, but having lived and spent many holidays in the UK, Ms. Buckley feels a kinship to the British Isles that play a major part in her 'Rachel O'Neill' novel series: *Midnight at Trafalgar, Midnight at the Eiffel, Midnight in Brussels, Midnight in Moscow, Midnight in Malibu*, and now, *Midnight in Vegas. (*Next and seventh novel in the series will be *Midnight in Monte Carlo.)*

Ms. Buckley's primary protagonist, *Rachel O'Neill*, lives in Cornwall and strives to celebrate a festive, meaningful New Year's Eve in major cities around the world – hence 'Midnight' in the titles.

To keep it real, the author has celebrated and experienced her characters' New Year's Eves in most of the major cities depicted in the novels she's written, and she has spent considerable time in all the cities.

In addition to the contemporary romantic suspense novels, she's written a novella, and collections of short stories and plays in four volumes, *Love has a Price Tag, Bits & Pieces of Me, Shoe's on the Other Foot*, and *My Dramedy*. These are comprised of fact and fiction - she doesn't say which is which, leaves it up to the reader to wonder.

This is dedicated to the memory of my oldest son, James Barry Isom, who suffered a fatal heart attack at the age of fifty-two.

I miss you, my son, and my heart breaks again every single day as I remember the very special relationship we had. Your death created the saddest of sad voids in my life and in the lives of your brother and sister.

Since Vegas was one of Barry's favorite places, it seems apropos to dedicate this book to him. Not only did he love the gaming, but being a true gastronomic, he loved the food in Vegas, the non-stop ample buffets.

So ... here's to you, my dear, dear child.

Books by Rebecca Buckley:

NOVELS - Rachel O'Neill Series
1. Midnight at Trafalgar
2. Midnight at the Eiffel
3. Midnight in Brussels
4. Midnight in Moscow
5. Midnight in Malibu
6. Midnight in Vegas

NOVELLAS – Honey Ray Series
1. The Christmas Diary

COLLECTIONS - SHORT STORIES & PLAYS
1. Love Has a Price Tag
2. Bits & Pieces of Me
3. My Dramedy (*six plays*)
4. Shoe's on the Other Foot (*digital only*)

I CHOOSE TO BELIEVE

So many changes in our lives
Whether we expect or ask for them.
Who is it that dictates what comes our way?
An age-old question.
Are lives navigated by religion's God?
Or are we thrust into motion
By self, soul and spirit?
Are happenings preordained?
A reward or punishment,
As pious ancestors droned?
Or are we isolated beings upon this earth,
Living and evolving to greater selves,
From one Lifetime to another,
Till we reach our destinations?
Are we truly tested, cultivated,
Scrutinized by a God on high?
Or do we harbor within, that higher power?
Do we control what befalls our existence?
I choose to believe God is within me,
He is my spirit and soul
Pressing me onward to happiness
And fulfillment.

Rebecca Buckley

MIDNIGHT IN VEGAS

PART ONE
Jessica Sanford

Rebecca Randolph Buckley

1

Ten-year old Jessica stood outside the gate of the most beautiful Victorian house in town, a far cry from the mountain shack where she lived. The Victorian sat back from the lush, tree-lined street and a weathered white picket fence marked the property's perimeter. To others the house might seem average and less desired than the larger, majestic Victorians in that part of the neighborhood, for its gray color with faded green shutters and chipped peach-painted bric-a-brac trim contrasted all the renovated, brightly painted street-lined historical mansions.

"What do you want, child?" a tall, slim, silver-haired woman barked from the screened porch of the big gray house. An imposing, stern figure standing firm and straight, she held open the screened door with a look on her face that would scare goblins. She wore her hair slicked back into a bun at the nape of her neck, a few wispy tendrils framed her lined leathery face.

The gangly, goggle-eyed young girl stared at the intimidating old woman, and bravely shouted, "Are you my grandmother, ma'am?" One hand gripped her bony hip as she stood her ground, cocked her head to one side, and squinted at the old woman up on the porch.

The woman squinted back at the impertinent child outside her gate. "Come in closer, child, so I can see you better, and then I'll tell you if I am your grandmother or not."

Jessica inhaled a deep breath, and lifted the gate latch. Hesitant at first, but with bold determination, she opened the gate. She collected her wits, took a deep breath, and marched in aggressive optimism up the sidewalk towards the woman, then stopped. "My daddy was your boy. Did you know that, Missus Carter? Your boy was my daddy. How come you never come see me?"

Roberta Carter admired the girl's grit, reminded her of someone else. She could see the blue eyes of her dead son glaring back at her from Jessica's face. "What's your name, girl?" she said gruffly.

"I'm Jessica Sanford. My mama told me you are my grandmother. She got married after your boy passed, so I carry the name Sanford after the man that came along and married my mama. Did you know that Sanford ran off and left mama with eight more kids and my mama works her fingers to the bone, night and day, to take care of all nine of us so we can go to school and graduate one day? What do you think about that, Missus Carter? And here you are living by yourself in this big old pretty house with lots of rooms in it. For just one person. In town. Makes no sense. Just think about it." Jessica placed both hands on her hips, a statement-making gesture, and stood erect and proud in the middle of the sidewalk bordered by red and pink rose trees.

"Why should I think about it?" Roberta Carter held back the chuckles. *She's a Carter alright - a chip off the old block.* She stepped down off the porch to get a better look.

It took nerve for Jessica to approach the most disliked and feared woman in town. Most children would cross over to the other side of the street rather than take the chance of meeting up with crotchety, old Missus Carter. Her reputation of being a mean, miserly widow kept people at bay.

"So, are you going to tell me why I should think about it, or not?" Roberta Carter asked, matching Jessica's glare.

Jessica leaned her head to the other side and steadied her young eyes on the old woman. "Because it's your responsibility to provide for me and my mother, that's why. Your boy was my daddy!"

"Git on out of here, you impertinent little brat! You are not my

4

responsibility and neither is your mother, by God. My son didn't marry your mother, and I will never claim a child of a nigger as my grandchild."

Jessica clapped her hands over her ears. Tears formed.

"So, go on, now. Git!" She motioned her hands towards the picket gate as she false-started towards Jessica. "Shoo, go on, now. And don't you come back here ever again."

Jessica couldn't believe what she had just heard. Tears rolled down her face. She couldn't move.

Mrs. Carter hesitated, struggling with feelings of empathy and wishing she hadn't said such cruel words to the little girl. She reached for Jessica, but the girl backed up, tears streaming, hands still over her ears.

Jessica turned and swiftly ran from the yard. Sobbing and running till she reached the outskirts of town. She finally stopped and bent over. Chest heaving and out of breath, she wiped her nose with her skirt and then stood up straight again, taking deep breaths. For as long as she lived, she would never get used to being called a nigger. A bad, nasty word. She didn't even look like one, she told herself, not dark like most of the Negros she knew. She had light-colored skin, like the Kraft caramels her mother sometimes brought home. And her features were just like her daddy's, her mama said so. Her mama didn't look like one neither.

She kicked at the dirt road, mumbling curse words while she wiped her nose and eyes with her hands, more determined than ever to hurry and grow up and get out of North Carolina and away from the name-calling prejudices. She knew without a doubt, no matter how impossible it seemed at that moment, one day she would put the town of Skyler behind her, and she'd go where being a colored girl didn't matter, no one would ever have to know.

"My days of being poor and called a Nigger are numbered," she repeated over and over every day after that. She would go to a big city where no one knew she had Negro blood in her, where it didn't matter who or what you were, and she would make some big, big money. Yes, that's what her young mind of ten told her. She would show them all. She knew she would do it even better than she knew her times-tables past the twelve-sies. Not only the times-tables champ, but also the smartest girl in the little one-room country schoolhouse outside of town.

There were two elementary schools for Skyler children, one outside of town in the country for the mountain kids and one in town for the town kids. The mountain kids were made up of mostly poor white hillbillies and black kids. Segregation, but townsfolk denied it. The poor versus the not so poor. The kids in the town school belonged to the townspeople who had a bit of money in their pockets and the rich country-folk. Those kids were considered the most popular and cultured for their ages, college hopefuls. Jessica and the likes of her eight brothers and sisters and others like them were not considered candidates for college.

But then most kids weren't like Jessica. She had a steel determination and mindset even at the young age of ten. And the more people slung nasty names at her, and criticized her mama's bloodline, the more she dug in her heels and plotted her way out of there.

2

Jessica graduated from eighth grade at twelve years of age, a year early from the country school. Her mother finagled favors of her rich employers so Jessica could go to the town school that summer for additional classes, preparing her for the first year of high school. The country school teacher also put in a good word for Jessica, her prize pupil.

In addition to being smart, Jessica was a dreamer. That's what her younger brothers and sisters, all eight of them called her, a dreamer. They would run around the yard, singing and chanting "Jessie is a dreamer, Jessie is a dreamer."

Her school teacher called her a dreamer. Sometimes it embarrassed Jessica, but she knew her teacher nor her siblings meant any harm by it. From her teacher, she took it as a compliment. Most people didn't understand Jessica, and she knew it. Her mama, barely in her thirties, called Jessica a dreamer too, also in a nice way. She smiled when she said it, once a dreamer herself. Her mother wanted the best for Jessica, wanted her to go to university and have a career, not have a passel of kids and be a housecleaner like her.

Uncle Sawyer, not her real uncle, but Jessica's biggest fan who encouraged her to keep right on dreaming. If she had known her real father, Jessica knew he would have most likely called her a dreamer too, and she wondered if he would have been like Uncle Sawyer, a white man too.

So, everybody knew Jessica was a dreamer, teased her about it. But she didn't really care what they said, the consolation that she would be leaving Skyler as soon as she could, kept her calm and happy. And, besides, in addition to being smart and a dreamer, she was a planner.

As far back as she could remember she had been a planner, she knew how to chart it out and get it done. Since the first grade as soon as she got home from school each day she would sit down and plan every single minute left in the day till she would have to go to bed. She would make a list in fifteen minute increments, a schedule. She'd list times for homework, chores, activities, supper, and private time, even when she would turn out the light to go to sleep - to the minute. And she stuck to it.

Being the oldest child and oldest girl, she had her own bedroom. It had been a storage closet for the previous tenants. She would plan for ample 'private time' to squeeze in precious reading of the books Uncle Sawyer gave her from his library. And at night she would scrunch into the pillows on her bed and read, sometimes going past the scheduled time for turning out the single light bulb, dangling from the ceiling in her closet bedroom. But most times she stuck to her schedule.

Sawyer Mason Skyler, a rich middle-aged bachelor, lived up the hill above his namesake town. A tall, thin, lanky man, who loved children, but had never married. He had tended his own mama till she died at the age of ninety-nine.

Jessica thought he resembled the pictures of the Ichabod-Crane character depicted in the Washington Irving book – "The Legend of Sleepy Hollow" – one of the books he had given her to read.

He had a gentle countenance, but a prominent Romanesque nose like Ichabod's that didn't seem to make her stare and snicker like most people.

She loved the ceramic sculpture of Ichabod Crane and his beloved Katrina Van Tassel that Uncle Sawyer let her hold and admire.

8

"It's a replica of the 1868 original," he told her. "A collector's item."

Uncle Sawyer, sole survivor of the Skyler family, owned most of the property in and around the township of Skyler. At one time the Skyler family owned the whole mountain.

He had first noticed Jessica after she started going to the town school that sat two-hundred-fifty feet below his big log cabin. While he sat on his porch, he could watch the children on the playgrounds below, and one day Jessica caught his eye because she would stay apart from the other kids and find a tree stump or a boulder to sit on and would read till the bell rang. He even watched her every day as she ate her sack lunch by herself, her nose always in a book.

The first time she caught him watching her, she had lifted her eyes from a book, in deep thought about what she had just read. She looked up at the sky and then at the trees, and then saw him on his porch staring at her. She stared back at him. After a few moments when she couldn't stare him down she laughed and waved. He waved, showing a big toothy grin, and then she continued reading her book. From then on, each day she would check to see if he was sitting on the porch.

Then one noon time, after reading a few minutes, she walked to the edge of the schoolyard and yelled up to him, "Hi, how are you today?"

"I'm wonderful!" he said. "What are you reading?"

"A novel called 'Jane Eyre'. Do you know it?"

"Yes, I do. Written by one of the Bronte sisters. Charlotte wrote that one. Have you read her sisters' novels?" He stood up.

"No I haven't, don't know about them."

"I have all their books. Anne wrote two novels, Charlotte, only the one, and Emily wrote one. After school today, why don't you come on up, and I'll give them to you."

"I will, I will. Oh, my goodness, thank you so much. I'll see you after school, then. What's your name?"

"You can call me Uncle Sawyer." He was beaming.

"I'm Jessica Sanford. Bye." She turned and ran to her class; the bell had rung.

That day after school he stood on his porch, waiting for Jessica to come up to his cabin. Thus, the beginning of an unusual, special

9

relationship between the skinny, curly-haired, bi-racial girl and the middle-aged man, an Ichabod Crane lookalike.

Jessica loved spending as much time as she could with Uncle Sawyer in his seven-room log cabin. She'd never seen such a fancy log house, stuck up in the woods like that. Oh, there were fancy houses in town; the judge's house, the mayor's house, the doctor's, where her mother worked, but none like Uncle Sawyer's house. She told him she admired his uniqueness and personality. She visited him regularly. His extensive library, the result of years and years of collecting books and studying them, overwhelmed her. She learned he hadn't always lived in Skyler, and quizzed him every time she saw him.

Sawyer told Jessica stories of all the places he had been when he was a young man traveling the world. He had artifacts from England, France, Belgium, Italy, Switzerland, Austria, Russia, and most other countries in the west and eastern parts of Europe and Asia. The Skyler family had interests in copper, tin, and gold mines in the U.S., he told her, as well as around the world. Sawyer had been the family procurer and overseer of all their investments in his younger days. He was the only one who had gone to university, had an accounting degree, as well as a law degree. So, he was the family's anointed one while they were alive.

And now, in his sixties, his primary pleasure of making sure the children of Skyler were exposed to the possibilities the world presented to them kept him busy. Many were the benefactors of his generous scholarships. He had great plans for Jessica too. A very special young girl. The level of conversation and intelligence in a young girl of her age, surprised Uncle Sawyer. Most grown women in Skyler couldn't hold a dialogue on subjects Jessica discussed with ease. He even began visiting her mama at their small house in the country and he showed an interest in all Jessica's half brothers and sisters. He would take them food, books, and gifts when he visited once a week on Sundays, the only day Jessica's mother didn't work.

As impossible as it may have seemed for a girl Jessica's age, while others played kid games, running through the woods playing hide and seek, or swimming under the water falls and diving from the granite boulders, Jessica preferred to sit and listen to Uncle Sawyer's stories and to read about his world away from the Blue Ridge Mountains.

On Saturday afternoons when her mama would let her walk to town, sometimes instead of bothering Uncle Sawyer, Jessica would spend the day at the town library to read and look through books for hours. She considered it a treat to get lost in the pictures and the stories she read.

3

Just before Jessica turned thirteen, the Sanford family moved into town. They moved into the big, gray, faded green-shuttered Victorian house that had belonged to Roberta Carter.

The old woman died and left the house with everything in it to her granddaughter Jessica Sanford, according to her Last Will and Testament. Uncle Sawyer being her attorney and accountant, broke the news to the family.

Old Mrs. Carter had given instructions that the taxes, insurance, and maintenance would come out of a family trust, but no cash or additional provisions would be made for the struggling family of ten. She also wrote a brief note to Jessica's mother, Evangeline, saying she left the house to her granddaughter Jessica because she reminded her of herself and her dear beloved son, Arnold. She wrote an apology for the unkindness she had shown to Evangeline and to Jessica, felt it was disrespectful to her dear son's memory.

Arnold Carter had died of a brain tumor when he was in high school and only seventeen years old while his girlfriend Evangeline was pregnant with Jessica. It was a sad time for both his mother and for Evangeline, but even then, Roberta Carter would have nothing to do with her son's teenage sex-mate, and wouldn't allow her to visit him on his sick bed or come to his funeral. Her public deep-seated prejudices stuck 'till her own death.

After Arnold died, Evangeline married Bert Sanford, a charming scoundrel and womanizer. She had one child a year by him and before Bert's eighth child was born, he disappeared, never to be seen or heard of again. The rumor was that a jealous husband over in Ashville must've killed him and buried him in the woods. Evangeline figured he just ran off with one of his women and headed west, responsibility was never his heaviest suit.

Now after all those years of trying to provide shelter, food, and clothing for her nine children in a small shack in the country, they owned and lived in a luxurious Victorian home in Skyler's upscale neighborhood. A dream-come-true for Evangeline who had struggled so long to provide the best shelter for her children.

Mrs. Carter also left a box of family photos for Jessica, and two automobiles in mint condition to Evangeline: a 1992 Cadillac Seville and a 1996 Buick Station Wagon. It seemed to Evangeline that now the good luck over-weighed the bad luck, but she had never complained through the bad; she had just kept on plugging away day after day, her priority being her dear children. She drove to and from work all those years in an old, banged up pick-up truck, and when they all went to town, the children rode in the open back, rain or shine. When it rained, they pulled a large canvas tarp over their heads. She wanted to prepare them, to the best of her ability, for the lives ahead of them. Now it would be easier. They had a beautiful home to live in, with enough rooms and lavish furnishings to enjoy, and nice cars to ride in. She could earn enough money to put food on the table and clothe the children, and because of Jessica's grandmother, she could do that easily. Good times ahead.

4

When Jessica turned thirteen, three days before her first day in high school, her mama gave her a globe of the world; Jessica's interest in the world hadn't escaped her mama's notice. A well-worn globe, not new, had been tossed in the trash bin behind the town mayor's house, where Evangeline worked as a housekeeper on Thursdays. Every Thursday Evangeline would go through the trash-laden barrels in the alleys behind the neighborhood houses before the trash collector came to haul it all away. She called it shopping.

When she saw the beautifully multi-colored globe sticking out of a box, it couldn't have come at a more opportune time. What could be more special for her eldest daughter than a globe of the world on her thirteenth birthday? At one time Evangeline possessed the same dreams and desires as her daughter, long before she became pregnant and quit school to take care of baby Jessica.

"Jessica, baby girl, you come in here right now," Evangeline called out from the steps, her mulatto face lit up with excitement about the Sunday afternoon surprise birthday party for her daughter.

Jessica sat Indian style on a flat rock in the middle of the flower garden, in the same front garden where at the age of ten she

14

bravely gave grandmother Carter a piece of her mind.

"I'm almost done, mama. Only one more chapter to go, then I'll come in. Mama, did you know that Queen Victoria had nine kids just like you?"

"She was the queen of what, baby?"

"England, married to Prince Albert. It's a beautiful love story."

"With all those kids? Don't see how I can believe that, baby. Hurry on up now, and come in the house."

"I want to go to England, Mama. That's going to be the first place I go when I'm old enough."

Evangeline turned to go through the screened door that had recently been trimmed with a fresh coat of emerald-colored paint. She looked back at Jessica and said, "You know, if I were you, little girl, I'd close that book and would come on inside the house right this minute, if you want to open your birthday presents." Evangeline smiled broadly, her coal black wavy hair brushed back from her face into a tight knot. She let the screened door slap and bounce into place behind her.

It had been hard keeping the secret from her special daughter for a week. She knew Jessica would be surprised about the globe and the other presents the kids had made for her.

Jessica's twelve-year-old brother Adam, already six-feet tall, had repaired and refinished the broken wooden stand, probably the reason the Mayor's household trashed the globe, but nothing wrong with the globe itself. Just a bit of fixing and stain made its stand good as new.

Her eleven-year-old sister Ginger had painted roses on a strip of construction paper and created a bookmark, with a fringe of embroidery thread looped across one end.

Ten-year-old brother Lenny had embroidered a piece of muslin his mama gave him, a handkerchief for Jessica. Lenny loved to mend and sew. He set himself up as the family seamstress.

The two youngest boys in the family, Joe and Phillip, had hand-written a story they made up of fishing and camping in the woods, and had drawn a picture of the two of them on the cover, calling the story 'Jessica's Brothers'.

Her other sisters, Mya-Lisa and Leia, worked together and made her a party dress. Each one added their own special touches:

embroidery, ribbon, ruffles. Even three-year-old Martha had sewn on a bow.

To top it all off, Uncle Sawyer brought a fancy cake made especially at the bakery for Jessica, with her name on it, and he brought ice cream, punch and orange soda. The kids had made party favors and decorations that they had hung all over the spacious living room of their precious Victorian house.

Sawyer had picked up on Evangeline's special outlook on life from the moment he first met her at the Mayor's house during a cocktail party. She was one of the servers. He knew she was Jessica's mother before they met, he'd seen her at the school. At the Mayor's house, he had asked questions about her. After that he made it his business to watch over the fatherless family of nine children, always showing up when they were in dire need. A complete mystery to Evangeline.

Comparing Evangeline in her thirties, and Sawyer in his early sixties, he knew nothing could come from it, but nevertheless, he fantasized about Evangeline since the day they met. Her caramel-colored skin shone with smoothness, and her huge, dark brown eyes were magnetic. Tiny, under a hundred pounds, she showed no sign of having birthed nine children. He could understand why Arnold Carter fell in love with her. Of course, he would never impose or tell her what he felt, for he knew that one day some handsome young man would come along and ask her to marry him, someone nearer her age.

But no one came. The nine children might be a deterrent, he told himself, not quite understanding why it would be. To him it would be an exciting challenge, but he kept his feelings to himself. His connection with Jessica had kept him close enough.

Jessica snapped her book shut and hurried up the porch steps, reaching the door just as it had settled shut behind her mama. She opened it and hurried into the house and stood facing the beaming faces of all her brothers and sisters with Uncle Sawyer and her mama. They were standing around the big mahogany dining table in the center of the room. On the table, sat a cake ablaze with thirteen candles. Next to it were piled a few wrapped presents, one a large odd-shaped one, shaped like a hot-air balloon.

"Surprise!" they all yelled amidst laughter. "Surprise, Jessie!" Then they sang happy birthday to her.

Stunned, tears gathered in Jessica's eyes. "Oh, Mama, Uncle Sawyer, all of you, I love you so much." She hugged and kissed every one of them even before opening the presents. "Thank you, thank you, thank you. I didn't expect a party."

That day Uncle Sawyer presented Jessica with a generous trust account for her college education. His kindness overwhelmed Evangeline, but it wasn't the first time he'd offered money to help her family. Many times, he'd offered cash to her, but she always refused. In a small town like Skyler, a man paying a woman's way meant only one thing. She didn't want to risk any cruel gossip about her or her children. A proud woman, and so far, she had been able to support her family by herself. Not easy, but she managed.

So, when Sawyer handed the bank book to Jessica for her birthday, and explained to her how it worked, Evangeline cried. She didn't stop crying 'till Jessica took her into the next room and held her, stroking her hair, promising to always be there for her and promising to make her proud. Already taller than Evangeline, at thirteen Jessica appeared to have exchanged roles with her mother - the taller one, the mama, the shorter, the daughter.

Evangeline held her daughter's shoulders squarely, facing her. She stepped back, "You're growing up so fast, baby, and soon you'll spread your wings and fly away ..." Her voice cracked as she became emotional.

"It's alright, mama. I'm not going yet. I have four more years of school here. And when I do leave to go to college, I'll always come back to see my family."

Sawyer stood in the doorway, looking on, moved by their loving relationship.

"But that's not the main reason I'm crying, baby. It's just that I'm happy for you." She reached up and held her daughter's face in her hands, "Now you'll have the money to be able to go to college like you've always wanted to do, and you'll be able to see all the places on your globe. You won't have to clean houses like your mama. I'm crying cause of all that. And I'm crying cause I always wanted to go to college myself, and now my baby's gonna do it for me." She hugged Jessica for a long moment, and then she pulled away and took her hand. "C'mon, now, let's go and thank Uncle Sawyer for the wonderful gift he has given you."

17

Sawyer had already stepped back into the dining room, holding another package. "I have one more present for you, Jessica."

Jessica's eyes widened in surprise, "You don't need to give me two presents, Uncle Sawyer."

"Here, you'll need this for your studies." He grinned cheerfully like a proud papa and handed it to her.

She removed the lid to the wrapped box and looked inside. "Oh, my gosh! Will you look at this, Mama! It's a laptop computer. I've been wanting one of these forever." She dropped the lid and ran to Uncle Sawyer, hugging him tightly and squealing with delight.

Jessica spent the rest of the day in a daze. Uncle Sawyer had made it possible for her to leave Skyler when she graduated from high school and go to college. Just four more years. Her prayers had been answered. Then she would set out to see the world after she finished college; she would get a job with an international corporation, in whatever field she chose to take her around the world. She'd been searching vocations on the Internet at school. Now she could do her Internet searches at home on the computer Uncle Sawyer gave her for her birthday. She loved her life.

5

Three years later, when Jessica turned sixteen, her dreams were shattered. A high school girlfriend, daughter of Judge Cramer, whose home Jessica's mother cleaned, invited Jessica to her brother's graduation party at the Cramer mansion. Jessica had a secret crush on her friend's brother, a senior upper classmate. She didn't date, although she loved to dance and would do it whenever the occasion called for it at school. Her contact with boys was limited to school and school events, but no one-on-ones, no dates, no boyfriends.

Evangeline encouraged her daughter to go to the Cramer party, even managed to find a dress at the Goodwill that could be repurposed and made to look current and fashionable.

Jessica had blossomed into a beautiful young woman with ample breasts, tiny waist, narrow hips, and long shapely legs. She had shiny blonde hair, long and thick, natural curly spirals that made her the envy of most. With her glowing golden skin against the light blue lacy party frock her mother overhauled for her, she attracted plenty of attention at the Cramer house - her first dance party, first private party.

That year, her junior year of high school, she enrolled in a jazz dance class for girls, and became one of the best modern jazz dancers in the class, even had the lead in a dance recital and the school's musical. But even still she had never dated. Her aloofness and grand composure seemed to keep the boys at bay. She spent all her spare time studying and reading the books that Uncle Sawyer gave her. She kept to herself, not because of shyness, oh no, known as a gutsy girl and outspoken. She chose to be in her own private little world, always dreaming and planning her future. After high school graduation, local college in Ashville would come next, and then one of the best business schools in the east to get her MBA. Uncle Sawyer talked up Harvard in Boston, and she loved the idea.

But in just one night at the Cramer party, in the back of a pick-up truck behind Judge Cramer's mansion, Jessica's life changed forever.

Halfway through the party, Wylie Cramer, the judge's son, led Jessica to his parked truck out back by the barn, carrying a six-pack of beer dangled in one hand, his other arm around her while smothering her with kisses as they walked. He told her how long he'd wanted to be with her but hadn't the nerve to ask. Said his sister told him that Jessica had a crush on him, and he thought he loved her and wanted to marry her as soon as they graduated high school. Wylie easily coaxed and led naive Jessica outside and away from the house.

Of course, Jessica loved the attention from Wylie, they hardly knew each other, hardly spoke in school. But the sudden attention and amorous behavior confused her. His kisses on her neck made her feel good. She'd never had those feelings before. She'd never been kissed or touched by a boy.

As they approached the truck behind the barn, two of Wylie's buddies appeared out of nowhere. Together the three of them forced her onto the bed of the truck, muffling her screams with their hands.

Her knight in shining armor quickly stuffed a dirty, oily rag in her mouth so she could not be heard over the faint din of party goers in the distance that stretched between the main house and the barn. The teenagers held her down, each battling with her, each taking what they wanted.

When they'd had enough and figured they should get back to the party before anyone came looking for them, Wylie warned a terrified and wounded Jessica if she ever told anybody what they did, they'd do the same to her baby sisters, and besides nobody would ever believe a nigger. And her nigger mother would not be able to work anywhere in town, especially not for his daddy.

In a terrorized, painful, violated stupor, Jessica believed him.

6

As she made her way down the back alleyways, Jessica didn't feel the blood trickling down the inside of her legs leaving a red, speckled trail on the ground behind her. She moved stoically, there were no tears, no expression. Everything seemed a blur, her mind groggy and empty. Not aware of the missing buttons down the front of her dress, and the threads hanging where the buttons once were, she soon became aware of the pulsating, burning pain emanating from her vagina and anus, spreading throughout her abdomen and back. It became difficult for her to walk. If anyone saw her, they would see a lone, disheveled girl, walking straddle-legged, doubled over, holding her lower torso with both arms, and stumbling in the darkness.

It seemed like hours had passed, like she'd been walking all night when she finally reached the back porch of her Victorian haven.

She opened the screened door and stood inside for a few minutes, not knowing what to do next. She couldn't tell her mother what happened. She couldn't think. Her thoughts were fragmented, nothing made sense. She didn't see anything familiar. The wicker furniture on the porch didn't belong there. When did her mother put that there? She lay down on the braided rug that covered a portion of the oak-stained wood-planked floor, pulled the rug around her, and drew up into a fetal position.

7

Around three in the morning, Evangeline woke up with a start. A foreboding feeling came over her. Her heart began pounding hard. She slipped her feet into slippers and pulled on her robe as she headed down the hallway towards Jessica's room. She'd meant to stay awake till her daughter got home from her first party, but had fallen asleep.

Jessica's bed hadn't been slept in.

Evangeline's heart quickened. She turned and ran to the stairway and down to the ground floor. After making a quick round of the rooms downstairs, she looked on the front porch sunroom. Then she rushed through the house to the back porch.

She stared for a moment without moving. There on the floor in the moonlight lay her oldest child, rolled up in an old braided rug. Evangeline's heartbeat stabbed her brain. Both vital organs were vying for the fastest and hardest throbs.

She knelt next to her daughter. "Jessica, baby, what are you doing here on the floor?" Pulling back the rug to uncover her face, she said, "Come to bed, baby. What you doin' down here?" Then she saw the missing buttons, the dress torn open.

Jessica's red-watery eyes opened and stared blankly at her

24

mother as if she didn't see her. Her pale face appeared to be hardened porcelain instead of her usual golden soft skin.

"Honey, what happened?" Evangeline cried. "Baby, are you alright?" She quickly unwrapped the rug from her daughter and saw the blood on her dress and on the rug. "Oh, my baby, my baby. What have they done to you?"

She searched her daughter's limp body to see the source of the bleeding. When realization struck, she drew Jessica to her chest and held her tight, sobbing as she caressed and rocked her daughter, who still hadn't uttered a word. "Who did this to you? Who did this to my precious baby girl?"

8

It didn't take long for Evangeline and Uncle Sawyer to put the pieces together and approach Judge Cramer a week later about what had happened to Jessica at his home. Jessica still didn't talk, she remained silent and stoic. She hadn't spoken to anyone or gone to school since the party.

When Evangeline and Sawyer took Jessica to the doctor the day after the ordeal, the doc had corroborated Evangeline's worst fear, yes, her daughter had been raped and injured. Possibly gang-raped. He told them the abrasions and injuries that happen when a young girl is still a virgin, would make it more difficult to penetrate causing damage by forcible entry and continual invasion. He also said she'd been sodomized. The doctor told them it could be extreme. And in Jessica's case the violent rape by several perpetrators had increased the damage, physically and emotionally. The police were called, as required on all rape cases.

There had been several witnesses that told the detectives they saw Wylie Cramer carrying a six-pack of beer and his arm around Jessica. Others said Wylie had been dancing all night with Jessica and it appeared the two of them were attracted to each other. But no one

26

saw what happened after the two of them left the house.

One young girl told Jessica's sister Ginger, how Wylie returned to the party that night with two of his buddies instead of Jessica. They all figured Jessica had gone home.

Everyone knew that something terrible had happened to Jessica Sanford by the beginning of the second week.

No one could say Wylie raped Jessica. Wylie's story was they'd gone out to the patio and had a few beers and then Jessica left and went home. He and his buddies had a few more beers and smokes and that's all he knew. He swore by it. However, Judge Cramer pulled some strings and sent his son to his brother in New York City to finish out the summer and enroll in college in the Fall.

Jessica still wouldn't talk and no charges were filed.

After a month, no one spoke of it or thought of it again. No one except Jessica's family and Uncle Sawyer who witnessed her slip deeper and deeper into depression

Uncle Sawyer asked Evangeline if he could bring in a psycho-therapist from Ashville, a friend of his that could possibly help her. He said his mother had been her client during a period of depression, and it had worked. Evangeline gave permission for the therapy sessions, hopeful it would help Jessica.

9

After a long silent summer and fall, by Christmas Jessica spoke again, not of the rape - no word about that - and not in the exuberant, youthful manner she had always communicated, more subdued than before, and not as much light in her eyes.

Sawyer saw to it that Evangeline's family had a pleasant Christmas. He invited them to his cabin for an old-fashioned Christmas dinner with all the trimmings, brought in a crew from Ashville to prepare and serve it, and under a gigantic decorated Christmas tree that reached into the rafters there were gifts for all. It seemed like Evangeline and her nine children were Uncle Sawyer's family, while he sat back, absorbing every single precious minute of it. His heart overflowed with joy. It almost broke his heart, however, when at one point he glanced at Jessica and saw her sitting alone, staring into space with tears in her eyes.

He moved to the sofa next to her and rested his arm across the back of the sofa. "Is there anything I can do for you, Jessica, dear? Anything that will make you laugh again?"

She looked up at him, smiled, and said "Thank you for being here, Uncle Sawyer. That's enough for me." Then she leaned her head against his chest as he pulled her towards him. He stroked her hair and looked across the room at Evangeline picking up gift wrapping, tidying the place.

"I want you to keep the trust account, Jessica, if you go to university or not. The money will be available to you when you turn eighteen. It's yours for whatever you choose. Of course, I'm hoping you'll choose college like we planned. I'm hoping by the start of the spring semester you will be your old self and ready to finish high school."

"I can't go back to Skyler High," she said quickly, still leaning on her uncle.

"You don't have to, honey. I have a friend who is headmistress of a private high school in Ashville, an all-girl school. You can live there and come home on weekends, if you want. And you'll be there to continue your therapy with Audra."

Jessica sat up and for the first time in weeks her face brightened. "I could do that? How would I get back and forth? Mama can't take me and come and get me."

"We'll see about a car for you. You don't have to worry your pretty little head about anything. We can come visit you on Sundays in Ashville too, so you won't have to come home to Skylar every weekend." He loved her sudden excitement. He had stumbled upon the magic button. The best Christmas present he could ever have wished for. He adored his adopted family; he literally, genuinely adored each of them.

From across the room, Evangeline saw Jessica's reaction to something Sawyer said, saw her sudden excitement. She immediately joined them.

"What's going on over here? Do I see a familiar great big grin on my dear daughter's face?" she asked.

"Mama, Uncle Sawyer says that I can go to an all-girl high school in Ashville. I can go back to school now." She hugged her mother with more strength than she had displayed in months.

"But, Sawyer, I can't afford a private school, you know that." Hesitant to burst her daughter's bubble, still she didn't want to encourage her any further, only to let her down later.

"Evangeline, it is my idea, so I'll pay for it."

"But—"

29

"No buts. You are my only family, if you haven't noticed." He waved his hand towards all the children playing with their toys, laughter ringing throughout the cabin. Kids running up and down the stairs. Then his fingers touched Evangeline's shoulder, while his long arm still stretched across the back of the sofa behind Jessica. "Please, let me do this."

Evangeline stood up and walked around to kiss his cheek. "Thank you so much, I don't know why you're so kind to us."

When she kissed him, their eyes met, and for a moment, Evangeline's heart fluttered. She caught her breath, then immediately straightened and hugged Jessica before heading back to her cleaning chores.

Sawyer stared after her, his heart fluttered too. In that moment, he wished he had youth and good looks. He'd been dealt a different look and had never felt women were attracted to him. Too tall, too lanky, and his aquiline nose had always been embarrassing, and he felt destined to be a forever bachelor.

At twenty-five he fell in love with a woman in Italy. His nose didn't seem to be an issue in Italy. But she didn't show up for the wedding in Rome. He never saw her again, didn't know what happened to her. Her family said they couldn't shed light on her whereabouts. But he did hear rumors the following year that she had gone back to an old boyfriend; they married and were living in Sicily. By then he buried himself in his work and business, steering clear of relationships with women entirely. After he returned home to care for his mother, he mellowed and began to feel compassion again.

Now, forty years later he had fallen in love with a woman thirty-five years younger with nine kids in tow.

I'm certainly screwed this time, he told himself.

10

Jessica settled in at the secluded Oaks Academy for Girls in Ashville. She was to attend straight through the spring and summer and then begin the senior year in the fall. She liked the school, and was grateful to her mama and Uncle Sawyer for helping to make the transition a smooth one. For the first time in her life she had more than one friend, four of them in the dorm: Janelle, Chauntelle, Carissa, and Tiffany. The five young ladies stuck together like glue. They studied together and played together - tennis and volleyball. They even took modern dance together, Jessica being the most natural dancer of the five.

But something about Jessica the others couldn't quite put their finger on; at times, she would withdraw into herself, almost cowering. More reserve than the rest of them, she seemed to hold herself in check, never letting go, never talking about her family or her life before Oaks Academy. They didn't know much about her other than the rumor that her rich family lived in Skyler. Rich wasn't out of the ordinary, they all were from wealthy families, they had to be to be able to afford the Oaks.

Carissa, the serious dancer, wanted to pursue it after she

graduated. She'd already done the research and discovered there were two primary places to break into the dance world - New York City and Las Vegas.

"You guys want to go to Vegas with me this summer after graduation? For a week or two to check it out?" Carissa asked, out of the blue one Sunday evening while they were watching TV - they were hooked on "Doc Martin", a weekly popular British series on public television. They had discussed going to Port Isaac in the summer when the show was filmed.

Tiffany spoke up first, "Now you're wanting to go to Vegas? I thought we were going to England to see Doc Martin filmed?"

"We can do both. First to Las Vegas to see what's there and how to go about applying for a job as a dancer."

Janelle added, "You know, I saw a TV show about showgirls last year, and all that they go through to make it as a dancer. They dance topless, you know. Are you willing to do that?"

"Well, if that's what it takes, I am. Nothing wrong with showing my boobs. It isn't like it's a big deal in Vegas. Everybody does it," Carissa laughed. "I'm in good shape, shouldn't be a problem."

Jessica hesitated. "But won't you be embarrassed?" Being the quietest of the five, although she befriended them easily enough, she always took a back seat when it came to conversation. So, they were surprised she'd spoken up.

"No, why should I be? It isn't the same thing as showing your fur piece." They all laughed.

"Fur piece?" Jessica said with a major blush.

"Well that's what it is, isn't it? I don't particularly like the other words for it. They all seem crass and nasty. The C word especially. Any boy ever call me the C word, I'll bat his ass, and I mean that."

"You're right," Janelle said. "I hate it when my dad calls my mother the C word. That's the most horrid word in the world."

"He says that to your mom?" Chauntelle said, frowning.

"Among other things." Janelle got up to get a coke.

They looked at each other in silence, shaking their heads.

"Of course, mom comes right back at him, calling him a prick or a dildo," Janelle added. "She doesn't let him run over her like some women do."

"My mama says a woman should be respected by her husband," Jessica said. "He shouldn't be mean to her."

"That's one reason I want to become a dancer and make a fortune so I don't have to have a man support me," Carissa said.

"A dancer makes a fortune?" Jessica shifted on the sofa, unfolding her long legs and placing her feet on the floor, suddenly interested in the answer to her question.

"They make anywhere from $700 to $1700 a week, girlfriend. That's more than a bank teller or a school teacher makes. Works for me," Carissa said.

Janelle perked up. "Really? Hey, maybe I'll just stay in Vegas and be a dancer too." She grinned from ear to ear, her perfect teeth radiating.

Tiffany, the thinnest and tallest of the five, weighing in at 120 and standing at 5'11", perked up with a big grin of her own. "Me, too."

"Why don't we all do it then? I mean, we're a team, aren't we?" Carissa said.

"Well, I'm expected to go to college in Boston." Jessica frowned as she stood up and walked to the diamond-paned bay windows looking out over the well-lit manicured grounds and gardens of the Oaks. She thought of the trust account Uncle Sawyer had given her, and she thought of her mama and brothers and sisters, all stuck in Skyler. She didn't want to go back there for the summer. "But I'd like to go to Las Vegas to visit; I don't see anything wrong with that, wouldn't hurt to go see it for at least a couple weeks after graduation. I haven't been anywhere other than Skyler and Ashville in my whole life."

The girls jumped up and joined hands and danced in a circle while chanting in unison, "We're going to Vegas, we're going to Vegas, we're going to Vegas . . ."

11

Graduation Day at The Oaks Academy in Ashville had the reputation of being a glorious party. Southerners do know how to throw a shindig.

All the parents arrived before two in the afternoon on Saturday after the final day of school. The expansive lawn surrounded by gardens of magnolia trees, wisteria vines, and climbing roses created the perfect setting of the annual event with rows of white slatted chairs placed on each side of a wide floral lined aisle. Assorted colors of gladioli and Iris were in tall, free-standing, white wicker baskets placed every three rows on each side. White satin ribbons streamed from the arrangements. It looked more like a wedding than a graduation. Women in pastels and matching designer hats, men in summer suits, straw fedoras and boaters, and white shoes ... all displayed the grace of the southern gentry at the annual afternoon celebration to watch their darlings graduate from high school. As the proceedings took place, Evangeline and Uncle Sawyer sat on the front row of the center section, proud of Jessica and what she had accomplished. All eight children were there too, dressed to the nines, with huge Cheshire cat grins on their faces, gawking at the grand spectacle, the likes of which they'd never seen before.

Jessica received top honors, top of her class. She could conquer the world. She heard the words repeatedly from her teachers, the world is yours to conquer, words that were more to be heard than believed. Her self-esteem suffered despite the words, for she didn't feel any different than she had the year before. The same person, the same half breed, the evil words stuck in her soul, still the same nigger. She'd always be a nigger, no matter what anybody said.

She thought of when her mama told her it had been difficult tracing their family's lineage on her side. Evangeline was born in Louisiana, she knew that, and she knew her daddy who she'd never met was half black. Her mother, Alba, was three-quarters white, Evangeline had been told. Alba didn't know who her parents were, said she'd been raised by a white family in Baton Rouge, and was a servant as far back as she could remember. That's all Evangeline knew about her family.

Uncle Sawyer explained to Jessica and her mother, that the Americas - North, Central, and South – at one time were populated with Europeans, American Indians, and Africans. The Europeans mixed with the Indians, Indians with Africans, Africans with Europeans, and so forth. And the hard-to-find pages of early history of the three cultures inter-breeding, would surely provide how the three races helped build the Americas together. He said that their relationships are surely depicted in many books and novels, if one would only do the research to make the connections. He even had suggested it to Jessica as a subject for her college thesis when the time came.

As Jessica stood on the graduation stage, reminiscing while waiting to accept her awards and her diploma, she thrilled at the sight of Uncle Sawyer holding her mama's hand resting on his leg. That made her day, not the diploma, not the award, seeing her mama happy and knowing Uncle Sawyer would look after her warmed her heart. Now Jessica could leave North Carolina without any regrets. Her family would be alright.

12

"But, mama, I'm only going for a few weeks. I'll be home before I go off to college. Tell her, Uncle Sawyer. I just want to go to Las Vegas with my friends. And then we're going to L.A. and San Francisco to see the sights before I come back and get ready to go to Boston. I don't know when I'll get the chance again to see the west coast. This is a trip of a lifetime, so what is so wrong with that?"

Evangeline looked across the room at Sawyer, a frown deepening on her face, a broad smile on his. She wondered what made him so happy, and then returned her attention to Jessica, touching her arm.

"Honey, you're too young to be going off by yourself with a bunch of girls. Those are big towns and lots of bad stuff goes on out there. Tell her, Sawyer," she pleaded.

"I think she's ready, Evangeline," he said.

"But it's only been a year since—" Evangeline covered her face with her hands.

"Mama, I'm alright. I really am." She looked nervously at Sawyer. "I am."

Not convinced, Evangeline knew better. The vile violation of her daughter would always be there to haunt them all. She would never forget how Jessica looked that morning when she found her on the back porch rolled up in a braided rug.

"She'll be going to New York and Boston by herself in the fall, Evangeline, and those are big cities too. You must turn loose. It's time. You can't protect her. She has to learn how to protect herself." He walked over and put his arm around Jessica. "Our little Jessie has grown up to be a very strong young woman. She's smart enough to know what to watch for, she knows the difference between right and wrong, and she needs to get out into the world to recognize those differences. It will only make her a stronger person."

Jessica hugged Sawyer. "Thank you, Uncle Sawyer. Thank you for everything. I couldn't go anywhere if it weren't for you."

"Well, you just be frugal with that graduation money, my dear. It's easy to let it slip through your fingers if you're not careful. Always ask yourself if what you want to spend it on is necessary. If it's just a whim or just something you want, but don't need, think twice about it. And always pay your bills first."

She kissed him on the cheek. "I will, I promise."

"I know you will; you're a true champion." He loosened his hold and reached for Evangeline. "And you, my dear lady, you have eight other children to raise. This one is done."

"No, she isn't. She's just beginning." Evangeline's eyes were sad, but a faint, proud smile glimmered.

Jessica ran into her mama's arms, holding her close. "Mama, I'll be okay. You gotta trust me. I must do this. I must go. I can't stay here this summer. Everybody comes home from school for the summer."

Evangeline saw fear in her daughter's eyes. It dawned on her that Jessica didn't want to be home when Wylie Cramer came home for the summer. Now she understood. "Okay, my sweet. You can go. I'm just sad I'm losing my baby to the world. But I know it's out of our hands now. All I've ever taught you, all your Uncle Sawyer has taught you—" She couldn't say another word; she buried her face into her daughter's shoulder and wept.

"When will you be leaving?" Sawyer asked as he gulped his coffee, trying to change the mood.

"Tomorrow. I've gassed up the car, had the engine checked and the tires. I'm packed. So we'll be leaving early in the morning."

"How many cars are you taking?" Evangeline said with a shaky voice, lifting her head and wiping her eyes.

"Three. I wanted to take mine, because I'll be coming back on my own. Janelle's taking hers, Tiffany's riding with her. And Carissa is staying in Vegas, so she'll need hers."

"You're going to Vegas first, right?" Sawyer asked.

"Yes, Vegas for a couple weeks, then on to Los Angeles to see all the sights and go to the beach. Tiffany has an aunt there, so we're staying with her. Mama, I'm going to see the Pacific Ocean!" she radiated excitement. "Then we'll head up the coast to San Francisco where her brother lives. I'll send postcards so you'll always know where I am."

"I'll pack a food basket for you, honey. So you won't starve to death before you get to Vegas."

"We're not going to starve to death, mama. We'll be stopping along the way to eat and sleep. You needn't do that."

"I'm going to anyway," Evangeline said as she turned away, wiping her eyes.

Jessica and Uncle Sawyer shrugged their shoulders in unison.

"She loves you very much," he said. "This is hard for her."

"I know."

He would worry about her too. "Now here's a little something to tide you over till your eighteenth birthday." He reached into his inside pocket and handed her an envelope. "Just put it away before Vangie sees it. You know how she is. And be frugal, my dear, be frugal."

13

It had been two weeks since Jessica left North Carolina for Vegas. It took the girls four days to get there with no mishaps.

When they arrived in Sin City, Jessica telephoned her mother and then called Uncle Sawyer, telling them both about the trip and how much fun she was having. She told them she drove through Tennessee, Missouri, Kansas, Colorado, and Utah. She said she typed in her journal everyday on her laptop and would send them day by day segments when she settled in, when she could sort through the notes.

She told her mother they had rented a furnished two-bedroom apartment, had just finished unpacking, and she'd call again in a few days.

Evangeline felt relieved to hear from her daughter, that she had made it safely to Vegas without any mishaps. She had worried from the moment the girls drove off. Worry, not only of the trip, but much more. Her daughter had changed. She could see pretense. Jessica wasn't as focused and as curious and eager about the world as she portrayed. Evangeline could see it in her daughter's eyes.

Sawyer had begun spending the evenings at the house with Evangeline and the children since Jessica left for Ashville and even more so since she went to Las Vegas. He helped wherever needed, sometimes cooked, cleaned, did the laundry for Evangeline. She seemed to be tiring more lately. Going to bed earlier, napping.

He loved to cook for the kids, had become extra fond of the younger ones. In fact, he enjoyed being with the Sanford family. Most of all, he loved being with Vangie, as he called her.

"Did she tell you that she's staying in Vegas a while longer?" Evangeline said through a frown one night as they were listening to music in the parlor, the kids asleep in their rooms.

Sawyer looked at his hands folded in his lap. "She mentioned it. What else did she tell you?"

"Said she's thinking of becoming a dancer, too, like Carissa."

Sawyer looked up at Evangeline and saw the worry in her eyes. Jessica had been in Vegas three weeks.

"How can she do that, Sawyer?"

He thought of how to answer her, not wanting to make matters worse. "Well—"

"I can't get any information out of her. Did she say anything to you about going on to California? I thought that was what she wanted to do. Everything's changing."

"No, she didn't mention California," he sighed. "But we should trust her, Vangie." He reached for her hand and cupped it in both of his. "She has to find her own way. It might not be the route we've planned for her, but we have to trust she'll arrive at the same destination, eventually."

"But she wanted to go to college? Travel the world? Now I don't think she's going to go, you know? She's stuck in Vegas with the silly notion of becoming a dancer. They dance naked there. What are we going to do? I think we should go get her and bring her back, Sawyer. That's what I think." Evangeline worked herself into a tizzy.

Sawyer moved closer to her and stretched his long arm around her shoulders, pulling her close. "Vangie, we have to admit that her dream was put on hold over a year ago, my dear. She's still working her way through it. We can't help her, for even though she says she's over what happened, we both know she isn't. So, we must give her some space, believe in her, be there for her when she wants us, and trust she'll do what's best. Can you do that?"

Evangeline leaned her head against Sawyer's shoulder. "I don't know. And I don't know what I'd do without you, I really don't."

"You don't have to do without me." He continued, "I've been meaning to talk to you—"

At that moment, a cry came from upstairs.

"Oh no, that's little Martha. I've got to go. She's having a hard time sleeping lately without me lying down with her. Kids can be a handful at bedtime. Sometimes they just don't want to go to sleep."

Sawyer stood and reached for his jacket on the chair. "I'll be going then, will leave you to it. Will I see you tomorrow?"

"Tomorrow, yes." She bounded up the stairs. "Bye. Lock the door behind you."

Sawyer walked to his car in a worrisome dread. He questioned Jessica's maturity to be out on her own, especially in a city like Las Vegas with a bunch of young girls, and especially so soon after what had happened to her. Yes, although he didn't admit it to Evangeline, he worried too. And he didn't know what to do about it either.

14

Wylie Cramer came home to Skyler from New York for the summer. His first year at Harvard had been a difficult one for him. Although he had a bright mind, it seemed as if he couldn't concentrate on school. He had all the signs of smoking too much dope, if anyone would have noticed; most of his friends did the same. He and his buddies seemed to be carrying their high school antics into college, it was all about 'fun and games' to them – sex, booze, drugs.

Lucky for Wylie, his father intervened and cleaned up after him again, got him through his first year by pulling a few strings, and Wylie pulled a few strings of his own by paying for answers to questions on final exams, a lucrative business that ran rampant among the students. Of late, investigations were taking place however, complaints had been made and a few students were ratting on the others.

So, his cheating days might be over, his second year might entail some serious studying. He was doubtful there would be a second year at Harvard.

The first week back in Skyler bored Wylie, all his buddies were off working in other cities as interns. One morning when he came down for breakfast, Evangeline Sanford and her helper were cleaning the foyer.

She had worked for Judge Cramer's family for years, same as her mother Alba had before she died. And although Evangeline had considered quitting after their son's attack on her daughter, she couldn't afford to lose the Cramer account. She worked for seven families in Skyler, spending half a day in each home every week. She did service for special dinners and events too, which happened to be more than what one would expect in such a small town.

Wylie walked past her in the foyer, but glanced back, remembering what she had said to him the week after the gang-rape. He'd run into her on the porch the day he left home for New York, a hasty escape some would say.

He remembered how she stood in front of him, blocking his way with raised hand and three stiff fingers pointing at his face. It had startled him. Then she had said in a guttural, forceful voice: 'Wylie Cramer, if you ever, *ever* touch my girl again or any one of my babies in your lifetime, you can kiss your fuckin' ass goodbye and prepare to burn in hell. And if you don't believe me, just you try it, you son of a bitch! I don't care who your father is or what he does; it means nothing to me when it comes to my family. You are the scum of the earth for what you did to my baby girl. I put a hex on you, here and now!' She gestured with outstretched hands and fingers, clapped her hands once, and walked past him and into the Cramer house to do her morning chores.

He hated to admit it, but it had put a bit of fear in him at the time, and it still raised his anxiety level when he thought about it. Her eyes had peered directly into his soul that day and hit their mark. He knew a bit about voodoo, had never really believed in it, but at that moment when she confronted him, maybe, just maybe, voodoo existed. If so, Evangeline just might be a practitioner, she had the look. Her words had chilled his bones then, and the memory of it still did.

When he turned and looked back at her that summer morning a year later and saw her eyes again boring into his, he decided it might be time to put some real effort into getting out of Skyler as soon as he could. Even if things weren't working out at Harvard, he had to go somewhere.

One of his classmates had taken a summer internship in Las

Vegas at one of the hotels; he could go there while he had free time on his hands before deciding about going back to school in the fall.

With nothing for him in Skyler anymore, the lure of Vegas 'hotties' helped him make the decision to fly the coop to Vegas the next morning.

15

A natural-born dancer, Jessica won top spot in a lineup of twenty-five girls in a new show opening at the Oasis.

Although not her idea to try out for a dance spot, she figured since being there with her friends who were also auditioning, she would do it for fun. Besides, she loved dancing.

Four of them were chosen: Janelle, Chauntelle, Carissa, and Jessica. Tiffany didn't make it. Jessica couldn't believe she had, and Tiffany hadn't.

She didn't know how to tell her mama and Uncle Sawyer she had become a show dancer in Las Vegas at $2500 a week. What would they say? They expected her to go to college in the fall. Maybe she wouldn't tell them just yet. Maybe she wouldn't last. Maybe they would fire her because she couldn't keep up with the professional dancers. Maybe she would quit and go to college in September. A lot of maybes.

Rehearsals were grueling. Jessica didn't expect it to be so hard. Most of the show girls had extensive ballet and dance training, some had been members of ballet companies. All of them were tall, long-legged beauties, and that's where Jessica excelled. She learned quickly, carrying herself regally, moving sinuously, and keeping an alluring look on her face, the rule. She had it down pat by the end of the second week. Her gracefulness astounded the choreographer and the dance instructors. Becoming a truly gorgeous showgirl, not a burlesque dancer, not vulgar or bawdy, the girls took their work seriously. Showgirls were not strippers or escorts. Showgirls provided glamour. It took practice and grace to accomplish the status of a classic showgirl, and Jessica fast became looked upon as possibly one of the best in the new crop. That's what they were telling her, and her paycheck reflected it.

She took pride in being the best, and being complimented. It became a way for her to throw herself into something to hide the fears that had been flooding her lately. She thought the memories of the attack were buried forever by the time she graduated high school in Ashville, but lately it all resurfaced. She found herself shying away from any man that would approach her when she and her friends were shopping or at the gym. Even when she jogged in the park, heads turned, and men would stare. It bothered her. But she knew she'd have to get over it. On a stage every night, dancing half-nude, she'd have to get used to the stares.

On opening night, everybody had an extreme case of nerves. They'd been rehearsing with the complicated headdresses and the elaborate costumes all week. For a young girl who had never been out of North Carolina, Las Vegas represented a world of incredible glamour and glitz. It mesmerized Jessica, and at the same time was frightening.

Halfway through the opening night, Jessica became totally caught up in the performance. She loved it. As she stood near the edge of the stage, posing while the male singer belted his last song of the night, she looked down into the audience. Many eyes were upon her, male and female. She was drawn to the dark eyes of one man staring up at her. He sat in a booth very near the stage. She'd never seen so much gold jewelry on a man. His hair was black, and skin was very tan. He was applauding. The applause crescendoed and filled the giant showroom. Jessica had never experienced anything like it before. Her cue came and she began to prance across the stage with the other dancers leading into another pose and more applause.

The curtain closed.

After the shows, the dancers would change into their street clothes or evening clothes, depending on their plans for the night. It had been two months since opening night, time for a girl's night out. Jessica and Carissa, along with a couple of the other dancers, new-found friends, were going to dinner and play some slots at MGM Grand. Tonight, they were going out to have their own kind of fun.

As they left the dressing room, security flanked the doors to keep unwanted male gawkers at bay. One so-called gawker yelled at Jessica.

"Hey, Jessica! Jessica Sanford! Remember me? Over here." The guy tried to break through the guards whose arms were spread to prevent him from getting to her. "It's me, Wylie Cramer. C'mon, Jessica. You know me. Tell 'em."

Jessica froze. She couldn't believe it. She screamed at the guards. "Keep that creep away from me! You hear me?" She ran down the corridor towards the stage door that led outside the building, her gal pals following, trying to catch up.

They burst through the doors where they saw Jessica bending over, holding her stomach, hysterical and breathless. "How did he find me? He's from Skyler," she screamed. "I can't stay here. I have to leave Vegas."

Carissa tried to cajole her. "Jessica, hold on. Calm down. C'mon, stop it. What's the matter?"

"Keep him away from me." With terrified eyes, she looked at Carissa and whispered, "That's Wylie Cramer. He and his friends raped me when I was sixteen. In the back of a pick-up truck." She began screaming again, doubling over. The other dancers surrounded her, not knowing what to do, telling her they wouldn't let him hurt her.

Also, outside, standing a few feet from the girls, the handsome man with all the gold jewelry, who had been a regular since the show opened, stepped forward. He frowned and said something to his cohorts before approaching Jessica.

"Excuse me; is there something I can do?"

Still shaking, sobbing, and terrified, Jessica jumped behind Carissa.

"It's a guy that hurt Jessica really bad, back in North Carolina.

47

In there waiting outside the dressing room. Scared the shit out of her," Carissa said, shielding her dear friend.

"What's his name?" the man asked.

"Wylie Cramer, in the corridor inside," Carissa said. "He's probably trying to get out here right now."

"We gotta go," Jessica cried.

"Wait, wait. How can I get in touch with you?" he asked hurriedly as they began running to their car.

Carissa yelled back, "At the show, we'll be back tomorrow night."

16

The next night Jessica had been assured by her manager and the security staff that Wylie Cramer would not be allowed in the showroom or anywhere near the corridors behind stage or outside the stage door. They assured her she wouldn't be bothered. Guards were everywhere.

A normalcy, stalkers and angry husbands and wives, jealous boyfriends and girlfriends of the performers were a common occurrence in the world of Vegas entertainers. Security set up strict precautions to defend their dancers, but occasionally, someone would slip through.

When Jessica arrived at the casino that afternoon they already had photos taken by the security cameras for her to identify and had immediately set up guards to keep him off the premises.

But still, when Jessica went onstage in the first number her eyes automatically scanned the audience to make sure she didn't see Wylie. Instead she saw the man who attempted to protect her the previous night, the good-looking man with the gold jewelry in the same seat he had the night before – a handsome devil, as her mama would say.

During the second number, he smiled up at her while she struck a pose downstage, and he nodded as she came nearer the stage's edge, stopping in another dance pose in unison with the other first-line girls. She flashed a super-wide smile back at him.

He nodded again, blowing her a kiss.

After the show a security guard delivered a business card to her in the dressing room. It read: Mario Russo at your service. Nothing else printed on the card. On the back the handwriting read: *Wylie Cramer is history. Join me for dinner? Meet in Casino?*

Jessica showed the card to Carissa. "What do think this means?"

"My god! I think it's clear what it means. Let's check him out, Jessica. C'mon. I'll go with you to ask some questions. You don't have to say a word if you don't want to. I'll do the talking. I'm curious about Wylie Cramer."

The two girls exited together, their other friends had dates and had already left for the night.

In the corridor leading to the casino, Jessica suddenly stopped. "I don't want to do this, Carissa. I'm not ready."

"What do you mean you're not ready? C'mon, I'm with you," Carissa said as she pulled Jessica forward. "You need to lose that fear. I wish you would have told me sooner what happened to you in Skyler. You must work through this, Jessica. Withdrawing isn't the answer. You don't have to go with him alone anywhere. I'll stick close. Okay? Let's just find out what this is about, okay? And what he did to Wylie."

As they entered the casino from the corridor, Mario stood, waiting. He immediately came towards the girls, and reached for Jessica.

He took her hand and held it up to his lips. "My dear, dear girl. I am so sorry you were frightened by that, that useless reprobate last night. I promise you he will never touch you or gaze upon your lovely blue eyes again. He is gone. I have seen to it."

"What do you mean, he is gone?" Carissa retorted, raising her eyebrows at Jessica.

One of Mario's henchmen stepped forward and touched Carissa's shoulder, "Just like the man says, he is gone. Your friend

50

doesn't have to worry about him showing up here. He ain't gonna bother her anymore. Okay? My name's Frank, would you like to join us for dinner?"

Jessica spoke up, "Yes, she would. Yes." She looked a little worried, but nodded approval at Carissa.

"That will work," Carissa said as she put her arm through Frank's.

"Jessica?" Mario said as he offered his arm. The four of them and two other men walked across the casino to the north side entrance where a Limo was waiting.

"This restaurant that we're going to was fashioned after its namesake in Paris, La Caupole," Mario said. "As you will see, it has a a dome in the center held up by pillars, just like the one in Paris. I've been to the original."

They arrived and made their way across the café to a table for four on a curtained platform in the corner.

He continued with the history, "It was a favorite haunt of Dali, Hemingway, Fitzgerald, Calder and Picasso. So in here they put up duplicate paintings, portraits, photos and other artifacts on the walls. Although the food in the Paris café isn't as good as it is here in Vegas. French Chef Boulud sees to that."

A super-elegant dinner, over and above what the girls expected, and Mario and cohort, Frank, were polite and cordial. The two-hour dining experience topped the charts for the ladies. When it came time to call it a night, they returned to the Oasis.

"Shall we walk you to your car?" Frank asked.

"Sure, if you want," Carissa said to the tall Italian man that had stolen her heart during dinner. No two ways about it, Carissa and Frank were both smitten.

They followed the corridor to the employee exit, flashing ID to the guards along the way.

Mario asked Jessica if he could see her the next day, since Mondays she didn't work. She gave him her telephone number and said she'd have to wait and see how she felt the next day, whether she'd be up to anything or not, she might want to rest. He said he would call.

That night as the girls got ready for bed, with Jessica's

permission, Carissa brought the other three up to speed on what had happened the night before with Wylie Cramer at the casino and told them of Jessica's rape back in Skyler.

The girls were mortified and encouraged Jessica to talk about it, not to keep it in. They were feeling so sad for her and told her so.

Jessica talked a little at first, remembering, then as she worked herself up to such an emotional state of crying and sobbing, she found it impossible to go on.

Carissa held her. "It's okay, Jessie. You're safe with us. And if it's true what Mario said, you'll not be bothered by that fuckin' asshole ever again."

Jessica sat straight up and wiped her eyes. "I wonder what he meant when he said never again. You don't think he killed him, do you? I mean, do you think that's what he meant?"

"Well, I don't know. But I think it's just like he said. You'll never see him again, whatever it means. I think we all agree he deserves whatever he got." Carissa said.

Jessica frowned, shrugged her shoulders, and then crawled into bed. "All I know is I'm dog tired, and I feel like I could sleep for a week."

PART TWO
Rachel O'Neill

17

Summers in Cornwall on the southwest coast of England brought perfect weather, according to Rachel O'Neill, not too hot, not too cold. Climate supplied one of the main reasons she chose to live in that part of the world. She always said, "Latitude of fifty degrees and above suits me just fine, nothing below."

It'd been twenty years since she moved to England from California, nineteen years of it in Cornwall. She still owned property in the States, however: a beloved log cabin in Montana that once belonged to her mother. She went there as often as she could.

In England, she bought the marvelous hillside home she lived in from her dear friend Paul, and she still had the first house she bought when she first moved to Cornwall - a charming cottage on the bluff overlooking Newlyn Harbor. She had rented the cottage to a pleasant elderly lady, a retired shop keeper from London, but now she wanted to sell it, had offered it to the renter.

Rachel had decided to downsize, not because of the money, but of the need to unclutter her mind. She even owned half interest in a handsome four-story house atop Montmartre in Paris, with her friend Janet. Rachel used it as a get-a-way when she needed inspiration for her writing or just a change of pace. But her preference of Cornwall, and where she lived most of the time in the three-story house on the hill with an unobstructed sea view, dominated her choices.

Already in her sixties, Rachel couldn't fathom being that old, and didn't like to think of it, but nevertheless each year brought her closer to the beginning of her seventh decade. Which was the reason she felt the need to get things in order so that whatever happened, a mess wouldn't be left for her son and friends to sort out. She felt the need to hurry before D day arrived.

Standing before the full-length mirror in her bedroom, walls covered with pink rose-bud wallpaper, she took a good, long look at herself. She saw an ordinary woman, not as curvy as she used to be, a bit on the short side, auburn hair pulled back to the nape of her neck, a black scarf knotted around the rubber band holding her thick hair in place. She inspected the smooth, clear olive complexion she liked. There were a few freckles still visible on her nose. A nose that didn't seem to be as turned up as it used to be. *Does aging make noses bigger?* She didn't wear face or eye makeup, only lipstick, always wore it. She wore lipstick day and night, believed it kept her lips from drying up and becoming wrinkly and thin like other women as they aged. Those who didn't buy silicone injections, that is. She could get fillers and injections for the wrinkles that were becoming more and more prevalent, but the fear of needles kept her from doing it, plus being afraid of not looking like herself, same as most women who had the procedures. Basically, her looks were okay, she just didn't care for the wrinkles. Not bad for her age, she noted as she preened and stretched in front of the mirror. She'd seen worse.

The house phone on the bedside table rang, interrupting her self-perusal. "Hello?"

"Rachel, you're home."

"Why, hello, Paul. Of course, I am. Where did you think I'd be?" she laughed. One of her favorite people.

Paul chuckled as he pushed his blond hair from his forehead, and stretched out across his leather sofa. "Well, I never know if you're traveling or not these days."

"Other than the short weekend trips up and down the coast, I haven't been anywhere lately. So, what are you up to?

"Oh, just been thinking about you. Any trips to London

planned? He said, crossing his fingers.

"No, haven't thought about it. Why?"

"Well, I'd just like to see you, that's all. Anything wrong with that?"

"Not at all. How are the boys?" Deliberately changing the subject.

"Not boys anymore. Jake is 19, Pauli is 17. They're in California rooming with their grandmother. But then she's never there, is in New York most of the time. They are so independent now that they are at UCLA. So I have an even bigger void in my life." He sat up and reached for the can of Diet Pepsi sitting on the glass cocktail table.

"I know it must be hard," she said, feeling sad for him.

"Yes, I'm missing Belinda more these days. What's her name filled that void for a while, but it was a mistake in marrying the nanny who was a Belinda look-alike."

"It all happened too fast for you, Paul. You didn't take enough time to finish grieving. You needed a nanny for the boys, and she resembled Belinda so much … well … you were looking for a replacement. But I don't need to tell you, you've figured it out by now. So what are you thinking these days?"

"I don't know. But I must make a change. Tell you what, come to London for a weekend. Can you? I need to talk to somebody."

"I can't right now, Paul. I'm sorry. I'm working on the last draft of a novel, trying to beat a deadline. But I promise I'll call you when I have a break, okay?'

"Okay, do try and come as soon as you can."

"I will, I promise. Gotta go now. Bye," she said and hung up. She plopped on the bed and put her hands over her face. Feeling guilty for lying to Paul. She could tell he still hurt, but she knew she couldn't console him just now. She was too busy consoling herself.

It had been three years since her husband, Maxim Ballenchine, had a fatal heart attack five days into their honeymoon. On a cruise ship in Barcelona, he died in his sleep.

After mourning his sudden death for three months in Moscow with the Balanchine family, Rachel returned to her own home in England, still grieving, but with every intention to recover from the devastation of losing yet another man with whom she had fallen so completely in love: first Pete several years before, then Maxim.

It had taken her a long time to dare to even think about marrying Maxim after Pete, and now she wished with all her heart she had done it sooner. Not only because she would have had more time with Maxim, but because she might have recognized early warning signs of the impending doom and would have insisted he go for a medical examination. Maybe she would have noticed something that would have helped to save his life.

Rachel stood up abruptly. She needed coffee. With her fingertips, she stroked the top of the antique mahogany chest on her way out of the room. She loved antiques and collectibles. Her houses reflected that. Didn't matter how many floors or the size of the rooms, she filled her houses to the brim with treasures from her wanderings and travels.

In her kitchen, she picked up an already poured cup of coffee and took a sip. Cold, she put it in the microwave. Rain pelted the windows and grounds outside, sounds of music to her ears; she loved the summer storms that pounded Cornwall.

She took the hot cup of coffee into the living room and sat in her favorite overstuffed floral chintz chair facing the huge picture window and a magnificent view of the tossing and churning sea. She figured she may as well continue with another morning of reflection, which seemed to be a habit these days. No use fighting it.

Rachel's own health had been shaky the first three months after Maxim died. She had to be aware of her health always, due to a serious bout of Pneumonia she'd had a few years prior, almost died. So, she normally plied herself with food supplements and vitamins to prevent it happening again. As a rule, she wouldn't let her system become depleted of the required nutrients and minerals. But after Maxim died, she bottomed out and became very sick, but luckily no pneumonia. In Moscow, Maxim's brother Valentin and his wife Della had insisted she stay longer so they could watch over her, but she couldn't do it. She returned to Cornwall to work through her own grief and health.

She wanted to be alone in her own thoughts and in her own beloved surroundings. It was the way she did things, worked it out alone. She knew how to survive pain, and by now she felt like a expert in overcoming whatever ill befell her. But mainly she always gravitated to her own familiar ground where she found comfort, where she could get a grip on reality, where she could heal while easing back into her own life. Alone, this time, meant getting back to life before Maxim. Or maybe more accurately put - life *after* Maxim.

Rachel felt she would never recover from the chain of deaths in the past years. First her father, before she came to England. Second, her precious mother died in Montana on the Blackfoot Indian Reservation. Then, not long after, her dear friend Ethan Philips, who had initially invited her to England, and who she almost married, succumbed to injuries from an auto accident on his way to visit Rachel in Cornwall. Fourth, Rachel mourned the death of her fiancé Pete Bell, murdered in Brazil by poachers. She barely had time to recover from Pete's tragic death, when her best friend Belinda Newland, Paul's sweetheart of a wife died of Lymphoma. Last was Maxim, her husband who died of a heart attack on their honeymoon.

Tragedies, one after the other – six of her beloved beings, gone.

Many times, she fought the feelings of being a jinx to those closest to her. For a time, she feared starting up relationships, she withdrew. But she knew, deep in her heart, that had nothing to do with it. Still, she couldn't understand why kind and good people died while the ruthless and evil lived on and on. Didn't make sense. Those were the times she questioned the existence of a higher power. Seemed unfair.

So, to Rachel no place suited her more to stabilize and revitalize than her own backyard, in her own nest, in Cornwall near the steadfast, strong sea and the age-old indestructible villages that were nestled into coves and green valleys along England's southwestern coastline. That consolation would always be there, she'd always have that, it would never leave her, the only constant in her life. The pull to Cornwall still had her in its grip, even after all the sadness and sorrow. And amidst it all, she had cozy camaraderie with the people of the land that quelled her soul. It always rescued her from the depths.

Now after spending three years of healing and nurturing herself once again in her favorite environment, with reading and writing, gardening, and gazing upon a unique creation through her picture windows high on the Newlyn Harbor hillside, and inhaling sea air as she strolled back and forth along the edge of the English Channel, and while visiting her pub friends at The Ship Inn in Mousehole and Swordfish in Newlyn, and driving to other villages up and down the Celtic Sea coast, browsing through antique shops, sitting in sidewalk cafes ... it all had been successfully therapeutic and brought her back to the land of the living.

That stormy, summer morning as she sat by the window sipping coffee from one of her favorite English bone china cups, she thought of hopping a plane to California to go visit her son in Malibu. She missed her son Devin and his son – her only grandchild, her only family. Being Godmother to Paul's two sons equated to family, she supposed, but they too were in California. She felt the urge to hold and hug her adorable grandson, nearly three years old. She would visit with her Godsons too. Yes, she needed family now.

Her cell phone rang. She set the cup on the Hepplewhite side table next to the chair and ran into the kitchen. "Damn, why didn't I have the phone with me? Dammit!" Out of breath, she grabbed it from the countertop and saw the caller on the led screen. "Anita, hi! How the heck are you?"

"Well, I'm hunky dory, so, how are you? Ready to get back to work?" Anita lay in her West L.A, bed, watching TV.

"Oh, I'm fine. Working on another one, a thriller I hope. But you know what happens every time I try a departure from contemporary romantic, it works its way right back. Are you sick? You don't sound right."

"Just a damn cold, can't breathe through my nose. A California summer cold. I'm so glad to hear you're writing, Rachel. What is it now, four novels in two years? Wow! Keep that up and you'll be churning them out faster than Daniele Steele. But that's not why I'm calling, honey. I'd like to put you out on tour this fall, are you up to it? Book festivals, conferences, book signings. Got some good possibilities for keynotes and workshops. Does that interest you at all? We need to get you back out there, baby. This agent's coffers are getting low."

Rachel picked up the French Press of coffee and took it with her back into the living room. "Well, I don't know about that. Is it necessary, I mean will it make a difference in sales if I go on tour? I hate doing those things. I had just decided to cut back on them." She poured herself another cup and sat in the chair. A sailboat crossing from Newlyn to Penzance caught her attention. The sun peeped through the clouds that were drifting away with the storm.

"It isn't about sales, dearie. You're a best-seller now, we don't have a problem there, that's taking care of itself. It's about keeping you visible, creating more interest, back list, movie deals, yada yada yada. You know what I mean? Movies equate more moola for you, you know, and of course more for me."

Rachel laughed, "I get it."

But Anita knew she didn't get it. Anita's ulterior motive to pull Rachel out of her house had been uppermost in her mind. She worried about her prized writer and dear friend, not because of the business entirely, but because Rachel had the tendency to become a total recluse and withdraw into herself. She had the tendency to do that anyway, and since the death of Maxim, she seemed to be folding up and disappearing into herself.

"Hey, I can always use more money, honey." Anita clicked the channel changer to a Lifetime movie, and shifted her shoulders up onto her pillows.

"Okay, what you got in mind?"

"I'll email you a potential itinerary in a couple of days. Look it over and let me know what you think. We're talking Los Angeles, San Francisco, Seattle, Vegas, Denver, and New York. Writers' conferences mostly. I'll send you the particulars."

"Alright. But I'm not promising anything. Really, not my cup of tea. And I especially do not like speaking engagements. You know that. I'll do panels, but not keynotes. Maybe workshops. Maybe. Those unnerve me too."

"Just take a look. Okay?" Anita reached for her glass of wine on the bedside table. "It'll be September through December – ending up in Vegas, maybe for New Year's. Might be fun. I might even join you in Vegas on New Year's Eve, if it works out. Call me after you look it over."

"Okay, okay." Rachel's pulse was racing as she ended the call. She knew she needed a shot in the arse and that certainly would be a big one. Maybe the kids could meet up with her in Vegas, she could invite her gal pals for New Year's Eve too, all five of them. They were family too. *Wouldn't that be fun, another New Year's Eve together*?

Born in Malibu the spring of the year Maxim died, her

grandson had to be how old now? She counted back and realized it had been two years since she'd first seen the baby, since Devin and his wife had brought him to England for his first birthday. Yes, time to make the effort. Time to go.

It might be a good idea to spend time at the cabin in Montana while in the States too. Her dear friends Allegra and Connie Brown had moved from Malibu to Montana and were living on Allegra's family ranch outside of Kalispell. They built their own log cabin, a few miles below the forest line, not far from Rachel's property.

Rachel missed Allegra. She missed all her gal pals, had been thinking about all five of them lately – Shellie in Switzerland, Amanda in Brussels, Janet in Paris, and Della in Moscow, and of course Allegra in Montana. They were all a great distance away from her, and from each other. She wished they were closer. Yes, it would be good to see them all again.

Rachel stared at her empty cup for a few moments, remembering. She thought about Allegra and Connie, who had both owned homes and had been neighbors of her son Devin in Malibu. After Allegra and Connie married they moved to the Montana McAdams family ranch where Allegra's brother ran cattle. It thrilled him that his sister finally made the decision to come home. But the Browns built their own gigantic log home, further up into the foothills.

Yes, Rachel would go to the States in September for her birthday, she decided. She'd stay through the winter. That would give her the rest of the summer in Cornwall to finish the final draft of her latest novel, a military thriller with a bit of romance - had to write romance, couldn't get away from it even though she tried. It came natural to her. This would be the first thriller though, if she could pull it off.

Picking up her cup and French press, she went into the kitchen and telephoned her son Devin in California to tell him what she thought. "Hi, Devin. It's yer ma."

"Mom! Been meaning to call you. I ... well ... I have something to tell you. Are you able to talk now, you got a few minutes? You alright?" Devin hadn't looked forward to having this discussion with his mother, but might as well get it over with. Better now than later, or her hearing it from somebody else.

"Something's wrong. I hear it in your voice." Rachel could

always tell when Devin had bad news. In fact, they both easily read each other's tones and moods, no covering up between the two of them. Didn't work.

"Hold on, let me get my coffee." He stalled. "Alright. Here it is. Uh … I'm divorced. Final papers signed last week. She left me. She took the dogs and the baby and left."

"What happened?"

"My fault. I lost my temper and we both said some things that couldn't be taken back. I stormed out and flew to Vegas for a few days. Have a home there I'm building with the construction crew, and decided to just stay there till things cooled down. Do you remember Jennifer? Jennifer Locke? She's one of my engineers. We got together one of the nights in Vegas and there you go."

"You're saying you hooked up with Jennifer in Vegas while you were married?"

"That's right. Had a few too many beers, and well … I felt bad about it, but didn't dare tell THE EX, that's what I call her now."

Rachel chuckled, his humor not lost on her. "So, what happened?"

"Well, when I came home, THE EX had disappeared, lock stock & barrel. She left me a note, said she was fed up with my temper and everything else. Said she knew I was fooling around, I'd be hearing from her attorney, she was filing for divorce and was going to take me to the cleaners. I knew she would, too."

Rachel didn't say anything.

"Mom?"

"So, it's done?"

"Yes, final last week," Devin said. "Signed sealed and delivered."

"When did all this start?"

Devin sighed, "The end began nine months ago. For a while I hoped she'd come back and I wouldn't have to go through all this and tell you."

"I knew something was off-kilter the last time we talked. Don't hold back when we talk, Devin. I worry about you and it's best I know the truth. I'm always here to support you no matter what, you know that. Never hesitate to tell me anything. So, she's not coming back? You don't think you can convince her?"

"Mom, truth is, I'll really miss my son, I really will, but to be honest, I won't miss her. She's high maintenance, and her over the top emotional roller-coaster moods, the loudness and crassness, well ... it got to me and embarrassed me in front of my friends and clients. I didn't enjoy being around her anymore. I see the difference when I'm with Jennifer. A world of difference. I need calmness in my life, mom. I really do. Like I said, I'm sorry about losing my son, but not about losing her. I hope you understand."

"Are you kidding?" Rachel returned to the living room. "I understand completely, having been there a time or two myself. But you aren't losing your son. You can keep that relationship going. It'll be difficult, but you can figure that out. What you must do is make sure your business is protected, hon. And fight against depression while you're going through this, so it won't affect you or the business, or your relationship with the baby. That's very important, keeping everything going. You know how it is, being a product of a broken home yourself. It's a good thing we incorporated the business. I think we'll be alright. I'll call my attorney in the morning."

"Don't worry about it, mom. I already talked to him. He's on it. Everything's taken care of. You just focus on what you're doing, and I'll take care of business. Okay?" He coughed, a loud, hoarse cough. "Dammit! Gotta stop smoking."

"That sounds terrible, Devin."

"Yea, got allergies too, I can't seem to shake it. Going to the doctor on Tuesday for a complete checkup. Now don't you start worrying about me. I'm okay. What I want to know is how you're doing?" He continued to cough, intermittently.

Rachel took a deep breath, sat on sofa. "Oh, I'm doing good. Writing up a storm, another novel, a thriller this time. Well, romantic thriller, whatever that is." She laughed. "And I'm coming to the States in September, that's why I called you. I'm staying till after New Year's."

"That'll be great. You can plan on staying here, for sure. Plenty of room, and you've still got your own wing. You can meet Jennifer." He coughed again.

"Devin, that sounds awful."

"It's okay, goes away."

"Well, I won't be in California the whole time, will be on a

64

junket. Writers' conferences, yada yada yada. Stuff like that ... stuff I hate doing. But while I'm in your neck of the woods, I'll stay with you. So, The EX won't be keeping the house?"

"No, she wants to live in Newport Beach, she's renting a condo on the beach right now, while looking for a house to buy. Go figure. If I didn't know any better, I'd think she has another guy on the hook. Who knows, maybe she does. I hope she does. I'm not angry. I like my calm life." He laughed, then coughed.

Rachel leaned back on the sofa, facing the window and the sea. "Well, just stay calm, give her whatever she wants that is reasonable. But, you'll share custody, right? You'll have to figure out all that."

"Got it covered, Mom. So, when are you coming?" He lit a cigarette and took a puff.

"First part of September, I'll let you know exactly as soon as I know all the wheres and whens."

"Okay, mom, I love you. And thanks for being the best mom in the world. For understanding and always being there for me."

"Hey, what are moms for? Love you too, honey. You keep me updated, let me know what's what, okay? Don't keep things from me. You're my only one, you know."

"I will."

Rachel stood up, "Okay, bye for now. I love you."

She stood for a few moments after ending the conversation, her hand on the back of the sofa, while staring out the window. *Changes ... always changes ... up to each of us, how we handle them ...* she remembered her mother Lily saying those words. *So true, Mama.*

18

Rachel woke up early, full of energy.

It had been a week since she agreed to do the tour that her literary agent Anita proposed. Just making the decision to do the tour seemed to give her a lift in disposition. It had always been that way with her. Travel raised her spirits. Planning and taking trips were partly engrained in her soul, same as having to be surrounded by flowers and being near the sea. Although it didn't have to be a sea, just a body of water. Even her cabin in Montana gave her that special fulfillment, by a lake. It made her feel one with herself, contented and whole, calm. At peace.

As she stood in the open doorway of her kitchen facing the expanse of blue as far as she could see - blue skies, blue sea - she closed her eyes and breathed deeply.

A vision flashed in her mind, the same one that had haunted her since a child. An elusive cabin in a forest. She came to learn that it had been her mother's cabin all along, in Northern Montana, not just an imagination. Before she discovered her mother, Lily, teaching at the Blackfoot Indian Reservation in Montana, before she realized the cabin on the edge of Glacier National Park was Lily's. Those early visions and dreams of a mountain cabin surrounded by trees and flowers beside a lake and stream, foreshadowed what was to come. How could she have dreamt it so exact and vivid?

Lily believed in dream interpretation, past lives and reincarnation, and she was a renown Native American spiritualist and teacher of religion and sacred rites. She believed their souls – mother and daughter - were connected in the spiritual world all those years, which is why Rachel had the visions. Nothing could destroy that.

When they met thirty years later, Rachel's spiritual education began, fueled by her mother's teachings and books. It continued in the years before her death.

Rachel remembered the two months she had spent alone in that same cabin the summer before she married Maxim. She'd gone to Montana to sell the cabin, to tie up loose ends before she married. But once there, what was to be for only two weeks, she knew she couldn't sell the place. How could she have even considered it? Too much of her mother remained within its walls; Lily's spirit permeated the cabin and the grounds. It was her legacy to Rachel, a haven and a reminder.

Rachel took another deep breath and sat down at the kitchen table. Her cell phone rang.

She quickly answered when she saw who it was. "Della, how are you?"

"That's what I planned to ask you. I'm glorious! What about you? You feelin' better? Doin' any travelin' yet? We're missin' you like the Devil, you know."

"Well, I am much better, I am. In fact, I'm planning to drive up the coast of Cornwall and spend a couple days in Port Isaac. It's my local get-away place, you know." Rachel giggled as she walked into the living room and stood looking out the bay window. She normally paced as she talked on the phone.

"Oh, I wanna go too, I love that charmin', little place. If we weren't flyin' to New York tomorrow, I'd come and go with you. Valentine is goin' to a restaurant convention and he's meetin' with some pretty famous chefs. It oughta be fun. I'll be callin' on some of my old friends in the publishin' world while he does his thing. Haven't done that in a bit."

"Sounds like fun, Della. Give my love to Valentine, I mean Valentin. You always foul me up by calling him Valentine," she laughed.

"He likes it, so I guess I'll be callin' him that forever. So what are you doin' besides taking weekend trips without me?"

"Well, I've been craving some heavy-duty travel, so I'm gonna be flying too, just like you. In fact, I'm going on a book tour, will be heading for the states in September, western part."

"Oh, that is grand, isn't it?" Her Irish brogue showed more than usual. "I'm so glad you're gettin' back into the swing of things, Rachel. Maybe you can fit Moscow in sometime after that. Will you promise me you will? Please say yes. I miss you so much."

"We'll figure something out. I promise," Rachel said with a glint of tears in her eyes. Talking to Della always took her right back to fresh memories of Maxim. She couldn't go back to Moscow yet. It would be too painful. But she would love to see Della.

"Okay, I'll call you when we get back and tell you all about New York. Got to run, loads to do between now and tomorrow. Love you, Rachel. You're still my sister-in-law, you know, and better yet, you're still my best friend … and sometime writing partner."

"I'm so grateful for you, Della. You make me laugh and smile all at the same time. And I can just visualize all that curly ginger hair bouncing around your head while you talk. And yes, I love you too. Bye …"

"Ta ta . . ." Della hung up.

Rachel wiped her eyes and picked up her jacket and the travel bag she'd packed that morning. She grabbed her keys and into the garage she went.

Off to Port Isaac for a change in landscape and mood. It always worked.

19

The picturesque coves along the western coast of Cornwall, in summer, drew hordes of tourists. Not that it didn't in winter, but the sunny, more colorful ambiance, and more people on holiday flock to the west during the summer season.

From March till August, film crews of the 'Doc Martin' television series inundated Port Isaac, the heaviest schedule in May and June. So, Rachel hoped she'd be able to find accommodations in the middle of June. If not, she'd go on to Tintagle, a larger town a few miles beyond Port Isaac, famous for its King Arthur Castle ruins.

She drove down the winding narrow road into the tiny cove village of Port Isaac. Pleasantly surprised she found it not as busy as she figured it would be. Too early in the day, maybe? Other than the tourist trade, Port Isaac was a lazy, peaceful little village, even with the fishermen going in and out for their daily catch. She figured the tourists were probably still in their rooms or at breakfast. The townspeople worked in the shops or in other villages, so they were all indoors somewhere.

She eased up the narrow one-vehicle lane that ran past 'Doc

Martin's office' to the grassy parking area at the top of the hill. Cars couldn't park in the village, but they could edge their way along the very narrow cobble stoned lanes to load and unload, or to get from one side of the cove to the other and up its steep sides to the roads above.

After parking at the top of the hill, she stepped from her car and took in deep breaths of the cool, sharp sea air wafting up the grassy slope from the rocky cove and stone breakwater wall below. A few people were at the water's edge picking up seashells and bits of sea glass. Gentle waves lapped up the meager beach where the small fishing boats were launched.

A few patrons were filing into Rachel's favorite café – The Mote. Didn't look like she'd be able to get one of the two outside tables, but she'd see how long the wait would be.

Finding sleeping accommodations topped her list. She'd try the Slipway Hotel across from the beach. Worth a try, although it probably was full, being the only hotel down in the cove. But there were others up the lanes, too.

She locked the car and began the trek down the lane to the heart of the village. No one at 'Doc Martin's office', a house where they filmed the show. No filming today.

Rachel learned that Port Isaac dated back to the 1500s when the pilchard fishery operated, and that fishermen still work from the Platt (a piece of land near the water's edge) in the tiny cove, unloading their catch of the day. She loved sitting at The Mote watching the small boats come in before sunset, listening to the men unload and kibitz before delivering their fish and then heading for their favorite pub.

At The Mote, situated right on the little beach of sorts, the Platt, and boat launch area, she stepped inside and asked one of the waitresses if she could put in her name for a table outside and asked how long the wait would be. At that moment the owner, Chad, stepped out of the kitchen to the bar.

"Hi, Chad. Busy busy, I see," Rachel said as she made her way to the small bar at the back of the house where he stood.

"You're back, Rachel. Good to see you."

"Can't stay away from this place for long, you know. My favorite getaway even though I live only an hour and a half away in another fabulous getaway town." She laughed.

"You here for the week?" He asked.

"Yes, in fact I'm looking for a place to stay, haven't booked one. Any ideas?"

"My buddy up the way might have a room." He touched her shoulder. "We all use him for overflow. Is that all you need? A room? Are you alone?"

"Yes, to all the above, I'm here to do some writing and nosing about, eating your fabulous food and drinking your wine. I'm easy to please."

"Have a seat on the bench over here. I'll give them a call. Want some coffee?"

"Would love some, yes. Black, no sugar."

20

Later that afternoon after a nap, Rachel showered, dressed, and headed for the Golden Lion Pub just a short walk down the lane halfway between The Old Schoolhouse Hotel, where she found accommodation, and The Mote. Chad had called the hotel and evidently there had been a cancellation and it hadn't been rented out yet. The perfect setting for Rachel, on the cliff to the right of the cove with an incredible view of the small harbor and most of Port Isaac.

So, her plan consisted of a happy-hour at the Golden Lion and then late dinner at The Mote. She'd made the eight o'clock reservation earlier with Chad. Then after dinner to the Slipway bar to finish off the night. A night of bar-hopping. She always found challenging conversations at the Slipway, although the Golden Lion had good ones too. One time she missed her dinner reservation, because she enjoyed the patrons so much in the Golden Lion, but tonight she would make sure she made it to The Mote on time. She craved the mouth-watering grilled salmon with apricot sauce and asparagus.

It was only a short downhill walk on the cobbled-stone lane from the hotel to the Golden Lion, less than two minutes. Her favorite bar stool was empty at the far end of the bar, backed by a tiny space of wall next to a window seat. She could watch, talk or listen to everybody that came in if she wanted and look down at the harbor if she wished. She had the view of the entire barroom, the small window seat next to her, and a booth by the double doors that opened onto the balcony, and another booth that flanked the other side of the doors near the entrance, plus the dining room beyond. Her barstool of choice was the perfect perch.

Late afternoon drinkers already crowded the balcony with an unobstructed view of the cove, its beach, and the sea beyond. The Old Schoolhouse Hotel could be seen from the balcony too, as well as Doc Martin's office up the embankment across the tiny bay.

When she stepped into the Golden Lion, there were a few locals on the barstools, mostly men, one woman. But, hallelujah! Rachel's corner stool remained empty. She rushed to it before any of the other patrons coming in the door behind her could grab it.

On her second glass of champagne, she thought how good it felt sitting on 'her' stool, that very minute, soaking up the local color, listening to and watching the mixed bag of Port Isaac people. She felt happy. Happier than she'd been in a long time.

One of the patrons got a bit loud. He and his mates were talking about the American gun control laws.

"What good does it do to take away all the guns?" he said to the bartender. "Tell me what good does it do? I mean they can't take them all away; there are millions in the hands of the people. I saw that on CNN today. No way, can't be done at this point in the game. It's a bit late, if you ask me."

The woman sitting next to him added: "I don't believe they want to take them all away, I think it's just the automatic weapons. Isn't it?" She looked down the way at Rachel. "Isn't that right, you're an American, aren't you?"

Rachel responded, "Yes, I think it's the automatic weapons and the cartridge clips over ten rounds."

The bartender spoke up. "I don't see how they're going to gather up all the illegal weapons and clips from those who already have them. There're 316 million people in the U.S. Impossible!" He picked up several beers for a previous order.

"You're right. I totally agree," Rachel replied. "I think the country's too big to take that approach, even if each state manages its own population and requires stricter gun registration laws. And if they stop future sales of weapons and clips, that'll only drive it underground, then we're in store for another crime wave, just like the thirteen years of prohibition back in the 20s, and now the drug wars. That's all we need. So, I don't know the answer. It's beyond me." She gulped the last of her champagne. "I'm glad I live in Cornwall."

The bartender reached for a bottle of champagne on ice behind him. "Would you like another?"

"That's affirmative," Rachel said.

"I remember you from before," he said.

"Yep, love it here in Port Isaac; come from Newlyn as often as I can."

"What's your name?"

"Rachel O'Neill."

The man nearest her on another barstool said: "An American Irishman to boot. Good God!"

The group laughed.

"A Brit, I prefer to say. Ancestors are from Scotland, Ireland, and England. They lived and bred in all three. I'm a byproduct, a mixture, if you will."

The woman laughed and said, "That's a great way of putting it. I would venture to say most of us Brits are a mixture, isn't that right, Teddy?" She hit the dozing guy sitting next to her. "Wake up, Teddy!"

"Wha— what's wrong? Time to go?" Teddy stuttered, suddenly bright-eyed.

Everybody laughed.

An attractive over six-foot man entered the pub, stepped up to the service end of the bar and ordered a beer. His accent sounded more Scottish than English, Rachel noticed. He wore a stocking cap, so she couldn't see his hair color, but his eyebrows were thick and black.

He glanced around the bar and dining room, then walked over to the double doors leading to the outside balcony, no seats. He spied the empty barstool next to Rachel and headed for it.

"Do you mind if I sit here," he asked, his penetrating eyes on her.

"No, not at all," she said, noticing his well-manicured, tan hands.

The barkeep set a beer in front of him.

Rachel ordered another glass of bubbly and smiled up at the man next to her.

"I think we have another Scot in our premises," one of the men down the bar said as he nodded at the stranger and glanced back at his buddies.

"Are you Scottish?" Rachel asked the newcomer.

"Northern England. Not Scotland. Although my ancestors were known to have lived on both sides of the border." He removed his cap, releasing a shock of unruly, curly black hair that fell to his neck and over his ears.

"Mine too. Originally from Scotland, way back. But I've never been there. England is my home now."

"You sound like you're from the states," he added.

"Yes, I'm a transplant. Love it here." She took a sip of the champagne the barman set before her. "Do you live around here or are you just visiting?"

"I live nearby. We have a family estate not far from here, near Tintagle. My mother is in hospital, just came from there. We're preparing for the worst. Sorting papers and all."

"Oh, I'm so sorry. Difficult to deal with that, I know. I've had to do it too." She remembered all she went through with her father's estate and then later her mother's - a trying time for her. Although her experiences were in the aftermath of her parents' deaths, at least his mother still lived.

Her mind flashed to Maxim's death, how smoothly Valentin had taken care of the estate and Maxim's wishes, making Rachel's transition almost seamless. A world of difference from what she had gone through in years past, even in dealing with her stepmother's death. She wondered if maybe men were better equipped at such things. Although Maxim had already created a will leaving Rachel his home and grounds in the country outside Moscow, which she signed over to Valentin. She didn't need another house to maintain, she had four already – one in the states, one in Paris, two in Cornwall. Besides it belonged to the Ballenchine family, she'd only been married four days to Maxim. But they insisted she keep the Trust he had left her.

"What brings you to Port Isaac?" the tall dark stranger asked Rachel. "Oh, by the way, my name is Stefan Evans. And yours is ...?"

"Rachel O'Neill." She offered her hand for a shake. "You've a beautiful name. It really is. Sounds almost made up. Is it? I mean you're telling me the truth? That really is your name? Stefan Evans?" She looked at him quizzically, squinting.

He laughed. "Yes, of course, that's what is on my personal papers. In fact, it reads Stefan Edward Blackbourne Evans. Is Rachel O'Neill your real name?"

"Sure is."

They both took a sip of their drinks, not seeing the raised eyebrows and grins from the patrons down the bar who had been eavesdropping.

"You didn't say where you live, Rachel?"

Rachel took another sip. "Not far from here. I live in Newlyn, near Penzance, you know where that is, right?"

"Yes, of course. I have business in Penzance on occasion."

"What is your business?" She looked at his tanned face and coal black hair, unusual for a Brit she noted.

"The wind turbine business. Manufacturing, selling, installing, servicing. I'm working with the Cornwall Council of Renewable Energy. We've installed dozens of wind farms throughout Cornwall, creating power and electricity without emitting hazardous waste and pollution into the environment."

"Oh my goodness. In my mind, England has always been years behind the U.S. That's incredible! You're improving, modernizing."

"I believe we are." He grinned. "We've a few turbines near Tintagle that I'm checking on while I'm here. Have you seen a turbine close up?" He leaned back and looked Rachel squarely in the face.

"No, I haven't. Haven't even noticed any over here. You can't miss them in the U.S. One of the largest groups is in California on Highway 58 near Tehachapi." She motioned to the barkeep for more champagne.

"Here, I'll get that," Stefan said to the bartender. "And I'll have another."

"Thank you," she said.

"As a matter of fact, there are 5000 turbines in the Tehachapi field. Around 3000 turbines near Palm Springs and 7000 near San Francisco. Those are the major farms," he said.

"So do you go there?"

"Have done, but I'm here mostly. This is new ground for us.

All of Europe is. Would you like to come out tomorrow to the turbines near Tintagle? We can go to lunch and I'll give you a tour."

"Sure, I'd love to. Where shall we meet?"

"I'm staying at the Slipway tonight, meeting people for dinner. Didn't feel I should be driving after imbibing. I wanted to relax for a night and take in the local color. We can meet at the Slipway in the morning, or here, wherever you want."

"What time?"

"Eleven?"

"Alright, eleven at the Slipway it is," she replied with a big grin.

"Now tell me what brings you to Port Isaac . . ."

21

When Rachel awoke at nine the next morning, she felt
energized. Considering the amount of alcohol she'd had the night
before, it didn't seem possible to feel as good as she did. However,
way too much to drink. A good thing she didn't do it all the time.

She slipped her nightgown from her shoulders, stepped out of it
and into the shower. Nightgowns were her passion. She collected
them, new and used. In fact, she shopped charity shops with a passion,
looking for long gowns of quality lace and silk, among other
collectibles. She had just taken off a pale yellow with wide ivory lace
straps and lace across the bodice, a vintage gown she found in a
Penzance charity shop. She couldn't understand how some women
wore flannel or jersey pajamas to bed - boring, hot, binding PJs. She
couldn't stand the warmness of them, would always get the sweats in
the middle of the night. She did own a flannel gown for cold nights,
but would always get up at one point and don a silk one.

As she showered she wondered if Stefan wore pajamas. Not
that it mattered one way or another, she certainly couldn't care less,
and she would never know anyway. She just wondered about it, told
herself it would be okay to wonder. But something about visualizing

him naked began to arouse her. It had been eons since she'd been aroused, she couldn't believe it was happening now. In fact, she had figured that part of her life had ended. But she felt a definite stir in her erotic zones, and laughed aloud. It might be nice to take a moment and masturbate to a climax, for she hadn't done it in a while. She laughed aloud again and as she shampooed, remembered when she first began masturbating.

At eleven years old, she had awakened one night feeling something happening down there, between her legs. It startled her. She had put her hand where the tingling took place and it increased when she touched herself.

As she remembered that first discovery she laughed again and quickly finished the shower. She decided she would give it a go when she called it a night. Right now, she had the promise of a delightful day before her and didn't have a moment to spare.

Rachel dried off with a towel and used the hotel's hair dryer to blow-dry her hair. Her new haircut took no care whatsoever. The most she would do to it after drying would be to use a flatiron to lift at the crown, to smooth and turn the ends under slightly. The straight A-line bob with bangs were the answer to her many years spent having to constantly style and curl her hair. She did none of that anymore. Very easy now, to just get up and go. She would also pull it back and secure it with a ribbon scrunchie into a short pony tail. It was all about easy. She didn't wear makeup either, only lipstick.

At 9:30, she checked her email and social websites, and all the rest she had to do to keep abreast of things.

There was an email from her son Devin, saying he couldn't wait to see her in September, but he might have to be away for three weeks. A new project in the Midwest had opened, and he would have to go if it came through. So, it would depend on that. If it came through, he suggested, maybe she should go on to Montana and come back through Malibu on her way home. Rachel answered that things had changed anyway. She would be doing book-signing gigs during the months in the States, so she'd work it all out as soon as she got her schedule. She told him she'd like to get up to Montana before winter anyway, maybe back to Malibu before Christmas, she'd let him know.

Then she read the email from her agent Anita listing the places she'd booked tentatively for Rachel's appearances. Newport Beach and Denver in September, Kansas City and Chicago in October, San Francisco and Seattle in November. Las Vegas the last week of December, putting her there for New Year's Eve. She'd never been in Vegas for New Year's Eve, so that interested her. It sounded festive. She'd invite the girls right away.

So, she'd go to Denver first after California, then up to Montana for the rest of the month until she had to go to Kansas City and Chicago. That would work. She'd have plenty of time to visit with Allegra and Connie, and she wanted to spend some time at the cabin. Then after Chicago and KC, back to Montana before she headed back west to those events. After that she'd play it by ear until Vegas. Sounded like a good plan, a bit scattered, but doable. She emailed Anita and told her to send the finalized trip details to her, ASAP.

The hour had passed quickly, she noticed. She closed her laptop and put on her jeans and rust-colored sweater, copper dangly earrings to match her hair and sweater, and brown boots. No black today. She opted to wear color instead, because she felt bright, colorful, and happy.

As she walked down the cobbled lane past the Golden Lion, she listened to the sounds of the sea sneaking into the cove. The breakwater buffered the waves that sometimes were quite large, sometimes spraying high above the rocks blocking their way, keeping the cove safe from catastrophe. Today it sounded gentle and calm. The birds were out for their morning feeding, their gull calls echoing down in the village rising from the sandy slope.

She loved the fresh smell of the ocean, nothing compared to sea air. Even from her house on the hill in Newlyn, she would stand on her grass and deep-breathe the pure air that surrounded her as she gazed from the far point of Mount's Bay stretching across to the opposite point of Newlyn Bay where she lived.

Rounding the corner by The Mote, she glanced to the right at the children playing in the low surf. The boats were already out, wouldn't return till afternoon.

Stefan drank coffee on the covered patio of The Slipway Hotel/Restaurant in the middle of Port Isaac village. He saw Rachel as she stood at the Mote looking toward the cove.

Other people were seated outside at the Slipway, some eating breakfast, some eating early lunch. He set the coffee mug down on the table in front of him and stood as Rachel came towards him. He gave her a welcome hug, then waved at the waiter to bring another cup of coffee for her. "You would like a cup of coffee, right?"

"Oh yes. Can't do anything without my coffee. I drink it all day long as a matter of fact. Thanks."

"So, did you sleep well?" he said as he sat across from her.

"Didn't wake up once till nine this morning. I feel very rested. Thank you." Memories of her shower filled her mind.

"I enjoyed the chat with you yesterday, was refreshing to hear the story about your family, your writing, and adventures. Makes mine seem staid and stuffy." He laughed, while reaching across the table and placing his hand on hers.

Rachel glimpsed into his gray eyes then averted her glance to the tinge of silver around his hairline that weaved its way back into the black strands, giving him a sophisticated, distinguished look. Stefan had all the characteristics of a romance novel Prince or Lord.

She chuckled to herself. She couldn't believe the men she'd met in her lifetime. Talk about fiction, no one would ever believe her. And now sitting here by this fictional romance character touching her hand, gave her goose bumps and tingles to the core.

"Rachel, I am undoubtedly pleased you are coming with me today. Would you be interested in going to the estate after lunch? I could give you a tour, it isn't far, is that alright? It might give you inspiration for one of your novels."

"Yes, of course," she gushed.

22

The drive up the Cornwall coast thrilled Rachel. Stefan's vehicle, a loaded Mercedes G-class four-wheel drive, rode like a dream. She'd never been in one so when she asked about it, he explained all the bells and whistles.

"This is the phone system. When an incoming call comes in, it appears on this dash display. I can push this button and answer it. No other equipment needed. Makes it perfect for me to conduct business while I'm on the road."

"I should guess so. Wow. I like that. You have the temperature controlled seats too, I see." Rachel said.

"It's a suitable vehicle for me, driving all over England, doing business."

"So, what do you drive when you're not doing business?' she asked.

"Obviously, I'm a Mercedes man. The SLS Coupe is my fun car. Have you ridden in one?" He glanced at Rachel, waiting for an answer.

"Yes. My agent in the states has one. She swears by it, says she wouldn't drive anything else. As for me, I'm a Jaguar and BMW fan, but right now I have BMWs. Didn't used to be as interested in cars, didn't matter what I drove or what anybody else drove. This has just happened over the last couple years. I drove my BMW M6 to Port Isaac, as a matter of fact. Guess I've become a car person in my old age." She laughed. "I've an X-5 four-wheeler to do my shopping and errands at home in Newlyn."

"I see. Seems we have similar vehicles, just different makes."

"Well, mine doesn't do what this one does. This is incredible. I may have to think about getting one." She smiled.

"Have you been to Tintagle?"

"Oh yes. Love to lunch at the castle." Rachel touched his hand resting on the seat beside him. "Well, not a castle, the castle hotel."

"Yes, yes. I know what you mean. Shall we have lunch there after we check on the wind field?"

"I'd love to, yes."

"Good. The estate is just a short distance north of Tintagle, so we'll go there after lunch. The windfarm is ten minutes southeast.

As they rode further inland northeast of Port Isaac towards Delabole, Rachel's thoughts ran rampant, from Maxim and how much she missed him to curiosity of Stefan – his work, his family – to her upcoming trip to the U.S. Her mind jumped all over the place. She finally shook her head as if shaking it out of her mind.

"Are you alright?" Stefan said as he witnessed the head shaking.

"Oh. It's nothing. I just sometimes fill my head with too much ruminating. Sorry. I need to stay in the moment, which is what I tell myself all the time. It's very perplexing." She smiled and touched Stefan's arm. "I'm okay. This is good for me, this ride, a departure from the norm. Thank you."

"I have the same problem, my mind playing games with me. It happens mostly at night when I'm alone, after dinner. That's when I over-think everything, wondering what if and how to. I dwell too much on the past and think too much about the future. Can't win either battle, you know," he said as he looked at her. "During the day, I'm so busy I don't have time to think. How do you spend your evenings?"

Rachel looked out the window at the green, hilly Cornwall countryside that she loved so much. "Oh, I read or watch movies; I have extensive collections of both – books and DVDs. And sometimes

I'll go to the pub to chat with the locals. I love doing that when the mood strikes." She turned towards Stefan, admiring his posture and how he gripped the steering wheel with determination, like a racecar driver. "I even write at night sometimes, but most of my writing I do during the day. On weekends, I take off to go antiquing or coming to places like Port Isaac. It's a simple life. Works for me."

This time he reached over and touched her hand. "Sounds divine. Have you heard of the AONB in Cornwall?" Stefan asked as he pulled up to a gate leading to the windfarm near Delabole.

"No, I don't think I have. What is it?" Rachel answered.

"It means Area of Outstanding National Beauty. It covers 370 square miles of Cornwall which is 27 percent of the county, separated into twelve separate areas considered National Park properties, of which eleven of the twelve cover the coastline. The twelfth is Bodmin Moor. Other counties throughout England have the same AONB designations as well. Delabole is part of the AONB region." He opened his door. "I'll only be a minute, need to check on something in the office. Are you alright here?"

"Of course, I'm enjoying the scenery," Rachel said as she smiled up at him holding the driver's door open.

"Will just be a minute." He shut the door and headed for the building.

She watched him go into the shed-type office, wondering if anybody else was in there, or if he was the only person. Surely there would be a watchman or someone on property to man the equipment.

Rachel opened the car door and stepped outside to get a better view of the fields stretching over the moor and to breathe in the air of the grassy terrain. She could only see four giant turbines and wondered where the rest of them were.

"Alright. We're set to go," Stefan said as he came out of the shed.

"I see four wind turbines, where are the others?"

"Only four at this farm," he said as he joined her. He motioned to the east, "About fifteen minutes further on there's another farm with twenty-two. But we won't be going there today. I just needed to check the instrumentation for this one. There are eight wind farms in Cornwall alone. My company has the management contract for them and for many in other counties, but I like to personally check those close to the estate when I'm in the area. Keeps my finger in the pie, so to speak. I like being in the field, gets boring stuck in the office all the time. Are we ready for lunch?" he said as he stepped to the vehicle and held open the passenger door, half bowing, gesturing for her to get in.

"Absolutely!" she said emphatically. Such a gallant man, she noted. She thought of the men she'd met since leaving the States in contrast with those she left behind. Of course, now older and wiser in the UK, it must account for the feelings, maybe her vibes had improved since her early years in the States. Also, one would think that experience had certainly added to her persona and improved her choices and decision-making processes in the past fifteen years.

"So, to the castle we shall go." Stefan interrupted her reverie, and at the same time wondered what kept her mind distracted from the moment. She seemed to be preoccupied, so he hadn't said anything after starting the car and returning to the road that led to Tintagle.

"Oh, yes. Yes. This is good," she said, realizing she'd been locked inside her head and hadn't noticed they'd left the farm. "I'm sorry. Didn't mean to ignore you. Sorry."

"No problem. We can't help it, you know. If we hadn't had a lifetime of experiences and events, we wouldn't do that, would we?" He smiled at her, noticing how her eyes sparkled when she looked at him. "Your eyes are green with little brown flecks in them. How unusual."

"It can be confusing, sometimes they appear to be brown and other times they're khaki."

"Khaki?" He laughed.

She returned the laugh, "Yes, that's really the color. I'm not kidding. That's what I put on my driver's license."

23

Inside Irina's Restaurant at Camelot Castle Hotel the view of the sea and ruins of King Arthur's Tintagle Castle below were breathtaking. No matter how many times Rachel came to Tintagle, it thrilled her every time. Just thinking of the history and the legends intrigued her.

"You know this is King Arthur's birthplace, right?" Stefan said, while Rachel sipped her wine.

"Yes, so the legend goes," Rachel tipped her glass towards him. "Do you believe the King Arthur story? You think it is all true?"

"Well, I can't imagine it not being true. His birthplace was here in Cornwall, or Camelot in Hampshire, or some believe near Winchester. Some feel Camelot was in Wales, some say Devon. It's pretty much a mystery, which only supports the possibility of fiction rather than fact. But I prefer to believe King Arthur existed. Most of the confusion is that he did have castles in Wales and in Hampshire and both were translated close to the word meaning Camelot. It seems the languages have caused the problem more than anything else. The early dialects in those times were easily misunderstood."

"I'd love to do a study of it, I really would. Maybe I will,"

Rachel said.

"I have several books on the subject if you'd like to borrow them when we get to the manor," Stefan said while signaling for the waiter. "Would you like some more wine?"

"Actually, I think I've had enough if I want to walk out of here on my own." She placed her napkin beside the plate and sat up straight. She looked up at the waiter when he arrived with the bill. "I really enjoyed the salmon, wonderful!"

"Thank you, madam. And you, Lord Blackbourne?"

"Delicious trout, very good. Would you like some coffee, Rachel?"

"Uh ... that sounds good," she was stuck on what the waiter had called Stefan.

"Coffee for both of us then."

"Shall I bring the dessert tray, your Lordship?" the waiter asked.

"Nothing for me, thank you," Rachel replied.

"Just coffee, please," Stefan added.

The waiter removed the plates and utensils, nodded to Stefan and then walked away.

"I agree with you about the salmon. I usually have that myself. Do you eat beef?"

"I do, as a matter of fact. Love it. Nothing like a good steak. Why do you ask?" Rachel leaned forward, resting her arms on the table staring intently at Stefan, wanting to ask him about the 'Lord' part of the waiter's salutation.

"Just curious. Most of the women I know prefer only fish or chicken. It's refreshing to meet one that has a penchant for beef. Are you alright?"

"Yes, yes. I ... uh ... like pork chops too, ham, sausage, bacon, meatloaf, hamburgers, hotdogs, venison, fish and poultry. But I'm not very keen on veal or duck." She felt him looking at her and turned to see his head tipped to one side, and squinting intently at her, as if to be reading her mind.

He spoke, "I must say, it's pleasant to meet someone who knows what she does and does not like, and has the fortitude to say so. I admire that very much."

"Well, I guess it's my age, as I get older the more honest and bold I become. It can be a detriment, however. So … uh … did I hear correctly? You are a Lord? Lord Blackbourne?"

"Yes. Some adhere to the formalities of one's station in life. I'd rather not. Embarrassing at times, totally changes the atmosphere."

"Are you related to Lord Evans of Charlestown, your name being Evans?" Rachel asked.

"No I'm not, just an acquaintance, a fellow Lord, however. Do you know him?"

"Yes, I do. In fact, we think I am connected to his family linage. I'll have to tell you about it sometime, but not now. It's a long story."

They both smiled, a bit more interested in each other as the waiter served coffee.

24

The drive to Blackbourne Manor passed faster than Rachel would have thought; conversation does that, causing all sense of time to fly into the wind. As they approached the country estate, consisting of 177,000 acres according to Stefan, the immense mansion perched on the rocky hill flabbergasted Rachel. It towered above fields of heather that swallowed up the grounds around it. From a distance the palatial dwelling could be seen easily, but as they traveled closer on the gorse-lined road through groves of Cornish Palms, only the gatehouse could be glimpsed directly ahead.

"This is incredible! Beautiful. I cannot believe this is your house, or manor, or country estate? Whatever you call it? Your home? Were you born here?" she said a bit weakly, open-mouthed and leaning forward, straining to take it all in.

"Yes, my home, my birthplace, yes. Amazing grounds so far, do you agree?"

"Amazing to say the least, an inadequate word, actually. There must be a way to say something that means more than amazing." She couldn't believe her eyes or the moment. Suddenly she panicked; she wanted to jump from the car and run back home to Newlyn as fast as she could. *It's too overwhelming*. She needed to keep her wits about her.

"So, what do you think, is Blackbourne as grand as Downton Abbey? You know the series is being filmed at a new location, at Alnwick Castle for the next few weeks, don't you? Belongs to the Duke and Duchess of Northumberland. It's no longer at Highclere Castle with the Carnarvon Family."

Rachel turned towards him, "I didn't know that. I wonder why they changed locations."

"I would imagine they are giving Highclere a break. You can imagine what an inconvenience it is, although the fees are very satisfying, I hear. Almost worth it to be inconvenienced. Here we are ... my very own Downton Abby." He laughed as he pulled to the entry of the Blackbourne Manor and honked his horn three times.

Rachel watched a young man dressed in grey slacks and a white shirt and black vest bound down the flagstone steps. Another man, dressed the same, waited at the door, holding it open.

The first man opened the car door for Rachel, "Good afternoon, madam. Welcome to Blackbourne."

"Thank you, very much. I'm glad to be here," she said, not able to think of anything else to say that would be appropriate. Her natural response would have been OH MY GOD! But she refrained from blurting it out.

Stefan joined them and gently took Rachel's arm. "Thank you, William. Would you please ask Walter to gas up the car for me right away? I'll need it soon to take Miss O'Neill back to Port Isaac."

He led Rachel up the fifteen steps and across the portico through the double doorway into an expansive entryway ... all the while her eyes wide with anticipation and bewilderment at what lay before her.

25

After a quick tour of the main rooms on the ground floor, Stefan and Rachel were served dessert and coffee in an elegant parlor near the entry room.

The twenty-foot domed ceiling in a gold and green fleur-de-leis design surrounding the Blackbourne coat of arms in the center took her breath away.

"This is a lovely room," Rachel said.

"It's my favorite, actually. Although the ceilings are high, the room is smaller and more appropriate for such intimate occasions as this."

"So, do you have other family members living here with your mother?" she asked after taking a bite of the strawberry shortcake covered with whipped cream.

"No, just my mother. I do have a younger brother who visits once a year from Canada, but there is no one else."

"No wives for you and your brother, so no children?"

"Oh, Arthur is married, yes. They have two daughters. But as for me, I've not ventured into matrimony. My work has been uppermost to me, not much time to nurture a wife and family, not that there weren't any women to choose from," he rolled his eyes. "There were plenty, as you can well imagine. Women looking for a title and a house like this to live in." He laughed. "But I must say, after growing up with a mother and father who never had a cordial word to say to each other up to the day father died, I just didn't want to take a chance that my marriage would go in that direction. I blame it on our wealth more than anything else."

"That's sad. It really is. But I can understand your decision, I can. I mean . . ."

He set down his cup and settled into the wingback chair while listening to and watching Rachel.

She continued, "What I mean is, well, my childhood was dysfunctional to say the least. I must admit it hindered and influenced the choices I made. My father was an alcoholic; my mother disappeared when I was three, so right there was enough to set me on the wrong track to familial bliss. I was raised by our housekeeper who, by the way, was the best thing that happened to me at that time. I left home when I was seventeen because my father married a money-grubbing, cruel woman, the proverbial wicked step-mother, and I enrolled in college. We had money too, not as much as you, but by that time my father owned several restaurants and was dabbling in real estate. After he sobered up he became a very successful real estate investor in Los Angeles. I married twice, one after the other, both total losses. But I had a wonderful son, he lives in California and I even have a grandson just three years old. I'm proud of my son, a successful builder. He's been the bright spot in my life through it all." She reached for the fork and took another taste of cake, feeling self-conscious for talking so much. She wondered what he thought about all she'd said, maybe it didn't need to be told.

"And your second marriage ended how many years ago?"

"Well, my son was five years old at the time, and now he's thirty-eight. So that makes it thirty-three years ago, doesn't it? My goodness, I hadn't realized it's been that long. But I did marry again. Just recently, three years ago to a wonderful man who I adored. We were married in my son's beach house in Malibu. But five days later he died on our honeymoon cruise. I—" She set the plate and fork down on the table between them and sat up straight in her chair, taking a deep breath. "Would you point me to the ladies' room, please?"

26

The drive back to Port Isaac felt awkward for Rachel, no reason for it particularly, other than she felt she talked too much and she let the memories of Maxim resurface. She wrestled with her feelings as Stefan talked, knew he saw the shift in her moods.

"I would like to see you again, are you up to that, Rachel?" He glanced over at her as they took the road down into Port Isaac village to the little fishing cove.

"Yes, of course. I'll be going back to Newlyn soon. When you're down that way, call me. I know a great fish & chip pub. Do you know Mousehole?" She hoped she didn't sound like she put him off, she didn't mean to. She just needed to put some time and space between them so she could sort it all out, maybe a couple weeks or so. Not that something would develop between them, it probably wouldn't. For God's sakes, he's a Lord! She looked out the passenger window at the stone cottages along the lane.

"That will be grand, yes. I should be coming that way next week; shall we say Friday afternoon? I'll take some time off for a change and after I see my mother that morning, I'll head down your way. Is that all right?"

She hadn't expected a definite time and day from him, on the spur of the moment like that. It rattled her somewhat, but she gave a pleasant answer masking her trepidation. "That will work. I'll take care of business during the week and will set aside some time for your visit. Yes, Friday afternoon. I have a business card here, with my phone number and email address. You can call or email and I'll give you directions." She pulled out the card and placed it in the divider cup on the console.

"And I'll give you mine when we stop." He drove up the narrow lane to her hotel. "Here we are." He pulled over and reached into his glove compartment, brushing his arm against her leg, while searching for a card. He found one and handed it to her.

"I'll just hop out, you needn't open my door," she said nervously as she pushed on the handle and feet were on the ground before he could respond. "Bye now, see you next Friday. And thank you so much for lunch and the tour. I never expected all that. Loved it. Oh, and the dessert at the manor. Wonderful time."

"Friday, then?" He asked, reaching across the seat for her hand.

She stretched and their hands clasped for a moment as their eyes connected and they sensed each other's vibes.

"Friday, yes," she said.

27

In the days that followed, Rachel couldn't help but think about the upcoming Friday meeting with Lord Blackbourne. During that week, she Googled him and found out as much as she could about him and his family. She wondered if he did the same about her. Probably not.

As much as she immediately felt an attraction to the man she couldn't help thinking about the perfect life she already had, and how she had struggled getting back to it once again after Maxim's death. Now it seemed like a replay of when she met Maxim. She reminded herself how she had doubted the relationship almost up to the moment it became legal, and here she had the same feelings again. Not fair. She didn't want complications in her life.

All week she went about her business constantly thinking about Stefan. She wondered if he planned on staying in a hotel in Penzance or an inn in Newlyn or Mousehole. Mousehole would be good since that's where they would be having fish and chips. Unless she took him to Penzance to her favorite pub. She might do that instead of The Ship Inn in Mousehole. The Ship Inn, where she and Maxim went the first time he visited Cornwall and where she would take everybody the first time they came. Right, change it up, they would go to Penzance. Or maybe to Marazion. She hadn't seen Margaret in ages. That would work. Who knows, Lord Evans might even pop in from Charlestown. Yes. That's where they'd go. She would call Margaret and have her save a table for early evening. The view would be perfect that time of day, a sunset with St Michael's Mount right in the middle of it.

With that decided, she felt better. If he stayed the night, which he might, for it would be too late to drive back to Blackbourne, she'd invite him for brunch the next morning, give him a tour of her own little palace. They could walk down to the sea where she loved to sit on the granite boulders and watch all sorts of activities.

She dialed Margaret's number. "Hello, Margaret. How are you?"

"Rachel. Where have you been? I've been wondering about you. Are you all right?" Margaret motioned to a waitress to take care of the register while she talked on the phone. She moved to a small table and poured herself a cup of tea.

"Are you busy? Can you talk?" Rachel said.

"Taking a break, your timing is perfect. So when are you coming in for your favorite fruit and cheese plate? We miss you, you know."

Rachel grinned, she loved Margaret. "That's why I'm calling. I'm bringing a new friend with me on Friday, early evening probably. Could you save us my table looking across the causeway to the Mount?"

Margaret took a swallow of tea. "Of course, I will. So, who is this new friend? Male or female?" She laughed.

"Male." Rachel waited for a response.

"You mean it? Business or pleasure?" Margaret's eyes were wide open with anticipation.

"How about pleasure?" Rachel giggled. "I mean, I don't know. I take that back. Just a new friend, let's leave it at that. I met him in Port Isaac a few days ago. He's another Lord. Can you believe it?"

"Oh my God, another one? You do realize how few commoners meet Lords in their lifetime, and here you're on your second one. Who is he?" Margaret stood and motioned to the waitress to seat patrons that entered.

"Lord Blackbourne. Blackbourne Manor, north of Tintagle?

Stefan Evans? And no, he isn't related to Lord Evans, I asked him, but he does know him. Amazing, isn't it? I can't believe it myself. No one would believe me. I haven't even told my son."

"Lord Blackbourne?" Margaret frowned.

"Wait 'till you see him. A real charmer. I couldn't have written him any better," Rachel chuckled. "Got to go, have to pick up a package at the post office in Penzance before it closes. I'll see you on Friday."

"Alright, I'll ask Felipe to come too, just to say hello." She wondered how her husband Felipe would react. Lord Blackbourne was an old friend. Emphasis on was.

"Good, I'd love to see Felipe. Yes. Bye." Rachel breathed deeply and felt much better. Margaret was good; she always lifted Rachel's spirits.

28

Rachel's nerves were in overdrive. Stefan would arrive at the Godolphin Inn Restaurant in Marazion at any moment. She drove to the parking lot and hurried inside. She got there later than she'd planned, because of more traffic than usual through Penzance, still she arrived before Stefan.

She entered and saw Margaret talking to a server, and headed towards them.

"There she is," Margaret said and flashed her usual smile, teeth glistening white. She reached for Rachel's hand and led her to the table with the view of the Mount. "Is this all right?"

"Perfect. I am so nervous."

"Is there something that makes you nervous about Stefan?" Margaret asked with a frown.

"Oh, I don't know. I just —it's just been so long since I've had a guest, a male guest. Remember the last time Maxim came before we were married? I'm just nervous, that's all there is to it." She sat down and took a deep breath "I'll have a big glass of champagne right now, Margaret. Before he gets here. In a water goblet, not a flute." She laughed. "I'm being silly, aren't I?"

Margaret laughed with her. "It's okay to be silly. In fact, I'll have a goblet of it myself. Be right back."

Craziness! Rachel knew it. She had no business being interested in another man. Her nine lives were already spent when it came to men.

"Honey," Margaret said as she returned to the table with two empty goblets and a bottle of champagne, "didn't you say you are going to the States soon?" She began pouring into the goblets.

"Yes, I'm leaving First of September. Will spend some time in Malibu, visiting my son, then my agent is lining up some dates for me. But as you know, signings and conferences are not my cup of tea at all and I'm not looking forward to it!"

Margaret sat across the table from Rachel. "So why are you doing it, then?"

"My agent talked me into it."

"Ah! Drumming up business sounds like. Well, it can't be all that bad. It'll be over before you know it." Margaret signaled to a waitress to seat the couple that just came through the door.

"True, and after it all, I'll spend New Year's week in Vegas. That ought to be fun. Omigosh! Here he is. Quick, pour me some more champagne." She stood up and motioned to Stefan to join them at their table.

As he approached, Rachel couldn't believe how stately he appeared. *Such a handsome man, looking like a Lord should look.* How in the world did she ever have the good fortune of meeting such a man? She couldn't fathom ever having another man in her life that equaled Maxim in stature and looks. And here, walking towards her, was a man that might, just might, equal Maxim in every way. How could that happen twice in one lifetime? Three times. Mustn't forget about Pete, she had loved Pete too.

Maybe she just got caught up with the newness and romance of it all, when the endorphins are working overtime. She'd never been in a long relationship. She either divorced them as she did her first two husbands – but those were different – one was a violent man, one a roaming bisexual. Pete and Maxim had died. Her involvement with men she loved never worked out. She needed to think clearly this time.

"So, good to see you, Rachel," Stefan said as he leaned and kissed each cheek as Rachel lifted her face to his. "You are as lovely as ever."

She blushed, unexpectedly feeling flustered and hormonal. "Glad you could make it. This is my very good friend and confidant, Margaret. She runs this place."

"Hello, Margaret, so nice to see you again," he said as he reached for and kissed the back of her hand. "This is a lovely choice, Rachel. I used to come here quite often, you know."

Rachel was surprised to know he knew Margaret, he hadn't said anything when she asked him to meet her there..

"He's not a stranger here, Rachel, not at all. May I bring you a drink, Stefan? The usual?"

Stefan pulled out a chair for himself and after Rachel sat back down, he sat. "I'll have the same as you ladies," he said, grinning widely, noticing the goblets rather than flutes. "Another goblet, please, and another bottle. I trust we can find a driver if we need one?"

"Well, we can always put you both up in the Inn, if need be," Margaret added without smiling. "Just like the old days."

Rachel shot a frown at Margaret, not believing what she'd just said. Her plans were for cocktails and an early dinner at the most, then she planned to home.

"Felipe is on his way here by the way, just arrived from Spain," Margaret added. "He'll be surprised to see you, Stefan. How long has it been?"

"A few months ago, in London." He looked at Rachel through sultry eyes and placed his hand on hers. "Staying here at the Inn tonight could be something I'd be very interested in. Thank you for suggesting it, Margaret," Stefan said, looking at Margaret, missing Rachel's discreet negative reaction.

"I—I— well, I ..." Rachel couldn't find the right words.

Felipe entered at that awkward moment and came straight towards them. "Hello, my dear Rachel," reaching for her hand and kissing it. "Lord Blackbourne ...didn't expect to see you again this soon?"

"Yes, the conservancy meeting. In London." Stefan stood and they shook hands.

"We're still trying to sort that out, you know. I hope you don't mind if I join you for a few moments. Then I'll be off."

"You don't mind, do you, Rachel?" Stefan asked.

"Of course not. I consider Felipe and Margaret as part of my family. I'd love to have them both join us." Rachel reached for her purse. "Would you excuse me for a moment, I'll be right back. Nature calls."

"I'll come with you," Margaret said.

In the ladies' room, Margaret touched Rachel's arm and gave it a squeeze. "Rachel, I need to tell you something. I hope you won't be angry with me."

"Why didn't you tell me you knew Stefan? I do have to pee, I almost waited too long to come in here. Go on, tell me what you want to tell me." Rachel went into the stall and closed the door. "I'm listening."

Margaret saw her own reflection in the mirror and smoothed back a loose strand of hair that had fallen across her forehead. "Well, I feel, as a friend, I should tell you. A very good friend of mine in London was engaged to Stefan. She caught him in bed with another woman in his apartment in London, which broke her heart and turned out to cause quite a scandal. They were to be married within the month, she called it off. He's quite the ladies' man, Rachel. Please be careful. You've had the best already with Pete and Maxim; don't need someone's leftovers now, do you?"

Rachel came from the stall with a look of disbelief and surprise. "When did that happen?"

"Two years ago. I wouldn't have even mentioned it if I hadn't seen how you looked at him a few moments ago. He's already got you in his clutches."

"No, he doesn't." Rachel retorted quickly. "I hardly know the man. Just learning about him, that's all. But thanks for telling me, it helps. I don't know if we're heading for a serious relationship and of course, like you said, I'll be leaving for the States soon. So, there's nothing to be concerned about, Margaret. Really. Not to worry." She washed her hands. "Let's get back to them, shall we? And remember, I'm a big girl, ran around the track a few times. I'll handle Mr. Blackbourne." She hugged Margaret and kissed her on the cheek.

29

Later that evening after a full dinner and several bottles of wine at the Godolphin Inn in Marazion, Margaret drove Rachel's car to Newlyn, and Felipe and Stefan followed in their own cars.

Margaret found it amusing and unusual to see Rachel in an inebriated state, so when Rachel said she didn't want to stay at the Inn, that she'd get a cab to take her home, they all drove the few miles to Newlyn for a nightcap.

Earlier, the evening had gone along cheerfully and amicably between Rachel and Stefan. They seemed to hit it off, despite what Margaret told her. Felipe had commented to Margaret in the kitchen at the Inn how their two friends seemed to get along remarkably well. Margaret had excused herself and her husband after cocktails and left the two alone to finish their dinner and take in the glorious crimson sunset beyond the bay behind the Mount.

Now, Rachel and Stefan were alone, lounging in Rachel's living room, sipping coffee and talking while looking out at the moon reflecting over the sea beyond Newlyn Bay. Margaret and Felipe had returned to Marazion.

"Such a lovely view you have," Stefan said softly, feeling more relaxed than he had in weeks. "I could learn to love this."

Rachel glanced at him wondering if he really meant what he just said. Hard to tell because of his charm and obvious ability to schmooze. She didn't know him well enough yet to accept him at face value.

She reached for the French Press sitting on the cocktail table, "I'll make some more coffee. Would you like brandy with your coffee?"

"That would be nice, yes."

Stefan watched her leave the room and sighed. Rachel fascinated him, and he didn't quite know how to advance, or if he should. She seemed so guarded and untouchable. He knew he had to tread lightly, for he'd heard most of her story in the past few days from her and from Felipe earlier that night. A thought occurred to him.

"Rachel," he called out as he headed for the front door, "I'm going to my car to get something, be right back."

When he returned, he found Rachel pouring hot coffee and brandy in their cups, he carried his guitar case.

"What is this? You play the guitar?" she grinned.

"Yes, I do. I build guitars, as a matter of fact. A little hobby handed down from my father. I have a workshop at the manor." He unlatched the case and took out a beautiful craftsman guitar of Brazilian wood. "I build two or three a year in my spare time." He began strumming and fingering the strings producing a mellow haunting sound that filled the room.

"That is breathtaking," Rachel said. "My two favorite instruments are the piano and the guitar. Spanish guitar especially. Incredible! Wow!"

He immediately began playing Malaguena. "You know this one, yes? One of Carlos Montoya's famous versions of Malaguena." Stefan quickly became absorbed in playing the classic piece.

Rachel was spellbound.

As he finished his shortened version he said, "The song was written in 1928 by Cuban composer Ernesto Lecuona and was originally the sixth movement of Lecuona's Suite Andalucía, to which he added lyrics in Spanish. I wouldn't dare bore you with my singing." He laughed. "You see, I'm a Spanish Guitarist music lover myself." He held up the guitar and twirled it to the backside. "I always have one of these with me, play it every chance I get. Practice, practice, practice. See the wonderful Brazilian wood markings? This is one of my prizes, I truly labored over this one. Worth a lot of money if I ever wanted to sell it. I'm so glad you like the music, Rachel."

"I love it! Especially your playing, and the guitar. I am impressed!"

"Well, it helps me stay focused and has helped me over a few rough spots the past couple years."

"Oh? What do you mean?"

"Well, Margaret probably already told you that I was engaged to be married a couple years ago, a friend of hers. It was something my mother wanted, she pushed us together. The woman wasn't right for me, and try as I might, I just couldn't fall in love with her. I went along with the engagement and then one night things took a dramatic turn and it was all off! I was sorry how it came down, but at the same time, I was glad. If we would have married, it would not have lasted. I've always believed in love, in marriage, but I have to feel a hundred percent. I have to be completely in love with the woman I choose to spend my life with, otherwise there is no point of it. Do you agree?"

"Ha! You don't know the half of it. I feel the same way. And I did fall a hundred percent, twice in my life. But death took them both from me. So, I do know that it is possible to feel a hundred percent. Although I do have to interject here, that you're never totally sure of the other person, you can only know how you feel, not how the other guy feels. That has got to be bad too, being in love but not having that love returned. Can you imagine how many people are in those relationships? That would be the worst."

Stefan stood his guitar up against the arm of the sofa. "The very worst. Do you mind if I use the toilet?"

"It's down the hall, second door on the right."

"I'll just be a moment," he said as he sauntered down the corridor. Rachel shook her head as she watched him walk away, the curvature of his buttocks pressing against perfectly fitting, thin slacks. *Lordy, Lordy, Lordy! This man is a hunk and not only looks good, he does everything right. I can't stand it. Save me, God. Get me out of here. He's too good to be true and like my daddy always said ... if it's too good to be true, it usually is. Beware.*

After another hour of imbibing and talking about each other's lives, it became apparent that both Rachel and Stefan were beyond Britain's standards for alcohol consumption – 2 or 3 drinks for a woman, 3 or 4 for a man. Not to mention the legal percentage of alcohol in the system.

"You are more than welcome to spend the night here, you needn't try to drive to a hotel in Penzance." Rachel said as she stood up, holding onto the arm of the chair for balance. She managed to carry empty glasses and cups on a tray to the kitchen without mishap, looking back over her shoulder at one point. "Is that alright with you, Stefan? Would you like to stay?"

"I don't believe I have any options. I'll just sleep right here." He stretched out on the sofa. "I don't even think I could navigate to my car in the driveway. Sorry about this." He stood up, losing his balance for an instance, catching himself by grabbing the arm of the wing back chair for support. "I'm worse off than I thought. Could you direct me towards the toilet again?"

Rachel went to Stefan and took his arm. "You can stay in the bedroom upstairs, on the floor above mine. The elevator is over here. I remodeled a suite of rooms for my husband Maxim, but he never got to use them. It's a beautiful floor. I hope you don't mind? I just feel it should be used." She surprised herself for suggesting he sleep in Maxim's bed.

"Yes, that will be good. I do think it's best, yes. Oh, my guitar!" Stefan turned to go after his guitar.

"Here, I'll get it," Rachel said.

They took the elevator up to the third floor and it opened onto a landing outside two double doors hewn of Davey Elm trees.

When Rachel designed the third floor for Maxim, she wanted it to reflect his creativity as a sculptor and artist. He sculpted in metal and wood as a hobby, sometimes leather and other fabrics and natural materials. So, the doors were made especially for the suite out of Davey Elm, a hybrid of Wyche and Cornish Elm, indigenous to Cornwall. The markings of the grain were striking, with shades of light to dark. It had been stained and sealed to protect the wood. Rachel's pride in the doors and design reflected in her manner.

"Here we are," she said as she opened the doors that lead to a suite of handsome rooms decorated in shades of brown, soft shades of gold and greens. The feeling of an outdoors wooded area. Like the Lamorna Birch painting hanging in her sitting room. Altogether she had created a restful and peaceful ambiance for the man in her life.

"This is superb, Rachel. How many rooms?"

"This den with the desk and leather furniture, bookcases, bar, entertainment center over there," she pointed as she spoke and led him through to the next room. "This is the master bedroom suite, huge bathroom, you'll like that, the shower especially, exercise room. Then there's this spacious studio in here, facing the sea. Wall to wall, ceiling to floor wooden blinds, opened or closed, depending on the amount of light an artist needs. A work space, if you will. Wooden floors, work tables ... it's all here." She laid his guitar on a sofa facing the windows and went back to the bedroom to turn down the bed.

"There are clean linens in the bath, and there are pajamas, if you'd like, in the closet. A robe. Spares, that I keep on hand for guests. Oh, by the way, you'll find a coffee maker and cups, some chocolate, and a small refrigerator with a few things in it in the studio cabinets. So please help yourself. I think that's it. Any questions?"

Stefan stared dumb-struck at Rachel, not believing what or who he saw before him. Another world, and it didn't compute. Blame it on the drink or blame it on the hour, blame it on the woman standing in front of him. He'd never had these feelings before and doubted that he ever would again. He must be dreaming.

"No, no questions," he said. "You've left nothing unsaid. A man could hole up in here for weeks and be perfectly comfortable." He walked to the bed, reached down and pushed on it, turned and went into the bathroom to inspect it. After a moment, he reappeared in the bathroom doorway. "Thank you, Rachel. I'm so sorry I'm not as together as I wish I were. Too much to drink and too many miles covered today. Suddenly I feel as if I must retire. Do you mind?"

"Of course not," she said as she smiled and began to walk towards the elevator. "I'm an early riser, so whenever you come down I'll fix your breakfast. I love the morning view of the sea. My favorite time of the day, sipping coffee while smelling the sea air. Good night, Stefan. Sleep well." She disappeared into the elevator.

Stefan stared at the closed elevator doors for a moment, and then he sighed and turned back into the bathroom, not bothering to close the double doors from the landing.

30

Rachel drank coffee at the wrought iron bistro table, outside the kitchen's open French doors, watching the daylight brighten. She woke up just before the sun rose, hopped out of bed full of energy, dressed and hurried downstairs to make coffee. She loved her early morning hours with only the sounds of nature, before the human element disturbed the solitude.

She had also adored her first little cottage down on the bluff, overlooking the boat harbor, where she would sit under the magnolia tree, watching and listening to the seagulls and the lines clanking against the masts of the boats below. Now that she lived farther up the hill, in a magnificent house, she could barely hear a muted version of the same sounds echoing in the stillness. But still lovely and soothing to the spirit.

Someone had told her that no matter where you stood on a beach, the horizon was twenty-seven miles out to where the sea met the sky. She'd meant to research that fact, remembered she hadn't as she took a gulp of coffee, waiting for Stefan to wake up and join her.

Thoughts of Stefan were interrupted by his voice, calling for Rachel. "I'm out here, Stefan," she answered. "On the patio."

He came through the door in the same attire worn the night before. "There you are. It's a grand morning, isn't it?"

"Yes, have a seat, I'll pour you a cup. Do you take sugar and cream?" she said.

"No, black is good. This is lovely out here. You've wonderful views from every part of the house."

"My little corner of the world. That's why I love it so." She poured and handed him the cup of coffee and saucer. "Did you sleep well?"

"Like a brick. Dropped right off in that comfortable bed. Haven't slept like that in months. The bed, the ambiance, the drink, whatever the cause, I need more of it, more often."

Rachel watched his mannerisms and overflowing energy as he talked. She smiled.

He continued, "Do you live here most of the time, or do you split your time between the States and your house in Paris and Moscow?"

"Oh, I signed off the Moscow property, gave it to Maxim's brother. I didn't need it, never lived in it. Besides, I'm house poor as the saying goes. Still have a cabin in Montana too," She laughed.

"Nice of you to do that for the family in Moscow." He raised an eyebrow, thinking how most women would immediately sell it for the money.

"Well, I adore his family, and it didn't make sense for me to keep it. I know Maxim would have wanted me to do that, he knew how I love England and would want me to live here anyway. As for the house in Paris, yes, I go there when I need inspiration. It's the best place in the world for a writer. I love to immerse myself in the crowded sidewalk cafes and the parks, people-watching and sipping wine in the interesting bistros and cafes at night. Great place. And the house atop Montmartre is wonderful. The girls and I did it up good. Let me know when you're going to Paris and I'll arrange for you to stay there. Anytime. Four floors. Bedroom suites on the top three. Just beautiful."

"I will. Maybe you would join me?" He squinted at her, watching closely for her reaction.

"Oh. Well, maybe so. We'll see. Excuse me." She stood up and took the coffee press into the kitchen for a refill.

Not the reaction he wanted. Obviously, wrong timing, he knew it. When she returned he said, "Let's go to Penzance for breakfast, on me, do you mind? Or better yet, St. Ives? It's just a 20-minute drive. Do you go to St. Ives much?"

"You know, I don't ever think of St. Ives. I drive by it when I take the A30 up towards Port Isaac, but that's usually my destination when I'm on the northern coast of Cornwall, Port Isaac. I don't know why I don't go to St. Ives, it's a very artsy town and tons of people flock there, especially in the summer to the galleries and cafes. Maybe that's the reason." She laughed. "But, yes, that sounds good. I'm up for it. You know it well, know a great breakfast place?"

Stefan shifted in his chair. "I do, I do. Plus, I've a few guitar clients there. In fact, I'd like to get in touch with one of them, brought a new guitar to deliver."

"The one you played last night?"

"No, that one stays in my hands. Wouldn't let it go for any amount of money. It's special and rare."

"Well, I just love hearing you play. I could have sat all night listening to you."

"I've always got one with me, so just say the word and I'll be at your beck and call." They both laughed.

"I didn't realize you come to this part of Cornwall as much as you do. Let me know next time you come, and please stay here at the house. You're more than welcome." She surprised herself with the invitation, wanted to take it back.

"That's generous of you. I'll take you up on it, if you're here."

"I'll be going to the States pretty soon, have a book tour and want to check on my cabin in Montana, see my son in Malibu, he just got a divorce, I found out. But doesn't matter if I'm here or not. I'll leave a key for you. You can use it while I'm gone." She lifted a floral planter from a window shelf. "The spare key is stuffed in here. Easy to get to." She pulled it out and showed him the earth covered key holder. "I mean it, do use the house."

"I'd rather when you're here," he said.

"That too, seriously." She placed the planter back on its shelf of pink and red geraniums. "My dear friend Dudley checks on the house when I'm gone, he lives in Mousehole, has the lapidary shop, and is a rock hound. He and I are Godfather and Godmother to my friends' boys. Paul and Belinda Newland, artists who had a studio next door to Dudley's shop, and who owned this home before Belinda died of Lymphoma a few years ago. Some very sad times. Paul and the boys live in London now. I see Dudley quite often when I'm home. We've got a lot in common, people we've known. So anyway, it'll save him the trip, if you're here. I'll leave all the information for you, if you care to use it."

"So, when are you leaving for the States?" Feeling sad suddenly.

"September third. Going to California to be with my son for my birthday on the seventh."

He brightened up. "A Virgo! What a delightful surprise! My birthday is on the eighth."

"You're kidding."

"Nope, not kidding. We'll have to have a mutual birthday celebration before you go. Shall we?" He perked up.

"Yes, that would be wonderful."

"I could drive you to London a couple days before you fly out, we could see the town, go shopping, maybe go to a show or to Ronnie Scott's, or both. Have you been to Ronnie Scott's?"

"Yes. I love that place. Love Jazz."

"And we could have a birthday dinner the night before you leave? How does that sound? I'll make all the arrangements," he added.

He's too good to be true. And British to boot. Love the British. Lord, help me.

31

The last week of August Rachel packed up a few things for the trip to the States. She didn't need to take a lot of clothing, for she had a closet full in the Malibu house and the Montana cabin, kept them stocked just for that reason, so she wouldn't have to tote much. She wanted to pack a couple evening gowns that Maxim's sister Anastasia had designed for her, however, to wear to special occasions. She thought maybe the few days in London with Lord Blackbourne, before the trip, also warranted an evening frock or two. And of course, the Las Vegas portion of her trip, New Year's Eve, certainly called for a special gown.

Stefan telephoned Rachel saying he'd booked a hotel for August 25th through September 3rd, he said he had some business to take care of and would need to arrive earlier. Rachel agreed to join him on the 27th, but would take the train instead of riding with him two days earlier; assured him she loved traveling by train. Besides, three days in London sounded perfect, not too much, not too little.

She hoped he'd booked separate rooms at the London Ritz - yes, the Ritz - a return engagement, the first since that very special New Year's Eve so many years before with Ethan and when she first saw Paul. *Poor Ethan*, she said to herself as she folded a pair of jeans and placed them into the traveling bag. *I wonder where we'd be today if he had lived.*

Her doorbell rang.

"Who could that be?" she said. Visitors were scarce in her world. Especially unexpected visitors. She hurried down the stairs and opened the front door.

"Margaret! What are you doing here? I mean, come in, so good to see you. What's up?" Rachel hugged her and stepped back.

"I'm sorry I didn't call. Knew you were due to go to the U.S. soon, and wanted to stop and wish you well on your tour. When are you leaving?"

"Come in, come in. Let's have a cup of coffee." Rachel led her into the kitchen. "I'm leaving tomorrow for London, will spend three days there before catching a plane out."

"That's nice. A little holiday before the holiday," Margaret laughed.

"Actually, it is. And are you ready for this?" she sat down at the table. "Please, sit down, Margaret."

"Okay. Ready for what?"

"I'll be spending the three days with Stefan in London. We share birthdays in September – 7 and 8. So it's a pre-birthday celebration. Dinner, show, Ronnie Scott's, shopping. He'll be there on business so we'll be doing a few things together and then he'll take me to the airport the morning of my flight. Sounds good?" She knew what Margaret thought about Stefan, but she tried to make it sound very nonchalant.

"Really. Well, that's interesting. Are you sure you want to do that?"

"It's nothing to worry about, we're just friends. I can take care of myself, Margaret. You know that. He's a very nice guy. Really."

Margaret laughed. "Okay, if you say so. And yes, he can be. So, I'll trust you to be on guard and not to do any foolish."

"Like what?" She was amused at Margaret's caution.

"Like jumping into bed with him, which I wouldn't blame you, he's to die for, but just be careful. We don't want any broken hearts around here. Okay? He has a reputation for that."

Rachel stood and reached for the electric teapot to pour the hot water into the coffee press. "Broken heart? Ha! It's already in a million pieces, don't you know that? How can it be broken any more than it is?" She laughed while she poured. "Besides, maybe I need a little departure from the norm, you know? It isn't everyday someone like Stefan walks into my life. So maybe this is something I need right now. Let's look at it that way. I'm stepping in with eyes wide open, my dear friend." She smiled at Margaret.

After a sip of coffee, Margaret looked at Rachel directly in the eyes, "Okay, hon. I know you are a very capable woman, and you are a careful woman, very smart, very savvy. So, we'll leave it at that. I'm for whatever you want, my dear. Truly am. Just don't want you to be hurt. Now, tell me about your trip to the States. That's what I want to hear."

32

Stefan was at the train station waiting for Rachel to arrive. She watched him hurrying towards her as she stepped from the First-Class compartment with her bag.

"Rachel, Rachel." He lifted her, gave her a bear hug. "I've been looking forward to this for days. Are you alright?"

Rachel laughed, "Of course I'm alright, why wouldn't I be?"

"I just meant, oh, I don't know what I meant. I'm just so glad you're here. Come, let's head that way. My driver's waiting outside. This your only bag?"

"Yes, only take one bag wherever I go. A hard-fast rule of mine. Learned early on not to over-pack. So how are you? Were you able to take care of business?"

"This way," he said motioning towards station exit. "Business done. Yes. Now my time is yours. And I've a few things planned for us, if you don't mind. I'll tell you about them at lunch. You haven't eaten, have you?"

"Not since a coffee and scone early on. I'm famished."

"Good, we'll have a light, leisurely lunch at the Rivoli Bar in the hotel and talk about what we'll be doing the next few days. And this afternoon, I thought a nice brisk walk through the park might be fun. Do you fancy that? I've wanted to do it for a long time with a special someone. Many times, I've strolled through Hyde Park, envying the loving faces and gestures of couples while I walked alone. You don't know how I've looked forward to this. I hope you don't mind. And it's a sunny day, perfect for a stroll."

"I love Hyde Park, and yes, I know what you mean. I've done it myself, envied the happy love-crazed couples walking hand in hand. So, I don't mind at all. We can pretend we're one of them. Yes, let's do that." She giggled and blushed.

Stefan had booked two rooms, connecting suites, at the hotel. Relieved, Rachel just wanted to relax and enjoy her time in London with Stefan without pressure before going to California and gearing up for the book tour.

She disliked book tours with a passion, didn't know why she agreed to do it. If she could get out of it, she would. She'd much rather just visit with her son in California two months and then go to Montana for a couple. Although she was excited about her plan for New Year's Eve in Vegas with her gal pals, had already booked the rooms and they were all planning to join Rachel there, another New Year's Eve together. It had been a while since the five of them had been together at her wedding in Malibu on another New Year's Eve ... Shelly from Switzerland, Della from Moscow, Amanda from Brussels, Janet from Paris, Allegra - now from Montana. They were all bringing their mates and it promised to be a fun week at the Oasis Hotel, the newest and most elegant on the strip that outdid all the others, including the Winn.

"There you are," Stefan said as Rachel came into the Rivoli Bar. He stood and greeted her with a kiss on the cheek, then took her hand. "I've taken the liberty to order a seafood salad platter and bread for two, I hope you don't mind. And some very nice sparkling white wine."

Sitting, Rachel grinned. "This is perfect, just perfect."

The waiter poured a Perrier Jouët Belle Epoque Blanc de Blanc and placed the bottle in a table-side ice bucket on a stand.

They both lifted their glasses. "To our holiday in London," Stefan said, clinking Rachel's glass. "May it be a special memory and preview of more to come."

"I'll drink to that," Rachel said as she took a sip. "Ummm, this is so good. One of my favorites. The enameled bottles alone are incredible. In my younger days, I collected them, used them as vases. Such beautiful florals painted on the glass."

"One of my mother's favorites, too," Stefan said after he took a sip.

"How is your mother, you haven't said?"

"She's home now, the worst is over. She is getting back into her usual routine – lunches, teas – the proverbial hostess to her garden club cronies and card-playing pals."

"Oh, I'm glad to hear that. Less worry for you." Rachel caught a sad expression on Stefan's face. "Are you all right? She is okay?"

"Oh yes, it's just that it's inevitable she'll one day pass on to another life, I know, and I sometimes think of that, like now. It saddens me. This time she escaped the grim reaper, but who knows when he'll be back and win. She's nearing a hundred. When it happens, the house will be empty." He gulped the champagne and poured more. "I'm sorry I put a damper on our day."

Reaching across the table and touching his hand, Rachel said, "Nothing wrong with loving our parents and dreading the day they leave us. I know exactly how you're feeling. I've lost both of mine, plus one of my step-mothers who saved my young life. I'd like to meet your mother someday."

"When you return, if she's still here, you most certainly will."

The waiter returned with their salad, heaped with shellfish – lobster, crab, scallops, and shrimp.

"Oh my. This is scrumptious looking. They certainly are generous with the shellfish, aren't they?" Rachel spread her napkin on her lap.

The waiter dished portions for each of them on plates and still plenty left on the platter. "Shall I bring you another choice of sauce? This is the chef's choice. I believe you will find it very tasty. Chef's own mayonnaise, made fresh every morning, mixed with a bit of chili sauce and sherry, Worcestershire sauce, finely chopped celery and shallots, salt and pepper to taste. His specialty."

"It's divine, Rachel. I can guarantee you will love it," Stefan added.

"Sounds wonderful."

The waiter spooned sauce onto their individual salads. "Will there be anything else?"

Stefan said, "I believe that will be it for me. Would you like anything, Rachel?"

"No, I'm happy. This is delicious," she said after tasting the dressing.

After lunch, they gathered their jackets from their respective rooms and headed out for the afternoon. It would be a few long blocks to the entrance of the park, so they hopped a subway from Green Park station near the Ritz on Piccadilly that ran the short distance to Hyde Park Corner station. Stefan surprised Rachel that he would want to ride the subway. She couldn't help but think how comfortable and natural it felt to be with him. He fit in.

After seating themselves, she said to Stefan, "It's interesting what the subways are called around the world, isn't it? San Francisco is Bart, Chicago is the L."

"London, the Tube. Paris, the Metro."

"Moscow has the Metro, too. So does Brussels," Rachel added.

"I think the Metro wins hands down," Stefan said as he grinned. "Here we are, Hyde Park."

A lovely day … practically clear sky, only a few fluffy white clouds dotted here and there, not a breeze in the air.

Stefan held Rachel's hand as they strolled. "Sometimes walking through Hyde Park can feel like a hurricane is coming at you. I think we're very lucky today," he said.

"Yes, you're right, And not a drop of rain can be seen. Can you believe it? I've been caught in the rain several times, forgetting to bring my umbrella. One time the rain soaked me clear through. Had to go back to my hotel off Piccadilly to change clothes and start all over again. Usually I'm heading for Harrods's back from where we started at Hyde Park Corner, down Brompton Road in Knightsbridge," Rachel said.

"Oh, so you like to shop in Harrods? We could go there tomorrow, if you'd like."

"I would like that, I always go when I'm in town. The Food court especially. Love to browse the bon-bon counter and the souvenir shop. I collect the totes. And of course, gotta see what's new in the purse and shoe departments, although I don't buy them. I usually carry the same purse till it wears out, then I'll buy another one, a good leather one though, one that lasts. As far as shoes go, I buy only what I need. I'm practical when it comes to shoes and purses." She let go of his hand and wrapped her arm around his, leaning against him as they walked.

Stefan looked down at her and smiled. "That feels good. I like having you lean into me."

They both laughed and continued walking.

"Shall we walk the entire 305 acres, or just traverse the Serpentine through the middle. Then to The Swan at the other side for a pint while we wait for a taxi?" Stefan asked.

"I haven't been to the Swan, but I've seen it."

"It's actually dated to the early seventeenth century, but is believed to have been an inn much longer than that."

"Oh, speaking of swans, look at those. Aren't they glorious? Some dear friends of mine, were married at The Abbotsbury Swannery in Dorset. An unbelievable wedding setting. And the bride's dress made her appear as if she were a dancer in "Swan Lake" ... I'll never forget it. That was Paul and Belinda. I'm sorry, hold on a minute." She reached into her purse and took out some tissue. "I miss Belinda, the Swan Bride. She died of Lymphoma a few years ago. They were the owners of my house in Newlyn. I told you a little about them, didn't I?"

"Yes, I remember. You're the Godmother of their sons," Stefan said.

"Occasionally, something reminds me of her, especially when I see a swan. And dear Paul. Sorry, forgive me for being emotional, I don't do that often in public." She put the tissue back in her purse and took hold of Stefan's arm again. They began walking.

"Shall we take a short detour across the lake to Princess Diana's fountain?" Stefan asked.

"We must. I had just come from the States to London, the night before she died. To visit a friend in the Midlands. He picked me up at the airport and we stayed overnight at his sister's home south of London. I couldn't sleep, so I stayed on the living room sofa, waking and watching television off and on. Suddenly a news flash came across the screen that said 'Di is Dead! We were here at Kensington Palace and placed flowers with thousands of others who were paying their respects. A sea of flowers. Such a sad, tragic week that was."

"Yes, it affected the whole world," he squeezed her hand resting on his arm. "Here's where we cross over. There's a café bar the other side of the fountain, we can go there and have a drink before we cross back over."

"Need I tell you I am having such a wonderful time with you? You seem to like the same things I like and it's so easy to be with you. But don't let it go to your head. I'm waiting for you to make that one mistake that will blow the whole thing." She laughed and he stepped back from her.

"Oh? So, you think I'm going to say or do something to scare you off or blow my cover?" He laughed too. "Maybe you'll be the one to say or do something that will send me in the opposite direction, did you ever think of that?" Still laughing, he reached for her hand.

"Could be, could be," she answered, still grinning. "You never know."

33

After a delightful afternoon and early evening together, Rachel and Stefan decided to separate, go to their rooms, and rest a while. Have some free time. The two of them would meet for dinner at eight in the dining room at the Ritz, afterwards they would catch the jazz at Ronnie Scott's, assuredly rounding out a perfectly wonderful day and night in London.

At seven Rachel's cell phone rang. In her robe, not dressed for the evening yet, she answered. The led screen displayed her son's girlfriend, Jennifer Locke's photo.

"Hi, Jennifer. How are you?" Rachel said. She sat on the edge of the bed.

"Are you at home?"

"No, I'm at the Ritz in London. I'll leave from here. Why? Is there a problem?"

"Oh, I'm so sorry, Rachel," she blurted out with a muffled cry. "I don't know how to tell you this ..."

"Tell me what?" Rachel's heart started pumping faster. She stiffened.

Jennifer began a full-fledged crying jag.

"What's wrong, Jennifer?"

Between sobs, "It's Devin ... he ... he's gone, Rachel."

"What do you mean he's gone? Where did he go?"

"Oh, Rachel," she couldn't stop crying. "He had a heart attack. I'm so sorry ... he died an hour ago."

Rachel's throat constricted, dizziness hit her. "You're joking, right? A heart attack?" She let out a cry.

"Are you alone, Rachel? Shall I call someone to be with you?" Jennifer could hear the hysteria building in Rachel's cries. "Rachel?"

"I don't believe it! No! Not Devin!" She began pacing back and forth, holding the phone to her ear while mumbling words mixed intermittently with whimpers and moans. She cried and sobbed, and finally fell on the bed in exertion, still holding on to the phone.

Jennifer didn't know what to do. "Rachel, could I call someone to be with you?"

Rachel reached over for the box of tissues on the bedside table. Weakly, she said, "A heart attack? He wasn't sick. When did it happen?"

Barely audible, "Just a little while ago, here ... at the house. I-I ... called the paramedics and ... and they couldn't revive him. I couldn't save him, Rachel. He just looked at me, said my name—" Jennifer couldn't talk anymore, emotions took over.

Suddenly Rachel straightened up with a wild look in her eyes. "I'll change my flight, take an earlier plane in the morning." Then she collapsed and wept hard again, letting the phone drop to the floor.

Jennifer could still hear Rachel's suffering. Her beloved son, gone. She could hear the hurt in her sobs and wished she could be there to comfort Rachel. "I'm staying at the house in Malibu, Rachel. I moved in two weeks ago. So, I'll pick you up at the airport when you get here, just let me know when. Okay?" She tried to control her own grief to support Rachel. Rachel had Devin all his life, Jennifer had only been a part of it during the past few months, so she could imagine how Rachel must feel. "Rachel, are you there?"

Rachel sat up, picked up the phone. "Yes, I'll call right now and change my flight. You take care of yourself, I know how much he cared for you." She began sobbing again. "I can't believe it ... gotta go, thank you ... thank you ..." She laid the phone on the bed, then held her hands over her face. "Devin, you can't leave me, not you ... anybody but you …"

She rolled over and muffled her sobs in a pillow. She didn't hear the hotel room phone ring thirty minutes later; she didn't hear Stefan knocking on the adjoining door.

The doorbell rang steadily, she didn't know how long she'd been lying on the bed, she'd fallen asleep. Her face and hair were drenched with tears. She had a throbbing headache and hadn't heard the previous pounding on the door, nor the voices calling out to her. She stood up and wiped her face and hair with a cloth.

Then a key entered the lock.

Stefan rushed into the bedroom, followed by security. "Rachel, are you all right, my darling?" he took her into his arms as she began weeping again. "Jennifer in California called the hotel, thought you might need someone. The manager called me; you wouldn't answer your phone or the door."

"My son ... he ... he had a heart attack, Stefan. He's dead. My son is dead ..." Saying the words hit her all over again. This time she cried as Stefan held her tight.

He motioned for Security to leave.

After Stefan helped Rachel remove her robe, she crawled under the covers.

Stefan sat on the bed beside her. "I'll call Virgin Airways for you and change your ticket for tomorrow. Is there anything else you'd like me to do? Shall I make some calls for you?"

Rachel opened her reddened, sad eyes and looked up at Stephan.

His heart sank, seeing her pained eyes tore him to pieces, too much for him. It took all his strength to keep from breaking into a sob himself.

Rachel took in a deep jagged breath, she said, "Would you please call Margaret and tell her what has happened, and ask her to call Paul? He has the keys to the house. Tell her to tell him I'll be all right and I'll call in a few days from California." Suddenly she sat up, holding onto Stefan's arms, "I don't know what I'll do when I get there and see Dev—" She broke down again, falling back and turning her face into her pillow. She couldn't say her son's name without weeping. "I can't believe it! I can't believe it! He finally found someone to make him happy ..."

When Rachel fell asleep, Stefan slipped out of the suite into his own to make calls. He left the adjoining doors ajar so he could hear her when she awakened and needed something.

He booked two first class tickets with Virgin for the 11:15 morning flight to L. A., and made a phone call to Margaret, briefly, to relay Rachel's wishes. Next, he called his mother to tell her he would be away for a week or two, said he'd be in the States to help a friend, and said he'd tell her all about it when he returned. The next call was his personal assistant, he left a message that he would be out of the country, could be reached by phone and computer if anyone needed him to answer any questions, otherwise, business as usual. With that done, he called the restaurant downstairs and ordered Brandy and a bottle of red wine to be sent up to his room.

Rachel awakened to soft music playing, dim lighting, and the French doors opened to the balcony. She could see Stefan standing, drinking wine, leaning against the railing looking out over the city.

"Stefan?" she said to herself as she reached for her robe and quickly put it on. "Stefan? What are you doing?" she asked.

"Ah ... she awakens. I'm watching over you, you see. Am playing the role of a guardian angel, although I'm a far cry from any angel. How are you feeling? Better?" He reached for her and pulled her close to him. "I worry about you."

"I think the sleep helped. It's been such a shock, you know. My baby. I'll never see him again, Stefan." She wept.

After a few seconds, he loosened his grip and reached for another glass to pour for her. "Here, have some Brandy. It has a way to soothe the soul and make everything better." He handed the glass to her.

She took it and sat in one of the chairs, leaned back, gazing out at the city. "It's a lovely night, isn't it?"

"Yes, it is. I'll order food for us when you're ready. I thought you might not want to go down for dinner. It's lovely up here and we'll have more privacy, if that's what you'd like," he sat across from her.

"You're right. I don't feel like dressing or going anywhere. I'm afraid I'll burst into tears if anybody looks at me."

Lifting his glass, he said, "Here's to a better tomorrow and fast healing—" his voice waivered. He'd done so well up to that moment, holding it together, but now, at the brink, he almost let go. "Sorry. If you don't mind, I need to take a sip, my throat's dry. Must be the night air." He took a couple desperate swallows.

She knew. His tears didn't get past her; his empathy got the best of him. What a wonderful man! She couldn't believe anybody could think otherwise of him. Thoughts of what Margaret had said in Marazion came to mind. She must not have known all the facts.

"I hope you don't mind, I changed your ticket for you. Flight leaves in the morning at 11:15, so we must be at the airport at 8:30. Will that be all right?"

"Yes, of course." She thought of arriving in Los Angeles and not being met by Devin as usual. She put her hand over her mouth as a new supply of tears surged. "What am I going to do?"

Stefan reached across and laid his hand on her arm. "You don't have to face it alone, I'm flying with you. I'll stay in California and help you with the arrangements; you can't be doing all of it yourself. It isn't right. I've friends in L.A., they'll help us, if we need them. So, don't give it a thought. You aren't alone. I won't leave you."

"Oh, Stefan." She gripped his hand, still holding her arm. "It's so overwhelming. Are you sure you want to do this?"

"I am very sure," he said as he reached for both her hands and drew her up from the chair to hold her. He gazed into her sad eyes for a moment, and then hugged her close as his own eyes teared up. "I am very, very sure. There's nothing I would rather do, than be with you."

There's no tragedy in life like the death of a child. Things never get back to the way they were.

Dwight D. Eisenhower

34

Jennifer waited at LAX airport for them.

Rachel had slept through most of the flight, she'd had a hard time sleeping the night before at the hotel, tossed and turned most of the night. By the time they landed and after orange juice and coffee on the plane, she almost felt normal.

Stefan had a hard time sleeping the night before too; his mind had been on alert to any sounds that might come from Rachel's suite. They had left the adjoining door ajar at his insistence. But, like Rachel, he slept on the plane, had plenty of rest by the time they landed.

"Jennifer is tall and blond," Rachel said as they walked towards baggage claim where they were to meet.

"She knows what you look like, right?"

"Yes. She sounds nice on the phone. Devin adored her." Her eyes teared up on that one, but she prevented a deluge. "You'll love the house; it's right on the beach." Her voice was shaky.

"It sounds lovely. From what you told me, it must be spectacular. And please, let me take care of everything for you. Just point me in the direction and I'll take it from there. I'll call your attorney in the morning and will contact the construction office too.

125

Then we'll go from there. Okay?" He rested his hand on her shoulder as they walked side by side, each also guiding a roller bag.

"I think I'm going to be all right now. I feel stronger and not so helpless. Between the two of us, I'm sure we can handle it. I really appreciate this, Stefan. I really do. It's because of you that I'm feeling stronger, you know."

"Just take it slow, and don't try to do too much all at once," he said. "And if you feel like crying, do it."

"Well, the first thing I'm going to do is call my agent and tell her to cancel everything. I am not going to do the book tour. No book festivals or conferences either. I didn't really want to do them anyway, and now I'm not going to. I've nothing to give." Her voice gave out on that one, and she reached into her pocket for one of the tissues she'd stuffed in it earlier. "I am not going to cry," she said as she straightened her shoulders and stood taller.

"Why not? Nothing wrong with it," Stefan added. "It's healing, as a matter of fact."

"If that's the case, I should be healed ten times over by now," she laughed. "Oh, there she is. See her, in the red top?"

Jennifer waved her white scarf at them. She recognized Rachel by the photographs Devin had shown her. He loved going through his albums, bringing her up to speed on his history. But at that very moment, seeing Rachel in the flesh, she didn't know how she could hold up at their first meeting. Extremely painful for her, too. The tears were already coming. Jennifer had loved Devin, right from the start. She fell hard and looked forward to a happy life with him. In an instant that life disappeared. She didn't know what to do now, she'd just found out about the pregnancy. Devin's baby.

"Jennifer?" Rachel said as her eyes began welling up with tears again.

Jennifer reached for her and they held onto each other for what seemed like a very long time. Both crying.

Stefan had one hand on Jennifer's back and one on Rachel's, feeling their grief.

Finally, they stepped back and wiped their eyes and noses.

"I am so happy to finally meet you, Rachel. Devin has told me so much about you. You have had an unbelievable life, he bragged about you all the time."

Rachel looked up at Stefan whose hand still grasped her shoulder. He gave her such strength. Just his touch reinforced her, a touch so new to her.

"And I can attest to some of it, what I've learned so far about this fine lady. She is incredible, and I hardly know her," he laughed. "And you, Jennifer, how are you holding up through all this?"

"Oh, I'm managing. It is still such a shock. I think I'm still stunned, it doesn't seem real. I'm just going through the motions. But come on, let's get out of this airport and get to Malibu. It's a beautiful afternoon, perfect at the beach. You'll love the views. But then, you know all about them, don't you Rachel? Devin told me you are part owner of the house, you're partners, right?"

"Well, the two of us formed a corporation and a family trust, all the property is in both our names. And the company. I don't know what we'll do about the company."

"I can help with that, if you want. I've been working with Devin nearly two years as a project engineer."

"A project engineer? No kidding," Rachel said.

"Yes, graduated with an engineering degree from Cal Poly San Luis Obispo after graduating from Cuesta Junior College. I worked for my father for nearly ten years in his construction company, worked my way up to Project Engineer III, and then Devin hired me as a IV."

Stefan raised his eyebrows. "That's quite an achievement, young lady." He looked at Rachel. "Sounds good."

"Absolutely!" Rachel said as they continued to make their way to a black SUV with D & R O'Neill Construction painted on the front doors.

"D & R?" Stefan asked.

"Devin and Rachel," Jennifer answered. "Rachel, I am so happy to meet you at last. I really am."

Devin's general superintendent, Mike, who Rachel knew, reached for the bags, "Here let me take those." He put them in the back of the SUV while Rachel and Stefan stepped inside in the seat behind the driver. Jennifer took the passenger seat.

"So sorry, Ms. O'Neill," Mike said as he fastened his seatbelt at the driver's wheel. "We all are shocked and so sorry."

"Thank you, Mike. How are you?" Rachel said, surprised to see him. "How's Elaine?"

"We're doing great, been handing out bids right and left, and Elaine's working for us now, too. She's Devin's— I'm sorry. I just can't believe he's gone. Doesn't make any sense." He shook his head and started up the vehicle.

Jennifer added, "Elaine was Devin's personal assistant."

"Sounds like he had a good support team in place," Rachel said as she wiped her eyes again, trying to hide the deepening hurt.

As they pulled through the gate to the estate in Malibu Colony, Rachel put her hand over her mouth, masking the quivering of her chin and mouth. But her eyes gave her away; she couldn't hide her whole face.

Stefan reached for her and whispered, "Go ahead, let it go. Just let it go."

She wept softly, couldn't get out of the car just yet. Seeing the home she and Devin loved; he had treated it like a prize of the Century. Rachel had been so proud of him and more than happy to help him buy the home and invest in his company. He'd never disappointed her. What a terrific success story, a sought-after builder, one of the best.

"I don't know if I can do this," Rachel whispered to Stefan.

"Yes, you can, and I'm here to help you. You can do it."

PART THREE
Las Vegas
Malibu
Montana
Skyler

35

With the blistering heat gone, the desert October weather had arrived in Las Vegas. Jessica and the girls were given a week's vacation from dancing at The Oasis Hotel in Vegas. They all decided to go home to North Carolina for four days. The producer of the show issued airline tickets to his dancers for vacations twice a year.

The Monday before the hiatus, Mario asked Jessica to go to dinner with him, just the two of them. By then she knew him well enough, and aside from the rough edges, he seemed to be harmless, despite the suspicions of what he had done to Wylie.

He took Jessica to his penthouse this time. Told her he wanted to show her where he lived. His wait staff had set a table of wine and antipasto dishes of pickles, olives, peppers, salami and cheese.

"Let's drink a toast to your vacation." He poured the wine and handed her a glass. "How about this view of Vegas, huh? Can you believe it? All the glitter and the fancy buildings, I like it up here."

"It's very nice," she said.

"Come with me, I want to show you something." He led her across the huge living room, then through a master bedroom, onto an expansive balcony with a pool. "Let's take a dip while we drink our wine and look at view of the city from here." He set his wine glass on a pool-side table, and removed his jacket and shirt. "Come on, it's just us. I've seen you practically naked already, onstage."

She laughed, and took off her little black dress, but not her lacy black bra and panties. She trusted him. Had come a long way from being sixteen and innocent. A big girl now, she could take care of herself, especially after all the defense classes she and the girls had taken.

"I'll hand the wine to you, go ahead. There are built-in stools in the water along the edge. See them?" Then he took off his pants, revealing a black speedo and a fabulous muscular body that stunned Jessica.

"Wow! Do you work out in a gym, or what?"

He laughed, "Yes, several hours a day. You like what you see?"

"I had no idea." She took the glass handed to her.

He joined her in the pool.

They talked about families, life in general, dreams. He had more substance than Jessica thought. Had an MBA from Harvard he didn't use, inherited a fortune from his father in New Jersey after he sold the trucking and boat-building businesses left to him. He invested all the money, and became a FOREX trader, spent a couple hours a day on his computers, building another fortune. His father's old style didn't suit him, he said, but he appeared to Jessica to be more like him than not, because he looked like Mafia, even though he claimed he wasn't. The Wylie disappearance, his buddies that hung with him, at times his behavior and mannerisms made her wonder.

"Miss Jessica, do you mind if I steal a kiss, just one. Just a kiss? Look at that moon up there, will you? Mustn't let it go to waste. Doesn't that stir something inside you?" He set their glasses on poolside and took Jessica's hands, pulling her towards him. "Just relax, baby. I won't hurt you, I promise. I love you, don't you know that by now?"

It struck Jessica's funny bone. The time, the place, what he said. She laughed. "Okay, but don't get carried away. If you weren't so cute, I'd say no."

A peck became two, then three. Their bodies pressed together, the water splashed against their legs and thighs. Jessica enjoyed what she felt, a sensual sensation in her lower extremities. She enjoyed the kissing, it seemed he couldn't get enough of her.

"Jessica, I have to have you. I do. I can't go on like this. Do you feel that?"

Yes, she did feel it pushing against her groin, but she didn't want to admit its effect on her. "Let's stop, please, Mario. Please." She drew back and got out of the pool. "I thought we were going to have dinner." She picked up the towel he had set on the chaise lounge, and dried her body. Then she slipped the little black dress over her wet underwear.

He pouted in silence as he drank the rest of the wine in his glass, before he got out of the pool and dressed. But he shook off the rejection and went on to provide a wonderful dinner and evening for the two of them. Jessica liked him.

After the last show on Sunday night the first week of October, all four girls—Janelle, Chauntelle, Carissa, Jessica—took a shuttle to the airport. Their friend Tiffany would pick them up at the Atlanta Airport.

Mario Russo and his side-kick Frank Rossi were waiting at the airport when they got there to say goodbye to Jessica and Carissa. They both adored the girls and relationships had blossomed, to some extent. Carissa's more than Jessica's. The other two girls headed for the gift shops after they checked in, said they'd meet Jessica and Carissa at the gate.

A bar sat near the last security checkpoint they'd have to go through to get to the gate, so Jessica and Mario grabbed a table and had a few drinks while waiting till boarding time. Frank took Carissa to a coffee bar, she didn't want alcohol.

"So, you are coming back in four days for sure, right?" Mario frowned as he asked Jessica.

"Yes, of course. Why? You don't believe me?" she laughed.

"I know you're going home to see your mama and she might talk you out of coming back. I know how that works. If I were her I'd do the same thing. In fact, I'd like to talk you out of going home. Why don't you just stay with me for your vacation. I'll take you to New York, wherever you want to go, the Bahamas, just name it." He leaned towards Jessica, the most beautiful girl in the airport, caressing her arm, petting her like he would a cat. "I love you, baby. I love you more than anybody I've ever loved. You know that, don't you?"

"You just think you do, Mario. You can't be in love with me. You don't know me. Besides, I'm too young to be in love. I'll be nineteen next month." He sat up straighter, "Nineteen, I thought you were twenty-one. You have to be twenty-one to be a showgirl."

"I lied about my age and have false papers to prove it. We all are nineteen. Just out of high school." She laughed. "Funny, huh?"

"But, Baby, you're not too young for me. I'm only twenty-eight. And I'm loaded; you didn't know that, did you? You won't find anybody as rich as me who'll be proposing to you anytime soon." He reached for her. "I'm asking you right now, Jessie, will you marry me?"

She laughed and leaned back from him. "I can't get married, Mario. Not yet. I can't get married, I won't." When she saw the hang-dog look on his face, it reminded her of her brothers, acting like a child sometimes. She reached over quickly and touched his hand. "What I mean is, let's wait a while, let's see what happens between us. It's only been two months since we've been dating, and you know I'm not like other girls ... the problem I have with ... well, you know. So, tell me, why would you want someone who won't go to bed with you?"

"Now that you bring it up, why is that, Jessica? Do you not like the way I look? Don't I turn you on? You not attracted to me?"

"It isn't you, Mario. It's me. There's something wrong with me, you already know that. I've told you before. I'm just not ready. Maybe— maybe after a few more months, if you're still interested."

A proud man, a handsome proud man, he leaned towards her, squeezing her hand. "Baby, I'll wait for you no matter how long it takes, for an eternity if that's what you want. But I'll bet money you'll be ready soon. I'm gonna start making plans, where we'll get married ... you wanna get married in New York? Where we'll live, here or New York, Jersey would be nice, have you ever been to Jersey?"

"I haven't been anywhere except on the road from Skyler to here. That's it."

"Okay. When you get back I'm going to propose to you officially, with a diamond and all the rest. Okay?"

She sighed heavily, shaking her head, knowing it was no use trying to convince him she didn't have an interest in marriage. So, she figured she'd just let it slide for now, she'd be on the plane in a few minutes, then she had lots to think about over the next four days.

36

Tiffany arrived with a van at the Atlanta airport and they headed to their destinations in North Carolina, a three-hour drive. On the drive, they brought Tiffany up to speed, told her everything. Then dropped off Jessica in Skyler first, in the south-western part of the state, didn't tarry, and immediately went further north to Ashville where the rest of their families lived.

Jessica hadn't told her mama about coming home. She giggled as she walked through the gate and up the rose-lined walkway towards the screened porch. She remembered the first time she stepped through that same front gate at the age of ten, when she didn't live there, when her grandmother denied her, telling her to go away and never come back. The memory of that day had been exonerated somewhat after old Missus Carter died and left her beautiful Victorian house and its furnishings to Jessica. Of course, Jessica figured that Uncle Sawyer had something to do with that. No one had said so, but she knew it had been to their advantage, Uncle Sawyer being Mrs. Carter's financial advisor and the executor of her will, and a good friend of Jessica's.

Now she was nineteen and on an early evening, she walked up the same rose-lined pathway. She knew her mother would be there to answer the door. She rang the doorbell, giggling and happy to be home. No one answered. Jessica pushed the doorbell again. Still no one.

That's odd. Someone should be home. At least one of her eight brothers and sisters were always there. Didn't make sense no one would be at home at that hour.

She picked up her suitcase and walked around toward the back of the house, through the gate in the hedge and along the stone walkway through an arbor. She heard voices and smelled barbecue. A breath of relief escaped her lips. *Now I'm home.*

As she rounded the corner and stood looking at the happy gathering on the patio, Uncle Sawyer saw her first.

"Jessica! My Lord, it's Jessica!" He dropped the barbecue tongs and headed straight for her before anybody else had a chance to react.

Evangeline squealed and ran past him grabbing her daughter Jessica and holding her tight. "You've come home! You've come home."

Uncle Sawyer reached around both of them and joined in the embrace. "We are so happy to see you, Jessie girl. What a surprise! Are you all right?" He stepped back and took a good look at her. "You okay?"

"Yes, I'm okay. Just needed a family fix. I missed you all so much."

By then the rest of the family jumped Jessica in a free-for-all, hugs and kisses galore for at least the next two minutes. Then they all made their way back to the patio for the meal that awaited them.

Jessica had brought presents for all – Las Vegas trinkets: sparkly combs for her mother and the girls, a palm tree key ring for Uncle Sawyer and assorted gadgets for the boys. Glad to be home again, she hadn't realized how much she'd missed her beautiful house and her loving family. She teared up as she listened and watched the children goof around with each other. She also noticed that her mother and Uncle Sawyer seemed to be laughing and smiling at each other more than usual.

Evangeline scooted closer to Jessica on the bench at one of the three picnic tables around the patio. "Honey, please tell me you're gonna stay home now, you are, aren't you? And then go to college like

Uncle Sawyer wants you to do."

Jessica glanced at Uncle Sawyer, their eyes met. He nodded.

"Well, I—I haven't decided what I'm going to do yet, mama. I'm gonna think about it this week and decide, if that's all right with you and Uncle Sawyer." Tears were welling up again. She didn't know why the sudden emotions, so she glanced away quickly and stood up. "Gotta make a pit stop, mama. Be right back." She hurried into the house through the patio French doors that she loved.

She loved everything about that house and had missed it as much as the family. When the contents of Mrs. Carter's will were revealed, she couldn't believe she now owned the house. Her grandmother had left it to her. No matter where she went it would always be there for her and her family. They would always have a home - a beautiful Victorian house in an upscale neighborhood of Skyler. If it weren't for the prejudices and what had happened to her at sixteen, she wouldn't mind living there forever. But she couldn't now. She just couldn't. She had to find her own way in the world, and if it meant going back to Vegas or going to college in New York, well, she would decide which direction to go by the end of the week. Marriage, out of the question, she did know that. Not a consideration. She didn't know how she would handle persistent Mario if she went back to Vegas.

A part of her wanted to stay home for a while. Maybe she could do that, maybe she'd request a leave of absence from the dance team, or even quit. That would give her time to equalize and figure out what she wanted to do. She knew she didn't want to be a dancer forever. Although she loved dancing, it had never been her ambition. She just went along with the other girls. She turned out to be one of the best, the producers told her. But now she must think about her future. And seeing her mama and Uncle Sawyer reminded her of that.

Jessica's brother Adam, now eighteen, had graduated high school and worked in construction in Highlands, an upscale resort town a few miles from Skyler; her sister Ginger just turned seventeen, a junior in high school, studying to be an artist; her brother Lenny, sixteen, was destined to be a homemaker, he loved everything to do with making a home for the family, cooking, sewing, cleaning; and her younger brothers and sisters were a little on the wild side, still children, cutting up and playing games in and outdoors, loved to tease each other. The youngest of the nine siblings, little Martha, ten years younger than Jessica, was a dainty little girl. Her mother had enrolled her in ballet classes.

"I want to be a dancer just like you are, Jessie. I'm tops in my ballet class, ask mama," Martha told Jessica on the bench in the backyard, eating her hamburger, looking up at her big sister adoringly.

Jessica couldn't believe how much her sisters and brothers had grown up. How did that happen? They seemed to be much older than when she left. She took the time to answer all the questions they shot at her, and returned all the hugs and kisses they planted on her. Jessica loved her family, and she had missed them more than she thought.

That evening she made up her mind as they all sat in the parlor, some talking, some playing board games, and some watching television. She had to find a career that would make her some money so she could take care of her mama and her family. And it wouldn't be done by dancing in Las Vegas. No way. It had to be something more substantial.

She moved over to Uncle Sawyer, sitting on a love seat looking through a book. "Uncle Sawyer, do you mind if we have a serious talk?"

He closed the book. "Why no, honey. Shall we go out on the porch?"

"Yes, let's do that. I'll get some lemonade and bring it out there."

Uncle Sawyer wondered what she wanted to talk about, he could see in her eyes that something troubled her.

Jessica joined him on the wicker settee and handed him a glass of lemonade.

"Thank you, my dear. Now what's on your mind?"

She sat next to him and set her drink on the table in front of them. "Well, I don't think I want to go back to Vegas. It's not for me. I want to do something with my life, like I always thought I would. Ever since a little girl, I knew there would be something out there for me that would help me take care of my family. But I don't want to live here, Uncle Sawyer, and I don't mean that I never will. It's just that I've always wanted to be someplace else. To see the world."

"Well then, first you need to go to university. You're smart and intelligent; it would be easy for you to go as far as you want after you finish school. Sometimes we don't know what our future will be until we take that first step. Somewhere along the way it happens. I've seen it happen many times. But are you absolutely positive you don't want to be a dancer?"

"I love dancing, I do. But how can that be a lucrative career for me? I can't dance all my life, I'll pique in my thirties. After that the next step would be a dance teacher. I feel like that would be a waste of my life. Don't you? Or I could become a sought-after choreographer, but that's a slim possibility." She laughed.

"True, but teaching can be a wonderful career. The way you take to history and the arts leads me to believe you'd be a wonderful teacher. And you love children; it's evident in the way you communicate with your family. You have patience. When and where you start is the question, it seems to me, and how far you take it."

Jessica sat up straight. "It's too late to start the fall semester, so what if I start school in the spring or maybe next fall? Probably next fall, that'll give me almost a year to apply and get ready for it. I'll be twenty. That's not too late, is it?" she frowned.

"As a matter of fact, it's perfect. You'll be older than the average freshman and will undoubtedly take it more seriously. The question is, where and which school?"

She put her hands in her lap and thought for a moment. "You know, I've been doing a lot of research on the Internet and, you aren't going to believe this, I'd like to go to Oxford in England. What do you think?"

"That's marvelous. I went to Oxford."

"I know. That's one of the reasons I want to go. Plus, prejudice is less in England. Although I feel I'm beyond prejudices, it still bothers me a little, can't shake it completely."

He hugged Jessica to him and stroked her back. "My dear, you have made such progress in healing from what that horrid boy said and did to you. That is all in the past. You deserve a blessed life, and you have one, as a matter of fact. If you never went to school, if you wanted to stay home forever, you could. I will make sure you and your mama and all the children are well-taken care of. You know I love you all." His eyes were tearful. It hurt his heart to remember when Jessica was raped and how it almost destroyed her. If it took him forever he would do all he could to help her forget.

37

"It's decided then," Jessica said to her mother the next morning at the huge breakfast table that seated twelve. She lifted her cup of coffee and took a sip before continuing. "I'll go back to Vegas and work till after New Year's. The show ends in January anyway, a new one goes into rehearsal next month, and that'll be a good time for me to fade out. That way I won't be leaving them in a lurch, although I'm sure they'd replace me in a minute. There are girls champing at the bit, lined up to get into the shows." She leaned back in her chair. "What do you think, Mama?"

Evangeline looked at her beautiful daughter, all grown up with a mind of her own, although she'd had a mind of her own since childhood. "Jessie, I have faith in whatever decision you make. You've got my full support. Uncle Sawyer feels the same way, you know. We're both behind you."

"Mama, when are you and Uncle Sawyer getting married?"

Blushing instantly, Evangeline's eyes opened wide, "What? Why you ask that question, child? Where did you get that notion?" Evangeline stood and began clearing the table.

"You can't fool me. I see how you feel about each other. It's

141

time, don't you think?" Jessica helped her mother stack the dirty plates that were left by the children who were already on their way to school.

Evangeline giggled. "You're a wise owl today, aren't you?"

"Well, it only stands to reason. He's over here more than he is at his own house. He might as well marry you and get it over with." Jessica chuckled to herself, loving every minute of making her mother giggle and squirm.

"Now you just mind your own business and get your own life in order, my little sweet pea. What we decide to do with ours is our business, and let's have no more talk about it. You hear?" Evangeline loved to talk about it, though. It had been on her mind more than usual. She wondered the same thing, but what would she do, ask him to marry her? What if he didn't want to marry her? So, no, she pushed it out of mind and went into the kitchen.

Jessica followed her mother with an armload of dishes. "You know, I'm thinking there's nothing wrong with being a dance teacher, is there, Mama? I mean, I could teach little girls like Martha, if I wanted to right now. I could do that. Set up a little studio and have my own business. I could start that right now."

"Yes, you could. But is that what you really want?" Evangeline turned and saw the frown on her daughter's brow. "Honey, it's something to fall back on, if you want. But I think that you should give your schoolin' a chance first. Go to college, see if there's something you'd like better, give yourself a chance before you settle on doin' something that comes natural and easy for you. Although they say that's what you're supposed to do. Something you love, that comes easy and natural. Do you feel that way about dancin', baby?" She rinsed off the plates and placed them in the dishwasher.

"Well, yes, it's easy for me, yes. But would giving up on my dream be the thing to do? Rather than tackling something out there I don't know anything about. I'm just a little scared, I guess. You're right. I can always fall back on being a dance teacher, yes."

Evangeline kept working, hoping her daughter would make the right decision and would finish her schooling. "That's my girl. You've always been a strong one, and you've always wanted to accomplish something. You haven't been reading and studying all those books for nothing, and not many have the chance to go, you know." She stood up and turned towards Jessica, "Don't be afraid, girl. Nothing's going to hurt you out there. You've got what it takes to tackle the world, baby. You've got my blood and the Carter blood in you. That's some strong, strong blood running in your veins. Can't beat that. And with Uncle Sawyer behind you, shoot! Nothing better than that."

"You're right, mama. I'll go back to Vegas and finish my commitment, then I'll come home and get ready to go to college in the fall. England, here I come! Easy as pie."

38

Stefan had been in Malibu with Rachel for over a month. October rolled around, and he needed to go back to England, he'd strung it out as long as he could, being away from his own business and commitments. But as he awakened on yet another bright sunshiny morning on Malibu Beach, he questioned the urgency to return to the damp, rainy weather of his homeland.

He threw back the covers and dropped to the floor to do his normal fifty pushups before starting his day. Then after doing the normal toilet routine he donned a jogging suit and left his suite of rooms, heading for the kitchen to have a tall glass of orange juice like he did every morning before his daily run.

Rachel sat at the kitchen island, looking at the newspaper and sipping coffee when he entered. "Good morning, Stefan. I poured your orange juice. Did you sleep well?" She couldn't believe the proximity of such a handsome man standing before her in a mansion on Malibu Beach, and they hadn't so much as had a sexy lingering kiss the entire month. Oh, they had a few hugs and kisses, sweet and quick pecks, but nothing more.

"Yes, I slept very well, indeed. And you?" Stefan reached for the OJ.

"Woke up early, tossed and turned all night, so I've already had a pot of coffee and have been writing. Started a new novel that's been rolling around in my head. I'm finally feeling able to get back to work."

"So, happy to hear that, Rachel. And now that we've handled Devin's affairs, I should get back to my work, head back to England."

"I know you have to go, Stefan, but I'll miss you, I will."

"It'll be hard for me to leave, but I must. You won't be alone, Jennifer is here. You can take this time to get your bearings. All is done. Do you feel that it's to your satisfaction?"

Rachel loved Stefan in that moment. She'd never been around a man as caring and sensitive and attentive. What a loss to the world that he never married and had a family of his own who would most certainly thrive on his kind of love.

"Oh yes, Stefan. You made it all very easy. Thank you so much. And I appreciate you handling Devin's Ex. I found it difficult under the circumstances, since she left Devin and filed for divorce. I guess I'm a bit resentful for her doing that to him. But then again, he said he loved Jennifer, and looked forward to a good life with her, told me so just a few days before he died."

"And of course, you still have your grandchild." He sat the empty glass on the counter and sat on a stool instead of taking off for his morning jog, sensing that possibly Rachel needed to talk.

"Oh yes, I love the little guy. He reminds me so much of Devin. Didn't look forward to the meeting yesterday, though." Rachel took Stefan's empty glass and rinsed it under the faucet. "She seems to be okay with the settlement, don't you think?"

"You were more than generous, Rachel. She should have no complaints.

"Well, like I told her, if she needs anything additional for the baby, all she has to do is call me. And when he's of age, he'll have a hefty trust account available to him. His dad saw to that. Plus, she has financial support and the house in Orange County."

"May I have some of that coffee?" Stefan asked.

"Oh, my gosh, of course. What am I thinking?" she laughed. She poured a cup for him. "There you go. It's a beautiful day, isn't it?" She set the cup in front of him. "Look at that ocean, will you? So calm and inviting. Makes a person want to just run and jump into it."

"Why not?" Stefan stood as he spoke.

"You're kidding."

"No, I'm not. Come on. Let's do something out of the ordinary. Here we have a gorgeous beach and we're sitting in the house." He reached for her and pulled on her arm. "Let's go."

Rachel hesitated and then set her cup on the counter. "All right, you're on."

They both shed their jogging pants. In shorts and t-shirts, they literally ran out the doors across the porch, down the steps, across the lawn to the beach, giggling like children, and didn't stop till they were jumping in the surf.

Later that evening as they sat on the veranda sipping Champagne, Stefan's last night in the States, they both were in a sad mood.

Jennifer hurried into the house from the garage and popped her head out the sliding doors for a moment. "I'm just going to run upstairs and freshen up, and pack a bag. In the morning, I'm going home for a few days, up north. Will you be ready to go to Moonshadows by seven? My treat for your last night in town, Stefan."

Rachel said, "Sure, we'll be ready." She glanced at the patio clock, 5:30 p.m.

After Jennifer disappeared Stefan looked down at his glass and said softly, "I will miss you, and all this, Rachel. More than you know."

She stared into her glass too. After a few moments, she turned and faced him, crossing her forearms on the table, "I'm afraid I'll be missing you too. Do you have to go?"

"Yes, it's time. I've put it off too long as it is." He leaned back and swallowed, still looking at her over the glass. "Have you decided what you're going to do?"

She thought for a moment, "Well, I have cancelled the tour; I definitely will not be doing it. I'm planting myself right here for a few weeks. Like I said, I didn't want to do the tour in the first place. I'll stay here for a while and then go to Montana to the cabin. Want to feel my mother's healing spirit, especially now. It is a spiritual place, you know. I told you about it. And of course, my friends are there, they're expecting me."

"Are you still planning to be in Las Vegas during New Year's Week?"

"Oh yes, all my gal pals are coming to celebrate, and their fellas. You are invited too, Stefan ... I do hope you will come, will you?

"I'll try, yes."

"I told my agent I would do the conference in Vegas that week. I'm a luncheon keynote speaker. And then on New Year's Eve, we'll celebrate the old and bring in the new." Tears welled up in her eyes.

Stefan saw the glistening in the corners of her eyes, he reached across and caressed her arm. "It hurts, I know."

"Yes, it does. I think of him a thousand times a day. How can he be gone? How could this have happened? Why would a child go before a parent? It isn't supposed to be that way. Those born first should die first." She dropped her face into her folded arms on the table, weeping.

Stefan rose and knelt beside her, pulling her to him, stroking her hair. She pressed her wet cheek against his chest.

"I don't know, Stefan. I just don't know if I can get through this. It doesn't feel any better," she whispered.

"It takes time. Grieve all you want, when you want. And remember the good times and all the love you shared with your son. You'll find that will outweigh the grief most of the time, will make you smile."

She pulled back, "But how do you know? It hasn't happened to you."

"Oh, but it has. When my father died, I thought I would never get over it. The day began and ended with him. It happened at a time in my life, eleven years old, when I needed him. He meant the world to me. My mother fell apart, even though they weren't the best of friends. She became a shell of a person, isolated herself. My brother and I had to learn to deal with it. If it hadn't been for a dear friend of the family, I never would have recovered. There should be someone you can lean on through this. Please let me be that someone, Rachel. You can call me anytime you want. I know what you're feeling, or at least a part of it. We're all different in our grief, but I do know it must be a part of recovery. It must be part of being able to go forward. Holding it in is not healthy. I think you're doing the right thing by going to your mother's cabin in Montana. It sounds perfect for you. I admire you for knowing what is best for you." He tipped her chin up with his finger. "I finally know what is best for me." He leaned towards her.

Rachel closed her eyes when their lips touched.

Stefan gently pressed his lips on hers, softly, and then drew back slightly, then they kissed again.

Rachel eased her arms around his neck as they rose together. Standing, she moved her body against his. They held the embrace, and a kiss that began as a soft touch now escalated to a passionate level.

"Rachel ... Rachel ... I—"

"Please, don't say anything." She held him tightly and nuzzled his neck with her nose and mouth. His aroma intoxicated her, and she wanted more.

They began swaying to the music of Natalie and Nat King Cole and their "Unforgettable" love song that was piped on the music system throughout the house.

When the song ended, Rachel broke away and headed for the door. "I've got to change clothes, Stefan. It's casual at the restaurant, but I want to put on something else, a dress maybe. Do you mind?"

"Not at all, I like you in dresses." He followed behind her. "I'll change into some slacks, been wearing these jeans all day."

39

When Jennifer pulled into Moonshadows' valet parking, and got out of the car, a valet took it from there.

Being in the Moonshadows Restaurant aroused fond memories for Rachel. During the month of preparing for their wedding a few years back in Malibu, Maxim and Rachel had frequented the dinner house. A romantic location resting on stilts above the beach, rocks and sand spread below, while waves rolled up beneath the restaurant. At night, spotlights were focused on the beach and boulders, adding to the unique ambiance. Little did they know Maxim would have a fatal heart attack a few days later.

Seated at a window table, Stefan marveled at the view. The sun fell lower and lower, changing the blue sky into shades of bright orange, purple, red, and yellow, surrounded by a dusty blue blending into the sea. A few sail boats were anchored in the calm water offshore, rocking slightly.

"Look at that, will you?" Rachel said. "I bet they're having their drinks onboard, listening to music like we are. Only they're in the middle of the water. Have you done that?"

"Oh yes. Many times. And you?" Stefan asked as he closed the

149

cocktail menu and placed it to his right.

"Yes. Dated a guy once who lived in Malibu, but docked his yacht in Marina del Rey. That was years ago, when I lived in Santa Monica. He owned the John Adams Life Insurance Company." Rachel laughed. "I don't mean to be specific, I'm just amused about some of my past experiences. Ben was a character. He asked me if I would quit my job and sail around the world for a year with him."

A waiter appeared.

"Uh, Rachel, would you prefer a cocktail or wine? Champagne?" Stefan asked.

"Champagne, please."

"I'll have the same," Jennifer said.

Stefan ordered and the waiter left.

"So, what happened?" Jennifer asked Rachel.

"What?"

"Did you quit your job?' Stefan asked.

"No no no. I didn't. I didn't go. Dumb me," she laughed. "I should've ... maybe ... but then, that's pretty close quarters, on a boat for a year in the middle of an ocean. No, I didn't go."

"I'm glad you didn't. Things could've gone in a different direction and I wouldn't have met you." He grinned at her.

"Could've . . ." She grinned too.

The waiter brought the champagne and poured.

"To us," Stefan said as he lifted his glass towards Rachel and Jennifer.

"To us," Rachel replied.

"I won't ask you to quit your job and sail around the world with me."

"Thank you for that."

They all laughed.

After dinner, Jennifer drove them back to The Colony, and then she went to Brentwood where she met friends. Thirty minutes later she telephoned Rachel, reminded Rachel she would be going Northwest with friends in the morning, and to call her on the cellphone if she needed anything.

Stefan excused himself to get into something more

comfortable. Rachel went straight to the veranda and set the mood ... music, lights, fire, bubbly. A huge moon made silver tracks on the sea, from the horizon to the beach. A beautiful and romantic sight.

After Stefan appeared in a sweater and jeans, Rachel excused herself to change clothes. He poured more champagne and sat in one of the lounge chairs staring out at the illuminated sea, thinking what a wonderful trip this had been, despite the tragedy. The thought of going back to England saddened him.

"Here I am ..." Rachel wore a flowing silk jungle-print caftan.

"Wow!" he said as he stood.

She held the sides and twirled, "I love my caftans. This time I'm going to take some of them home with me. Left them here from before."

"It is most becoming." He lifted a glass from the table and handed it to her. "Again, to us."

"To us."

"Well," she said as she sat facing the ocean. "I'll miss you, but I know you must return to your life and I to mine." After a few moments of silence, she turned towards him and said, "Thank you for all you've done. I truly appreciate you being here, I do."

He stood, took her hands and pulled her towards him. "I— I believe I've fallen in love with you."

She stepped back, "Oh no! You can't do that. You haven't. Why would you? I mean ... well ... I mean ... no, don't do that."

"Why not?" He slipped his hand across her shoulder and up into her hair, gently grasping while drawing her face closer to his as he bent and kissed her before she could say anything more.

At first, she tried to pull away, but then the sensual closeness and sexy kisses shot both their desires beyond the stopping point.

He picked her up and carried her to his room.

Their lovemaking became fast and furious, bordering on wildness with an abandon Rachel had never experienced. She let herself go; she lost control of her feelings and her body, and she didn't care. She just didn't care. She accepted and wanted to do whatever Stefan wanted.

Stefan wanted every single inch of Rachel's body. He wanted to taste, feel, and explore all of it. She didn't resist his touch, which

151

aroused him even more. At the same time, her arousal grew, seeming to accelerate with his. The moans and excitement heightened as the urgency increased.

When Stefan brought her to an orgasmic high by simultaneously titillating her with his tongue and fingers, he quickly pushed his erection deep inside her, then pulled it out. In and out, in and out. As their movements quickened involuntarily and in unison, they held each other in a grip that could not have been broken.

And then it happened.

The explosion racked them both and sent them scattering from the bed as the windows fractured and the ceiling caved. Plumes of smoke and builders' dust filled the air.

"Rachel, where are you? Rachel?" Stefan called out, trying to see through the darkness and sediment-filled air.

"I'm here, wrapped in the sheet." She scooted across the floor in the direction of his voice.

"Can you see me?" he croaked, spitting debris from his mouth.

She peered from the sheet, coughing, "Yes. I'm here, coming towards you. On the floor."

He reached for her, scooped her up in his arms as more ceiling fell, and swiftly carried her through the doorway into the main hall of the house.

They heard the sirens as he rapidly carried Rachel out the front entrance and down the driveway, with Rachel still wrapped in the sheet.

"Oh, dear God, we're naked," Stefan whispered. "Stay here." He adjusted the sheet tighter around her. "Don't move." He ran back into the house and within a couple minutes returned with jogging apparel for two. "These are too big for you, but it'll work for now."

They hurriedly put on the sweats as the police and fire trucks arrived.

The authorities and experts determined the explosion was caused by a faulty gas main that ran along the beachfront, servicing several of the opulent Malibu dwellings. The neighbors had reported a gas odor the day before, they found out later, but it hadn't been investigated yet. Luckily it wasn't connected to Devin's house, for his was an all electrical house, no gas hookups. Rachel's son had made sure of that before he moved in. If he were alive, he would say 'once again, mom was right,' for Rachel had always made sure their homes were all electrical, even though it was costlier.

Rachel contacted the construction office and repairs were underway almost immediately to fix the damage that had occurred to the west side of the house blown away by the explosion. They were lucky there hadn't been more damage or harm to anyone. The home next door was demolished, it had been hooked up to the gas main.

When Jennifer arrived the day after, Stefan reluctantly returned to England, and Rachel decided to go on to Montana.

40

The month of October passed quickly, gone.

Rachel transitioned into her Montana mountain cabin with ease. She took to it like yellow daisies to sun. Her mother Lily's spiritual 'footprint,' was all over the property, which gave Rachel added strength. It was the best place in the world for her to be, a spiritual solace to heal her heart and soul. As much as she'd mourned other dear ones, nothing compared to the pain of the death of her son. Nothing. Ever.

The first of November rolled around so fast, snow packed in, making it more difficult to get around. She had always dreamed of being snowbound, had written about it in her novels. Now it might happen to her, a delightful prospect, she thought to herself one morning as she sat on her porch, bundled up, and sipping hot coffee.

She heard the horn honking before she saw the vehicle coming up the driveway. Allegra and Connie. What a surprise! She hadn't seen them in two weeks, since the barbecue at the ranch when they'd invited all the neighbors and other people Rachel had met during her previous stays.

She stood up to greet them. "My Lord, are you brave or not?

Coming out in this weather. I'm glad I keep the drive plowed."

"We had to have our Rachel fix," Allegra said as they embraced. As tiny as before she had the baby. A hundred pounds at the most. As striking as ever.

Connie reached for Rachel, "Thought we should come out and see if you needed any help. Anything needs fixing or lifting? I'm your man."

"I do have something you can move for me, I do. The picnic table and benches out by the lake need to be brought up here and stored in the shed for the winter. You asked." Rachel laughed. "But first, how about some coffee? Come on in."

"Coffee sounds good to me," Allegra said.

"Where's the little one?" Rachel asked.

"With Arlie," Allegra said. "He adores his nephew, takes him to town with him, and wherever he goes. We've got a built-in babysitter."

"Arlie's going to turn him into a cattleman, for sure," Connie said as he laughed.

Rachel poured coffee, "Nothing wrong with being a cowboy."

"So how long you going to stay, you said you weren't sure when we saw you," Allegra asked.

"Oh, I don't know whether I'll stay here till December or go back to Malibu. I must be in Vegas the week before New Year's, you know, and then I'll be going back to England right after. You are coming for New Year's Eve, aren't you?"

"Yes, Arlie said he'd take care of Jody, so yes, we'll come a couple days before. Where are you staying?" Connie added, "On the strip or downtown?"

"The writers' conference is at the Oasis, so I'll be staying there," Rachel said.

'You said it's a romance novelist conference?" Allegra asked and poured herself some more coffee, she gulped the first cup. "You want some more, Connie? Rachel?"

Connie shook his head.

"I'll have some," Rachel said. "It's a bit different than the usual conferences, belongs to Jimmy Thomas, a male model and entrepreneur. And he hosts other male models at the conference, book cover models. Jimmy himself is on tons of covers. You can imagine

155

how the female romance authors flock to his conference, quite a gimmick for him."

"I can imagine," Allegra said. "Is he why you're going?" She grinned.

Rachel laughed. "Not! My agent lined it up. I'd rather not go. But you know me and New Year's Eves, haven't done one in Vegas. So, Jimmy Thomas is the ticket. The conference is his baby, started it himself and it's grown considerably, according to the reports. My talk is about what a publisher is looking for. Easy topic. Will only be there for the keynote luncheon. Thought about doing a workshop, but now, I don't want to. I don't have it in me. I think this will be it. I'm through with conferences, book festivals ... all of it! My head isn't there anymore."

"Not through with writing, I hope. Right?" Allegra asked.

"Oh no. That's who I am. I'll always write, till death do us part."

"Good." Allegra leaned back in the kitchen chair while she drank the coffee. "You said your other gal pals are coming ... Janet and the others?"

"Yes ... Janet, Shellie, Amanda and Della ... and their sweethearts." Rachel said. "We've celebrated quite a few New Year's Eves together, a recurring event for us when possible. I'm so happy you're part of our little group now. It's a special time of the year for me. Starting back on my father's deathbed, when he made me promise to see the world for him, and write about it, and celebrate New Year's Eves in all the major cities of the countries. Something he had always wanted to do. I've tried to, ever since. Not every year, but most. Of course, I do it for myself, too, not just for my father. It's something I love. He just gave me the idea." Rachel grinned.

Connie stood up from the table. "It's an admirable task, it is." He walked to the picture window and gazed out over the meadow to the pond.

"Yours was a glorious party, Connie. One of the best. Truly wonderful. I'll never forget it. On my wedding night." She turned away for a moment, feeling a bit sad, remembering. After the early New Year's Eve wedding, they all went across the lane to Connie's mansion and his spectacular party later that night. No, she would never forget her wedding day and that New Year's Eve.

Allegra placed her hand on Rachel's arm and said in a loving voice, "I don't know how you do it, Rachel. So many losses and you still seem to be able to go on. You're the strongest woman I know."

"I'm not all that strong. But you might say I'm resilient. I bounce back quickly. On the outside that is. I still feel it inside, but somehow, I'm able to focus on what needs to be done and can keep going forward. I've pretty much always been that way, no matter what. I think my release comes in the writing. I'll hole up in front of my computer and write write write ... I write pain into my characters. Good way to dump it onto them and deal with it through them." She laughed. "Seems to work."

Connie turned towards the two women sitting at the table. "Speaking of parties, we're having a Thanksgiving bash at the ranch this year, Arlie and his crew are smoking turkeys and he's invited practically the entire valley. You must come, Rachel."

"Oh yes, you have to," Allegra added.

"I wouldn't think of missing it. Absolutely. Shall I bring something?"

"Just you," Connie and Allegra chimed in unison.

"And invite your neighbor from up the road. What is his name? The artist?" Allegra asked.

"Sam Willis. I'll ask him. That's a great idea, he doesn't have family. Perfect. I'll call him later." Rachel had been thinking of Sam all morning. She couldn't believe such a nice man, a talented man, would be holed up in his cabin in the mountains alone. She could do it, but then she was different. She chuckled at the inconsistency. He was just as different.

"So, what is going on in that mind of yours that is tickling your funny bone?" Allegra asked Rachel.

"Oh, I keep thinking about Sam, wondering how he could live his life up here all by himself. But then I essentially do the same thing in Cornwall and when I'm here. Not much difference between us in that respect. We both have our projects and work to keep us busy, don't need much else. Yes, I'll definitely bring him Thanksgiving."

41

Rachel drove up the winding road ten miles north to Sam's cabin near the Canadian border. She loved the forest scenery in the mountains skirting Glacier Park on the road north. She took the drive quite often, but not always to visit Sam.

As she rounded the last turn on the snow-covered road before reaching his gate, she slowed to let a group of buffalo cross in front of her. *Nothing more soothing than witnessing nature in action.* Whether it be the animals in the woods and meadows, or the waters of oceans, lakes and streams, birds and wild flowers ... it all had a calming, happy effect on Rachel. No exception today.

When she had awakened that morning, she thought she had heard Devin's voice calling her. It came out of nowhere, as it did at any time of day or night, without warning. She couldn't shake it. So that morning she jumped out of bed, dressed, grabbed her jacket, and wiping her tears, she hopped into the pick-up truck and took off up the mountain towards Sam's place. She didn't want to bother Stefan with a blubbering phone call. She needed a face to face. Right now. Sam would have to do.

There he stood, by his gate, repairing the barbed wire fence. Sam's large log cabin lay at the base of a forested hill further up the drive. It reminded Rachel of the Lincoln Log home catalog she leafed through many times when she thought about rebuilding or adding on to her mother's cabin.

Sam's cabin had two stories: three bedrooms and two baths above, and the living space below – kitchen, family room, sunken formal and living rooms. It had a full wrap-around porch, and a detached three-car garage was to the right of the log cabin. His artist studio sat to the left of the house, with a barn beyond it. Quite an impressive property for a single man. Logs were of white pine.

He heard her coming and stood up and waved, setting his tools aside as he walked towards the gate to greet Rachel. The timing is perfect, he thought to himself. A bit lonely lately, but a new lady-friend from Billings had visited and left a few days before, hadn't gone well.

"Hello, neighbor," he said to Rachel as she lowered her window.

"Feel like having some company?" she said, noticing how fit and tall he looked in his fur-lined jacket, slim jeans and cowboy boots.

"You bet I do. Go on up to the house. I'll be right behind you." He swung open the gate and stood aside.

They had coffee in the breakfast nook that nestled in a huge bay window between the kitchen and the family room. The forest beyond the back garden glistened, wet from the melting snow on a sunny day. Deer were chomping the grass and flora in the open spaces around the trees bordering the thick woods that spanned up the mountainside.

"Don't you just love watching the deer?" she asked Sam.

"Yes, I do. In fact, I just finished a new painting of a family of them, I'll show you later." He continued to look at Rachel as she watched the deer, and he wondered what brought on this impromptu visit. She didn't do this without a reason. He wished she would, but of course he couldn't say that to her. He still thought it uncanny that her mother, Lily, had been his school teacher in the old days. Who would have thought that Lily's daughter would have found her mother after all those years of thinking her dead and would now be living part-time in the cabin her mother built? No one ever knew Lily had a daughter, she never spoke of one. And the mere coincidence that he and Rachel were both half Indian was amazing to him. His father was Blackfoot like Rachel's mother. Lily taught school on the reservation till she died. And after all those years Sam and Rachel ended up becoming neighbors in Montana near the Blackfoot Reservation. He liked that. Lily's daughter.

Rachel leaned back in the chair, lifting the cup of coffee to her lips, she drank the last of it.

"Here, let me get you some more, sis." Sam reached for her cup and took it to the kitchen counter.

"Sis?"

"Yes, I consider you my sister. Lily was like a mother to me. Got a problem with that?" He grinned.

"I always wanted a brother. How do you like your Keurig machine, bro?" she asked, noticing the chrome unit on his counter.

"I don't know why it took me so long to switch. You have one?"

"Not yet, but it's on my list. I'm getting tired of dealing with nasty coffee grounds. The Keurig makes it so simple and no mess."

"Yes, that it does. Mess be gone!" he laughed. "Here you go." He placed the tall turquoise-colored mug in front of her again. "Now, tell me what's on your mind. I can see something's bothering you." He had noticed her red-rimmed eyes, a sure sign of crying.

"You can, can you? Well, that doesn't surprise me. Even though we haven't been around each other that much to know our expressions, family just knows, isn't that right?"

He grinned. "We recognize moods, you're easy to read. Besides I have the knack. Your mother told me that, long ago. She was pretty intuitive herself, you know."

"That's what I found out in her writings and by other people telling me. We weren't together long enough to learn first-hand, but when we were, I could feel some sort of divine presence emanate from her."

"Gifted, same as you,' Sam added. "She said so."

"Oh no, I'm not. No way. I mean, I .... well ... I don't know what exactly you're referring to. Could you enlighten me somewhat?" Rachel leaned forward, her elbows on the table, wanting to hear more.

"She said you are creatively gifted. That you have undeveloped talents. I see that in you. In your writing, your sense of color and style in the cabin, your appreciation of nature ... you are a lot like Lily, she

160

just took it to greater spiritual heights. You can read people, and you have the capability to take it to a new dimension, if you want. Yes, that's what she said. So, what's on your mind?"

"I don't know, now. I forgot." She laughed.

"No no no ... c'mon, tell me."

"Okay. First, I'm missing my son so damn much. I wake up hearing him," her voice broke, she covered her face with her hands, giving in to the tears.

Sam offered her a box of tissues and squeezed her shoulder. "It's alright, just let it go."

After a few moments of letting go, she blew her nose and continued. "You know … it's pretty hard to get on a steady course this time. Because the moment I'm involved with something and am doing great, I want to call Devin and tell him about it, just talk to him, get his opinion like I used to do. He called me every week. He would tell me all about his work, his life in general, his marriage, we'd talk for an hour or two. I miss that, Sam. I don't have that anymore. I just miss him." Her chin began to tremble and the tears welled up again. "Oh, here I go again. I don't want to cry anymore. I didn't come here to cry." She took another tissue and wiped her eyes and nose.

"You're still grieving, Rachel. It's not even three months yet. You need to talk about him and your feelings. I'm here for you. I even have a phone, you know. You can call me anytime you want. Now that I'm family."

They both laughed.

Sam stood, "Here, let's have us a big hug. You need to be hugged, and I do too. We're never too old or too independent to be hugged."

His protective arms were warm and natural. She lingered as long as she thought it safe to do so, figuring past a point might be construed to be more than a friendly hug.

"Now, isn't that better?" He held her at arm's length, noticing the brown flecks in her green eyes, and the hint of freckles across the bridge of her nose.

She caught herself admiring his strong face, square jaw and tender eyes. His gentle touch surprised her, for a man of his size and strength. "Yes, thank you, thank you. Guess I did need that. Must have known you'd have a good shoulder to cry on."

"See, you do have a sixth sense, just like your mama said." He grinned as she sat down. "Now, what else is bothering you?"

"Nothing. What makes you think there's something else?"

"There IS something," he said, and smiled. "I know these things."

"Well ... well ..." She took a deep breath and let it out forcefully. "Okay, Okay! I've met somebody in England. Believe it or not, he's a Lord. Good God Forbid!"

"What's wrong with a Lord?"

"That isn't who I am. I could never live that lifestyle."

Sam frowned, leaned back and folded his arms across his broad chest. "Has he asked you to live that lifestyle?"

"No." She thought for a moment and realized how dim-witted she must seem to Sam. "But, I feel like it's going in that direction and it's really stressing me out, and I don't need another man in my life. Does that make any sense?"

"Yes, and when the time comes, and it will, you'll know whoever the lucky guy will be, you won't stress over it. It will feel right without questions. Right now, you're here, so there's nothing to bother about. He's not here. Relax. Mustn't waste time on something that doesn't exist in the present. You're in control of this moment. You're in the driver's seat. Or as your mother would say, 'Live in the moment. Only this very moment."

"You are so right, Sam. What's the matter with me? Dang! I'm dense."

"C'mon, I want to show you my latest painting. I need your input ..."

An hour later Sam watched Rachel drive down his driveway towards the main road leading back to her place. He considered the invitation to join her at the McAdams ranch for Thanksgiving. It appealed to him, for it had been a few years since he'd been invited to such an event. Holidays for him were next to nil as an adult. His family had long since died away, other than a few distance cousins who'd left the reservation to parts unknown, and he had chosen a solitary life over being part of the hub bub of the outside world. He'd had enough of that while out there. Every so often he'd meet a woman in Billings on business, but even with the ones like Darlene Stokes, who had come to visit the past weekend, it never worked. Always something wrong with them, or unacceptable in the mix. He had never met a woman who captured his heart.

But Thanksgiving with Rachel and the Arlie McAdams bunch and with Connie and Allegra Brown seemed like a doable proposition. Yes, he could do that. He liked them all.

Amused at the thought, he went back to his studio to work on another project.

42

There had to be over fifty people at the McAdams ranch for Thanksgiving. For some a three-day affair like theirs ... horseback riding, fishing, hot-tubing, card-playing, music and entertainment, gorging on wonderful food ... highlighted the holiday season, in spite of the winter weather. Arlie McAdams knew how to host a party. His sister Allegra and her husband Connie were great party-givers too. So, with combined forces they outdid themselves.

Sam and Rachel arrived on Thursday morning, just for the day of the actual Thanksgiving feast. They both separately decided that would be enough for them. So, they rode together, Sam picked up Rachel on his way down the mountain.

They brought along their dinner contributions. Sam was loaded with squash, tomatoes and apples, Rachel walked in with a huge cranberry-blueberry cobbler - her son's favorite.

"Oh, my gosh, Rachel, that looks delicious! Here, let Jeremy take it," Allegra said motioning to Jeremy, one of the house-helpers.

"I'll take these on into the kitchen," Sam said, walking past the women with the bags of apples and squash.

"I'm glad you came, Sam," Allegra called after him. "Thank

you for all your garden goods. Terrific!"

"So, you got a house-full, I see," Rachel said.

"Yes, we do. The McAdams always do it up good, you know." She laughed. "Come on in here, in the parlor, so we can talk a little bit before all the hullabaloo begins."

"How's the little one?" Rachel asked.

"He is the love of my life."

"Yes, I know how that is." Rachel said with a half-smile.

"But I've got some terrific news, Rachel. I'm pregnant. Can you believe it? Connie's so excited, his own baby. I'm happy happy happy! Can't begin to tell you how much."

Rachel grabbed Allegra's hands and squeezed them. "That is the best news ever. Do you know what it is yet?"

"We're talking about waiting till it's born to find out."

Sam walked into the room. "There you two are. Arlie is calling for you, Allegra. Says he's ready to start setting up the tables, he wants you to direct the helpers, he's busy with the barbecues."

"Okay, let's get to it. Come help me, Rachel."

43

Jessica and the girls went home for Thanksgiving. They had three days off, so they flew in to Ashland, North Carolina. Uncle Sawyer and Jessica's mother were waiting at the airport for Jessica.

Such a beautiful family holiday at the Sanford home in Skyler that year. More special than ever because Uncle Sawyer proposed to Evangeline Sanford on Thanksgiving Day at the dinner table in front of all nine of her children, and she accepted.

It didn't surprise anyone that Uncle Sawyer loved their mama, but it did give them a jolt when Evangeline grinned from ear to ear and immediately said 'yes, yes, yes' to his proposal. And it was an even bigger surprise to all of them, including Evangeline, when he produced an engagement ring with a diamond the size and color of a miniature pink rosebud in a rose gold setting.

The happiest Thanksgiving they'd ever had.

Later that night after dinner in Skyler, North Carolina, in their lovely Victorian home while listening to music, Jessica sat with Uncle Sawyer in serious conversation.

"I'm thinking I do want to go to college in England. Is that all right, Uncle Sawyer?"

"As opposed to?"

"As opposed to Princeton, Harvard, Yale, Columbia. I've done the research. Oxford has about 36 colleges to choose from, whatever you want to study, it's all right there. I'm interested in literature and business, so to me Oxford is the place to be. Do you agree?" Jessica said.

"Yes, I must agree. It's my alma mater. And if you find you might want to continue your business education in the States, then you can do that too. But for literature, you've chosen the right schools."

"So, I'm thinking after the end of the year. When our show closes, that'll be it for me. I'll come home and make my plans, but I won't be home for Christmas. It'll be after that."

Of course, Uncle Sawyer already knew this was coming; his bride to be and he had discussed Jessica's options earlier. Now it was a sure thing. She had made the final decision. He couldn't be happier.

44

Christmas Eve in Montana was a quiet one for Rachel. She holed up in her cabin, didn't want to go anywhere. Earlier in the day, she called Paul in London to wish him a Merry Christmas. No answer. Then she called Margaret in Marazion, Cornwall. No answer.

Around 5:00 o'clock in the afternoon, she telephoned Jennifer in Malibu. "Did you get the packages I sent to you, Jennifer?"

"Yes, I loved the boots. They fit perfectly. How did you know my size?"

"Just a guess. I'm glad you liked them. What about the jacket?"

"Oh, Rachel, it is wonderful! I've always wanted a fringed, suede jacket. And it fits too. For now, that is."

"What do you mean, for now?"

"Well ... now is as good a time as any to tell you. I'm pregnant, Rachel. With Devin's baby."

"What?" Rachel was instantaneously half excited, half worried.

"Yes, and I'm happy about it ... Grandma," she laughed. "I'll raise him to take over his daddy's business – if that's alright with you."

"I don't know what to say, honey. Of course, it's alright. I ...

when is he due? You already know it's a boy?"

"Yes, I was two months along when you were here, so now I'm five months. I just had a sonogram. He's a boy! Devin's boy. He would be so happy. I miss Devin every single day, and now I'll have his baby to love."

"Two grandchildren. I don't believe it. Both boys." Rachel was dazed. She reached for a can of Diet Pepsi in the refrigerator. "Now if you need anything at all, you will let me know, will you?"

"I sure will, and thank you so much for the Christmas presents. I've got family here, Rachel. We'll have to cut this short. They're waiting for me to go out to dinner."

"Oh … that's okay, go. I'm so happy to hear the good news. I love you, Jennifer. Bye now." She was stunned.

An hour later she telephoned Devin's Ex and talked to her dear grandson for a few minutes. Then she called her agent in Los Angeles. No answer.

All her gal pals would be meeting her the next week in Las Vegas, so she'd be able to celebrate with them first hand. The prospect of seeing them helped her get over the loneliness and depression that had overcome her in the past couple days. Although now, with the news of Devin's baby, she didn't feel as depressed as she'd been.

She decided to open a bottle of Champagne to celebrate Devin Junior, she wondered what Jennifer would name him. Rachel heard a vehicle come up the driveway. Sounded like a pickup truck. She set the bottle on the counter and went to the door. It was so dark she couldn't see who it was for a moment.

"Sam. Dear Sam. Wonderful Sam. What the heck are you doing here? Are you crazy? The roads are dangerous. Come on in. What a surprise!"

"Thought maybe you might want some company. Ran into Allegra in town today and she said you were going to be home alone tonight. So here I am. Figured we'd be alone together." He laughed as he reached for Rachel and hugged her.

"Come on in, come on in. I just took out a bottle of champagne."

"Well then, let's get at it. Sounds good to me. I carry a case of it in the truck, so if we need more, I'll bring it in," Sam said as he removed his jacket and gloves.

"In the truck? You're kidding?"

"Well, actually, I forgot to unload it today when I got home from the store. So, hey, how lucky can we get? It's our own natural refrigerator in the back of the truck. It's freezing cold out there." he laughed again. "Shall I do the honors?" He pointed to the bottle.

"Of course." Rachel took two flutes from the cabinet. "I am so glad you are here. You just don't know."

"I think I have an inkling." He smiled as he popped the cork. "Success." He poured two glasses.

"What are you doing without anybody on Christmas Eve?" Rachel asked.

"What do you mean? I'm here with you, aren't I?"

She laughed. "You know what I mean. Surely you have women friends. You mentioned one before."

He sat at the table across from Rachel. "Oh, I don't know. I just don't have it in me to expel the energy it takes to court any woman. It's so much easier to do what I want when I want, with who I want."

Rachel burst out laughing.

"Why are you laughing?"

"You sound like me, that's why. I've said that so many times in my life I can't count how many. I'm serious. That's my line. You can't have it." She gulped the drink.

"But you've married and I haven't, how many times is it?"

Rachel thought for a moment, "Twice divorced before I moved to England, married once in England, to Maxim. But then you know that. Almost married two others in England before that - one for business reasons only, chickened out on that one, and then fell in love with Pete from Liverpool. A few months before we were to be married, Pete was killed on an expedition in South America. Three times married is the answer. Have I confused you enough?" She giggled, gulping the second glass of Champagne Sam had poured for for her.

"No, I keep up with you. And the last one, from Moscow, died of a heart attack on your honeymoon. I remember. You've told me several times." He grinned.

"That's right. I do repeat myself. Sorry."

Sam saw the sudden sadness in Rachel's eyes even though she tried to cover it with flippancy and humor.

170

"I don't know where the two exes in the States are. One cheated on me with other men, the other beat the crap out of me. Who cares what happened to them. I'll have another glass, thank you. Another drink, that is," laughing as she held out her glass.

"Here you go. The last of it. Okay, I'm off to the truck for more. Be right back." He picked up his keys from the counter and went through the doorway. Returned in a few seconds, under a minute.

Rachel hadn't taken one sip of the last drink he poured her. She kept staring into the glass.

"You okay?" he asked as he popped the cork on the second bottle.

"I guess."

"These bottles are cold from being in the bed of the truck. It's freezing out there. Have you eaten?" he asked as he poured himself a drink, noticing she hadn't touched hers.

"Oh, dear me, probably not. You hungry?" she answered.

He opened the refrigerator. "You want me to make you an omelet? And some bacon, I see you have some. Or sausage? Toast, yes, French bread. Love French bread," he said as he removed the items to the cutting board.

Rachel watched him take control of her kitchen. She lifted the glass to her lips.

"Lettuce and tomato, some green onion, seasonings. Yep, you got it all." He turned to reach for his glass of champagne and their eyes met and held for a moment. "You have beautiful eyes, you know that?"

She sputtered, "What?" Then laughed.

"You do."

"You do too, so now what?" Giggles overcame her. "Will you be my new cook? Move in and cook for me in Cornwall? Part-time here, part-time there?"

He noticed the effects the alcohol had on her, and hoped she was temporarily forgetting her sadness. He had to admit, he certainly enjoyed the evening, so far for him it was the best Christmas he'd had in a long time.

She continued, "What else do you know how to cook?"

"Oh, I do steaks, I do spaghetti, meatloaf, chicken a hundred different ways, ham, pork chops. I do a mean Rainbow Trout

Almandine." He chuckled right along with her.

"So, you do mac n cheese?"

"Of course."

"You ... are ... hired! For sure! I'll have another." She lifted her glass.

He poured for her.

"I like cheese sandwiches too, with bread and butter pickles."

"So do I," he said. "And Mayo."

"Do you like to read?" she asked.

"Read all the time."

"So, do I," she said.

"In fact, I've read your novels," he said as he poured the omelet mixture into the pan.

"No kidding. You have not."

"I have."

"Amazing!" she said. "I like to paint too."

"I remember you mentioned that. We should go out painting together sometime when you're here in the summer. Plenty of scenery around here and lots of subject matter."

"I've noticed that," she said as she gulped the rest of the drink. "Oh dear. I'm very tipsy. Do you think you could make me some coffee?"

He heated water in the teakettle, knowing she had a French Press. In the meantime, he gave her a glass of water to drink. "Drink this to dilute the liquor in your system. We both should do it." He poured himself one. "Okay, bottoms up."

They both downed the glasses of water.

"Now coffee coming up and then dinner. Are you ready?" he asked.

"I sure am. I'm hungry."

Rachel managed to stay upright through dinner, although Sam worried about it a time or two. She drank the Champagne so fast, and it hit her just as fast. But with dinner over, dishes done, and coffee in their mugs, they were surprisingly able to carry on a conversation in the living area. Sam put on background music at Rachel's direction, and with the fire ablaze and crackling, the atmosphere was festive, cozy and warm.

"Thank you for making a Christmas for me, Sam."

"You made mine too."

He reached over and touched her shoulder in a friendly gesture.

"I wonder if I'll end up here in my old age. Like my mother did. Alone with my books, like she did with hers," Rachel said.

"She had more than her books, of course. She had the children of a Blackfoot nation who she taught and who cared for her. I for one. Decades of them. Sometime when you're up here again, I'll take you to the reservation to meet the people whose lives she touched. Would you like that? Some are still here."

"I would, I would. I haven't thought about that in years. Yes, I would like that."

He reached for the French Press to pour more coffee.

"Here, let me pour it, you've done everything tonight. I can do something," she smiled at him. "I can't thank you enough, Sam. Oh! Did I tell you I'm gonna be a grandma again? Jessica is pregnant with Devin's son. Now that makes me happy."

PART FOUR
Las Vegas
New Year's Eve

Rebecca Randolph Buckley

45

The day after Christmas Rachel flew to Las Vegas, Nevada. A thin sheet of snow covered the desert floor and rooftops, with a temperature in the mid 40s, even with the sun shining, still chilly. One thing about Vegas, the people flocked to it regardless of the season or the temperature.

Rachel checked into the conference hotel, the Oasis Hotel. She had agreed to speak at one of the luncheon events, changing her topic from the original. She agreed to talk about creating characters and giving them voices that rang true. An easy thirty minutes for her. The rest of the time she would prepare for her friends coming from all parts of the world for the New Year's Eve Celebration.

In her room the first night she ran a hot bath, sprinkled perfume in the water, poured a glass of champagne and slipped out of her satin robe as she stepped into the oversize Jacuzzi tub.

This is the life! Her thoughts took her back, as usual, to other times she soaked in her own perfumed 'pond' and imbibed her favorite bubbly. It always relaxed her, sometimes too much though. That night while soaking in the bath, she thought of the Grammy week when the mega star Whitney Houston died. She had done the same thing - ran bath water, poured a glass of champagne, and stepped into a hot bath. A big difference, however. Whitney had also been doing drugs and pills all week, as well as booze. And when her feet hit the boiling hot water, as reported, her feet were numb to it and the terrific heat surged to her brain causing her to pass out and crumple in the tub, hitting her head and drowning. A tragedy of all tragedies.

Rachel set her champagne on the side shelf and reached for the pitcher of ice water she had poured earlier. She knew that if a person takes a very hot bath, ice water should be available to drink as well. Keeping the body temperature down so as not to produce a rush to the brain causing unconsciousness.

She leaned back against the waterproof pillow with thoughts of anticipating another festive holiday eve with her friends just two days away, but tonight she would go to a dinner show at the Oasis.

At 7:30 p.m. Rachel entered the Palm Room, a lavish showroom, booths of carved wooden palm fronds and green upholstery, carved wooden columns encircling the auditorium and framing the stage reflecting its name. Greens, gold, pinks, blues and tans were the predominant colors in the beach island-themed room.

Rachel asked for a seat near the stage. She chose one near the right side of the right ramp where the dancers were sure to prance and perform. That's what she needed, to be entertained, to experience something different.

First came the dinner, she'd chosen filet mignon, vegetables and salad. She ordered a bottle of Champagne for the duration of the dinner and show, figured if she didn't drink it all, so be it. It was a short walk to the elevator to go to her room. It didn't matter, anyway. Being free to do whatever she wanted, intrigued her. She passed on the dessert, drank the bubbly, and had an interesting conversation with the people around her about the meal. Most everyone enjoyed the dinner except an overweight man who complained about the small portions, and a woman who complained about the chicken as she continued to eat every bite.

Rachel loved people, observing them around her wherever she went, their quirkiness, hearing what they had to say. She found them amusing most of the time, and usually took notes. Loved eavesdropping too.

The show topped the list of all she had ever seen, in Paris or anywhere, London, New York, name it. It held her from beginning to end. All music and dance, fast and furious, not a pause or hesitation of any cast member. Vocals were so good she couldn't believe she'd never heard of the singers. Why weren't they recording artists? The beautiful dancers were mesmerizing. One stood out from the others, a tall Eurasian-type, or maybe South American, Rachel couldn't tell, but extraordinary in looks and dance. She couldn't keep her eyes off her. A real showstopper. Wow!

Rachel's mind raced with thoughts of a future character based on such a girl and a possible storyline for one of her future novels. She always spectated and speculated, always thinking of the next novel in everyone she saw that caught her eye. She loved this part of her writing, on the lookout for new people, subjects and plots.

After the show, she made her way to the in-house lounge show to have a Midori-soda and watch a fabulous group playing there. Perfect way to end the evening, she figured, a nightcap and then off to bed. Tomorrow she would be giving the luncheon talk at the conference.

She reached for her cell phone to make a call, but hesitated. Paul had flashed across her mind. She hadn't been able to reach him all week. Wanted to invite him to Vegas for New Year's Eve.

No answer, just a machine message.

46

Allegra and Connie arrived the day of Rachel's luncheon speech. Rachel checked at the front desk to see if they were there, after her speaking engagement. She called on the house phone to let them know where to meet for Happy Hour.

Stefan would arrive at any moment from England, so she wanted to hang out at reception for him. Della and Valentin would be coming from Moscow later in the day, Shellie and Adrian were flying in from Switzerland, Janet and Robert from Paris, Amanda and Richard from Brussels ... all arriving the same day. Thrilled to have her dear friends together once again for New Year's Eve, Rachel glowed with excitement. It warmed her heart that they all had accepted her invitations.

She hadn't heard back from Paul, so that most likely meant he either didn't get the message or had other plans. She was unhappy he wouldn't be there, for after all, Rachel's New Year's Eves had begun with Paul on the night she and Ethan celebrated in London's Trafalgar Square.

Rachel had also invited Margaret and Felipe from Cornwall, but as it turned out Margaret had been admitted in hospital for surgery.

Margaret told her not to worry, but Rachel worried anyway, and planned to go see her as soon as she returned to England.

Now Rachel sat on a settee in the smaller registration area facing the entrance so she could see Stefan as he arrived. He'd just texted her from the taxi leaving Las Vegas's McCarran Airport, and she told him where to meet. Any minute he would walk through the doors.

She couldn't say what she thought about Stefan coming. In a way, she still loved her freedom, especially around her gal pals. She didn't know how he would fit in with the guys, and didn't know if he would feel awkward. Her thoughts were making her feel guilty. She had invited him, for God's sakes, so she needed to shake off the negativity and get over it. *Stay in the moment. He's here, in Vegas, on his way to the hotel.*

At that very moment, he walked through the breezeway doors.

All the unsure questions and feelings vanished. Joy flooded her senses.

How could she keep going back and forth as she did and had so many times when it came to the men in her life over the years? What made her vacillate so much? She'd often wondered if she should see a shrink, had never had sessions with anyone but herself. Even after she'd been violently raped by the congressman those many years ago, and later almost murdered by him, she had worked through it by herself. Some of her trust issues and uncertainties still had been unresolved because her mother abandoned her at such a young age, she knew that. Although her father had run her mother off, threatening to kill her if she tried to take Rachel with her. She also knew that had affected her relationships with men. She never hated her mother, didn't even ask questions about her as she grew up. Her father wouldn't talk about it anyway. Most of her young life he drank, and didn't sober up till her stepmother Lee came on the scene when Rachel reached her teens. And when Rachel finally found her mother in Montana, she loved her instantly and vice versa, as if they had never been apart. So, she didn't really know why she had such a problem with freely giving a man her all.

And now, here Stefan rushed towards her, a rare specimen of the male gender, who seemed to adore her and who she adored when they were together. She must let go.

Stefan dropped his bag and took Rachel in his arms. He leaned back and looked straight into her eyes. They were on the same page, he just knew it. "Would you mind if I kiss you?" he said, glancing around not wanting to embarrass Rachel. He grinned widely, his perfect teeth sparkling almost as much as his gleaming eyes.

"Do you really need to ask?" she teased. She reached up and wrapped her hands around his neck and in one long tender kiss she felt loved and loving.

Of course, she had had that feeling with others, but now they were dead. It frightened her to think of it.

47

Everyone had arrived and were meeting at the Chart House Restaurant in the hotel where Rachel had made reservations for twelve. She decided to skip the happy hour, and left messages for everybody to meet for dinner at seven.

She and Stefan came down earlier to the restaurant to make sure her wishes were carried out, and that the waiters knew to put the entire tab on her hotel account. Her guests were to pay nothing. She chose wines and Champagne to be placed at the table, ready and waiting.

Stefan stood by, sipping a cocktail while watching her in action, impressed at her assertiveness and know-how in organizing the event. He admired her slim, simple black halter dress of satin and stilettos of black patent with cutouts along the sides. Very chic and elegant. Her only jewelry were ebony drop earrings with a bracelet to match. Black complimented her auburn hair which he loved. Her nails were painted a color that matched her lipstick and hair.

"Would you like a drink while we're waiting?" he asked after she finished with the maître d'.

"Yes, I would. I'll have a Kahlua and soda, if you don't mind.

For a change." She smiled.

"This is a switch, I don't believe I've ever seen you order Kahlua."

She laughed, "It's what Vegas does to me. I order Midori and Kahlua sodas, for some reason. Fun drinks, I guess. Fun town, maybe?"

"I shall definitely return with your Kahlua and soda." He headed for the bar.

She pulled out a chair from the table and sat down, her feet were hurting.

The table settings were stunning, exquisite china, glassware, silver, flowers. Bottles of Pink Champagne were in table-side iced buckets, one for each couple. Bottles of red and white wine were intermittently placed strategically on the table, reachable by all. She looked at her watch, fifteen minutes till seven. Although she knew all her friends had arrived and were in the hotel, she hadn't seen them yet, for she knew after such long flights they would all need to refresh and possibly nap before dinner. So notes had been placed under their doors with the plan for the evening.

"Here you go, Luv," Stefan said as he handed a glass of Kahlua and soda to Rachel.

"Thank you very much," she said. "Come sit by me and relax for a minute. We've got time."

He pulled a chair out from the table. "This is very lovely, Rachel. You are an accomplished hostess, very capable. And seem to enjoy it."

"Yes, I must admit I do. In fact, I love to give parties. Sometimes I have them catered, sometimes I do the cooking myself. Depends on the size, and the occasion."

Stefan reached across Rachel's back and squeezed her bare shoulder. "My mother used to be quite the hostess, too. But now she's unable to do much with her failing health. I do want you to meet her, Rachel, when you return to England. You will come to the estate for a few days, yes?"

"Yes, of course," she replied quickly and then looked towards the doorway, hoping to see her friends arriving. She didn't feel sure she should spend time at his estate and didn't want to talk about it. It seemed too serious of a request to her, serious in the sense that it seemed ... seemed ... it just seemed like they were getting too close. Committing maybe? But she didn't know how she could refuse after all he'd done for her and the time they'd been together. What could she say? 'I don't want to spend any more time with you because I'm afraid we'll get serious?' It already had gone too far. Regardless, after he'd helped with the arrangements of her son's internment, and stayed with her for a month taking care of her, she needed to be more resilient and trusting. She'd just take it a day at a time and not worry about it. It would go where it would go. She'd do as Sam suggested. Although, right now, she'd made the right decision in booking separate rooms.

48

Jannelle drove, Jessica and the other girls were talking a mile a minute as the van swerved through the traffic heading for the Vegas strip. "I'm going to take the freeway to downtown, it'll be quicker," Jannelle said.

"What time is it?" Jessica asked.

Carissa answered, "Quarter to seven, we're okay."

"I don't know why I let Mario talk us into meeting him for drinks and appetizers," Jessica said. "That's cutting it pretty close for the nine o'clock show."

"We'll be alright," Carissa said. "Just need to be in costume by eight forty-five."

Five minutes later they pulled into valet parking at the Oasis. Jannelle told the valet to have their vehicle ready and waiting at 8:15. He said he would.

The girls hurried into the hotel casino and headed for the steak house where Mario and his group were waiting.

Mario stood and ushered Jessica to the chair beside him, Frank did the same with Carissa, and the others took the rest of the empty chairs between Mario's other friends. Ten at the table. Another table of twelve were seated in the same semi-private dining space.

Rachel watched the girls file in and instantly recognized the one from the show she saw the night before. She couldn't believe it, what were the chances of ending up dining at the same restaurant in a city such as Las Vegas with showgirls she saw the night before. *Aren't they performing tonight? Maybe they have a night off.*

She couldn't keep her eyes off the one most exotic-looking of them all. Rachel's eavesdropping mode immediately clicked in and interfered with conversation with her own group seated at her table, catching up on each other's recent lives.

Connie and Allegra, from Montana, both dressed in black, were seated across from Rachel and Stefan. And since Connie and Stefan were both British, they were embroiled in talk about the politics of Britain.

"Do you know someone at that table, Rachel?" Allegra leaned and whispered.

"As a matter of fact, I went to a show last night here, and I think the girls were the dancers in the show. I know one of them is, couldn't miss her anywhere. I'm dying to know more, you know how my inquisitive nature kicks in," Rachel said.

"I certainly do, mine does the same thing."

They both laughed and downed their drinks while trying to hear the conversations.

At the other table, voices were getting louder.

"Yes, we're going to do it. We're going to do it. This coming summer we're going to Cornwall, England. We mean it. To Port Isaac to watch the filming of Doc Martin," Carissa said, to the table of showgirls and what looked like mobsters to anyone looking on.

"I can't wait!" Jessica said to Mario.

"How you think you gonna get there?" Maria barked. "You want I should charter a plane, you want me to do that?"

"Omigod, no!" Jessica said. "We're going on our own, Mario. It's a girl thing. No men allowed."

Jannelle spoke up, "My mother goes to England all the time, and she'll make the arrangements for us. We don't need your help, Mario."

"Well, I don't think I want to let Jessica go off on her own like that, without me knowing what's happening. She could get hurt, or get lost, you know. I can't let that happen," he said as he reached for Jessica's hand and put his other arm around her shoulders, pulling her towards him.

Jessica pulled away, sat up straighter. "I can take care of myself, Mario. I can. And I will."

Rachel immediately responded. She stood up and stepped to their table. "Excuse me, I couldn't help over-hearing what you said. I live near Port Isaac. Doc Martin is my favorite British TV series, have seen all the seasons. And I'd be happy to talk with you about going to Port Isaac, girls. Maybe I can help in some way, finding you a place to stay, giving you tips on transportation. I go there all the time. It's my get-away place. And I can assure you, you're gonna love it." Thrilled that she found a way to possibly get to know the tall, beautiful dancer that captured her attention the night before, Rachel held her breath.

Jessica squealed and her eyes widened, "You really live in England?"

"I sure do. And I want to say, you are superb dancers, I saw your show last night. In fact, I'm taking all my friends here to see it New Year's Eve," Rachel motioned to her own table of guests who were all focused on what she had to say.

"How many are you? We'll leave tickets for you at will-call. And we'll have to have lunch to talk about our trip," Carissa blurted.

The other girls chimed in, eager to hear what Rachel could tell them about Port Isaac in Cornwall.

"That would be wonderful, yes. There are twelve of us, but you needn't do that, I'd planned to take them anyway, we're from all parts of the world." She pointed at the couples as she named their home regions, "Montana, Switzerland, Belgium, France, England, Russia ... and we're all here for a special New Year's Eve get-together."

Tiffany, one of the dancers, spoke up. "My father just moved to Belgium. Ghent. My mother lives in Paris."

Jessica stood, reached in her bag and took out a pen and note pad and began writing. "My name's Jessica Sanford. Here, you give this to Will-Call, they'll take care of you all. We'll make sure you have the best table in the place. That's New Year's Eve, right?"

"Yes," Rachel looked back at her table of friends, "That okay with all of you? New Year's Eve we see the best show in Vegas?"

The response included an exuberant clapping of hands.

"Okay, I'll leave you alone now. I just couldn't help but say something since you were talking about some of my favorite things. My name is Rachel O'Neill, we're staying here at the hotel, and you can leave me a message saying when and where we can meet for lunch this week. I'll bring my gal-pals with me," she grinned at her dear friends, "and our guys can go off and do what they want." Everyone seemed to like the idea. "So, have a wonderful evening." She returned to her own table, feeling a surge of new energy and purpose.

49

After dinner, Rachel's group met in her suite for coffee and dessert. She knew they'd be suffering from jet-lag, so she planned nothing but the dinner on their first night in Vegas. She figured they'd want to call it a night rather early. But for those who wanted to linger and talk about old times, it seemed best to gather in an intimate setting without the noise and activities of crowds around them.

Her suite had two-bedrooms with a sitting room and a large living room and bar. The hotel had laid out a buffet of desserts with hot drinks and alcoholic beverages fully stocked and waiting.

Coming from one of the bedrooms, Rachel entered wearing a black paisley caftan, "Stefan, will you please pour me a Moscato? There should be bottles of it in the refrigerator."

"Anyone else want wine or spirits from the bar, yes?" Stefan called out as Allegra and Connie entered the wide-open door into the suite from the corridor. "I'm the designated barkeep, here to serve," he said as he uncorked Moscato for Rachel.

"I'll have a Brandy, please," Connie said, "and some Moscato for Allegra, while you're at it. Do you need any help, Stefan?"

"I don't think so, not yet. Here's two Moscatos for the ladies."

Connie took the drinks to them as Stefan poured Connie's Scotch.

Richard, from Brussels, joined the men, ordering a Scotch too. "Connie, can you tell me more about the cattle you broker?"

Richard's tall, slim wife Amanda, still in her dinner dress of pink lace, ordered a glass of Champagne and joined Rachel and Allegra, who were sitting on the sofa talking about their cabins in Montana.

Robert and Janet (still in her winter-white, knit dress), who flew in from Paris, walked through the door carrying two bottles of Champagne.

"More Champagne, everybody!" Janet exclaimed. "Hell, we're here to start us some celebrating!"

"There's the Janet I love so well," laughed Rachel. "Robert, there're other drinks at the bar, if you'd prefer. Stefan's in charge."

Robert grinned, "First I'll take care of our girl here, some champagne, Stefan. And then I'll have a shot of Vodka."

Stefan held up another bottle of Champagne at the bar, "Here we go, my man. Champagne for the lady. For you we have Stoli Elite, yes?"

"Yes," Robert said. "The best. Excellent!"

Through the door, Della and Valentin from Russia entered. Della had changed into a green jogging suit, which complimented her flaming red hair. She looked more Irish than ever, a stark contrast to her black-haired, dark-eyed, tall, handsome Russian husband.

"Where's Shellie and Adrian?" Rachel asked.

Della answered, "They'll be here in a minute. She has a headache and wanted to take some Aleve and rest a minute."

"I hope she's okay," Rachel said.

"She is. Just a bit jet-lagged," Della said.

A half hour later Shellie and Adrian joined the group and they all spent another hour catching up on life in all their fast lanes before they retired for the night.

50

Jessica left a message for Rachel that the lunch date would be the next day at 'Paris' in the food court. The guys were to go to the casinos to try their luck, while the gals lunched with the showgirls.

"I can't believe we're meeting up with those fabulous-looking dancers." Shellie said.

Amanda pointed, "There they are, over there at the entrance."

"Ah, there's Jessica. Look at her, will you? Wow!" Rachel said.

"We look like old mares compared to those young ponies." Janet said.

They all laughed.

Rachel led the way and took Jessica's hand when they came face to face. "You are so gorgeous. All of you are." she said.

They were grinning ear to ear as they said their hellos and meandered to a table that would accommodate them.

Janet opened the menu, "What would you suggest we order, girls?"

Janelle answered, "Everything is good, trust me. Whatever your heart's desire."

Amanda commented about the chicken Caesar salad.

"That looks good to me," Rachel said. "That's what I'm having."

"Me too," said Amanda.

The waiter and the cocktail waitress came to the table to take their orders.

Jessica ordered, "Champagne all around, Leslie, please."

The girls were in total agreement with Champagne. The noise level quickly rose with their chatter and laughter as they waited for the food.

"So tell us about Port Isaac?" Jessica asked Rachel.

"Well you already know how it looks since you've seen it on Doc Martin, right?"

"Yes, but does it actually look like that?" Carissa said.

"Sure it does," Della answered. "I love the place, myself. When I visit Rachel we sometimes go there to feel the history of Cornwall and all the spirits of those who've gone on before. You can actually feel the magic, you can."

"We're coming there, we honestly are. Next summer when they're filming. At least I am," Jessica said.

"I don't know if I can do it, Jessica," Janelle said. "I've got some plans on the horizon. Don't know yet."

"Well, I'm coming to England, Rachel. I am. for sure," Jessica said. "I've made up my mind."

Rachel reached for her glass. "Here's to the show tonight and to a wonderful New Year's Eve tomorrow. May we have good health and good luck ahead of us."

Della raised her glass, "May we get what we want, may we get what we need, and may we never get what we deserve."

The girls laughed and giggled.

Rachel couldn't help but notice that even though the young dancers were embroiled in a vocation that would tend to age them quicker than most and expose them to the dark side of life early on; at present they still had an innocence and child-like enjoyment of life going on. She hoped that they would escape the inevitable, she hoped that maybe they wouldn't stay in Vegas. That the newness of the adventure would be enough for them. They all seemed to be from another walk of life. She could only hope. She felt protective of them, at least of Jessica.

"So, what is your long-range plan in life, Jessica?" Rachel asked.

"That's a good question. My mama and my uncle want me to go to college, I have a trust fund. I could go anywhere I want." She took a sip of her drink. "All of us can do that. But I'm just not sure what I want to do. One thing for sure, though, I am not hooking up with Mario like he wants me to do." She looked at the girls. "I'm leaning towards entering college next fall at Oxford."

Carissa frowned. "I think you should go on to England before the summer, Jessica, if you can get away from Mario. The longer you stay the harder it will be," she said.

"You're more than welcome to come stay with me till you get your bearings, Jessica. I can show you the ropes, take you to Oxford to get all the information. I have a big house in Cornwall," Rachel said, feeling excitement rise within her.

Della chimed in, "It's a huge house. You could have your own floor! You really could. And it overlooks the water."

"Really? So ... so when could I do that if I wanted to?" Jessica asked reluctantly.

"Anytime. I'm heading home next week. You could come along then."

"Oh, my goodness! No, I couldn't do that, it's too soon. I'd have to go back to North Carolina first and see my family, tell them my plans. Oh, my goodness! Should I do it, you guys? I'm getting excited!"

Janelle grabbed her hands and squeezed them. "Yes, you should. Go to England, go to Oxford. Make a good life for yourself, Jessica, yes! See the world!"

All the girls agreed, telling Jessica they'd come visit her, and they wouldn't tell Mario. Said she should make her plans now before the new show came in. Said they were considering getting on with their lives too, away from the Vegas scene, sooner rather than later.

Rachel loved hearing that.

"And when you all come to Europe, you have to come up to Belgium too." Amanda said.

"Switzerland, too! Not far from Amanda," Shellie said.

"And Paris! Janet said.

194

"Well! Are we forgetting Russia here? Moscow isn't chopped liver, you know!" Della added.

Laughter all around.

"By the way, if you ever need a local hide-out, I'm just a short flight away, in Montana! Don't forget about me," Allegra said.

"We'll exchange addresses and phone numbers before we go," Rachel added.

"And vice versa," Jessica said with a very wide grin.

The food arrived on serving carts delivered by handsome servers.

"I love Vegas!" Della exclaimed loudly. "Just love it."

"Me too." Janet lifted her glass.

They all cheered, happy to be together.

51

NEW YEAR'S EVE! A happening night in Las Vegas.

Rachel planned a wonderful celebration for her guests from around the world. Always she had been invited to NYE parties hosted by others, this time it would be as she wanted it. She made all the arrangements her second day in Vegas, before and after giving her talk at the conference. Then the third day her guests arrived. Fourth day, lunch with the showgirls. Now the fifth day, New Year's Eve had arrived!

It began that morning with selecting a dress for the evening. Rachel and her five female cohorts spent all morning in exclusive shops at Caesar's Palace and in the Venetian. Prices fluctuated from affordable to not so affordable, all designs and styles.

"It is a day to die for," Della commented in one of the stores at the Venetian. Her eyes immediately zoomed in on the perfect green dress, her favorite color. "That's it. I've found my dress. I love the sequins. Please, please, please fit." She grabbed it and headed to the dressing room.

Amanda brought her dress with her from Brussels, a long, fitted, lacy pink one she had designed especially for the occasion.

"Look at this one, Rachel," Amanda said. "So, classy, as well as sexy. And all black. You'll love this. Look at the back of it." Amanda held it up to show the girls.

"That is perfect for you, Rachel," Janet said. "The sexy V in front as well as the back, wow! Stefan will pee in his boots."

"I hope not." Rachel laughed as she went for a closer look at the long black dress. She took it from Amanda. "It's pretty, I like it. The fabric is soft. I don't know if it's strong enough to separate my boobs, though."

They all laughed.

The sales girl reminded her of the special bras in stock that would solve that problem.

"Okay, I'll try it on," Rachel said. "Need a black bra too."

Allegra found a blue dress with pearls dotting the bodice, the skirt had a nice flare which complimented her tiny body nicely.

Shellie and Janet were still looking, and wanted to go on to the next shop.

"Let's meet at the café at the end of the corridor along the indoor canal, in about an hour, for lunch. Okay?" Shellie said as they were going towards the door.

Amanda said she'd tell Rachel and Della. She sat on the settee and drank the Champagne offered to her while waiting to see the choices that were being decided in the dressing rooms.

Later, in their hotel rooms, the gals were resting, waiting on their guys to return from wherever they were.

Although Stefan and Rachel had separate rooms, they were adjoining and the door left open between them.

Rachel heard someone opening Stefan's door, and called out, "That you, Stefan?"

He came to the adjoining doorway, smiling at Rachel. "Did you find a beautiful evening gown?"

"I did. Come in, let's have a glass. It's nearly New Year's Eve, you know." She started to get up from lying on the sofa.

He went to the bar, "I'll get it, you rest. I know how grueling it can be to shop all day."

"Oh, do you? Are you a shopper?" she asked kiddingly.

"As a matter of fact, I am. I love shopping. Especially for

women's clothing and jewelry. My mother has been the recipient of my extravagance for years."

"And your women too, no doubt," she said, still kiddingly.

"Yes, they too." He kept pouring, not looking at Rachel. Then he turned and delivered the drinks to the cocktail table in front of the pale blue brocade sofa.

"So, did you shop for formal attire for tonight?" Rachel asked.

"No, I brought it with me. I have suits for all occasions."

"I should've known," she laughed.

"Let's make a toast, shall we?" he asked, still standing.

"Go ahead." She lifted her glass.

He thought for a moment. "Here's to the loveliest woman I have met in such a long time. And to the possibility that she will eventually feel about me as I feel about her." He clinked her glass.

"And who might that be, pray tell?"

"You, of course, dear Rachel. Love of mine."

They both stared at each other, not moving, just holding up their glasses in mid-air. Both smiling.

She stood, facing him, "And here's to the man that is the most caring and attentive man I've ever met. The most observant and intelligent handsome man I know." She clinked his glass.

"And who might that be, pray tell?" Stefan asked.

"You, of course. Only you."

He set his glass on the table and took Rachel's from her. Then moved closer and put his arms around her and gave her a kiss, a kiss of sweetness and love. They clung to each other for a few moments, swaying with the goodness of it, feeling a natural desire grow between them, that captured their senses and emotions.

Stefan whispered, "I'm falling in love with you, Rachel."

Rachel leaned back looking up at him. "You mustn't do that."

He hugged her tightly, then let her go. "Okay, let's drink to that."

They reached for their glasses when the doorbell rang.

"Oh, who could that be? We're all meeting at six downstairs," Rachel said as she walked towards the door. "We have three hours yet."

She opened the door and there stood a hotel attendant with a huge bouquet of lavender roses. "Oh, my gosh! Who could these be from?"

The porter brought them into the room and set them on a table. Stefan tipped him and thanked him.

Rachel pulled the card from the arrangement, while counting the roses.

"Thirty-six roses, three dozen! My goodness." She opened the card and read, "Sorry I cannot be there, Love from your dear friend, Paul. Happy New Year!" She sighed. "Oh, I had hoped he would come. You'd like him."

Stefan frowned, wondering about Rachel's feelings for Paul. His name came up in conversation quite often. "I have something for you too." He quickly went into his room, returning with a gift box tied with a gold ribbon. "Something for you to wear tonight for this special occasion."

She untied the ribbon, lifted the lid to view an incredible single strand of giant black pearls and matching giant pearl drop earrings.

"Oh, Stefan! These are too beautiful! Oh my!"

"Do you like them?" he asked.

"Of course, I like them. What is not to like? Oh, thank you, thank you, thank you." She put her arms around his neck and kissed him softly.

"Will you wear them tonight?"

"I most certainly will, they're perfect for my new dress. How did you know?"

"How did I know what?"

"They are perfect for my dress."

"I didn't know."

"They are."

At six o'clock the twelve members of Rachel's party met in the hotel reception area and continued to the stretch-limo waiting outside. Only a short ride to the MGM Grand, where they were to be dining in a private room at the only Three Michelin Star restaurant in Las Vegas - 'Joël Robuchon'. Rachel had preordered the 14-course tasting menu degustation. She figured there would be something for everybody and no where would the food be better than at Joël Robuchon.

She had picked up a menu from the restaurant the second day there, and couldn't believe the offerings: the first course of Le Caviar

Oscetra served atop king crab and a crustacean gelee, extravagant and over the top, she knew. Next came La Salade de Pomme de Terre – Carpaccio of foie gras and potatoes covered with black truffle shavings, then came Le Saumon – Scottish salmon confit coated with wasabi cream, fourth would be Le Homard – Maine lobster in a thinly sliced turnip with sweet and sour dressing, and on and on including bacon, egg, frog legs, langoustine ravioli, sea scallops, soup, sea urchin, black cod, spiny lobster, and beef Chateaubriand. Of course, the accoutrements were lavish and gourmet prepared. A meal like no other. And the dining room luxuriously filled with flowers, crystal, and everything sophisticated.

When they were seated in the private room, they all expressed their gratitude to Rachel for being such a wonderful host, but agreed she had gone overboard with her graciousness.

"If not for my dearest friends, who else can I do this for? I love you all, and I want you to be happy this very special New Year's Eve. Most of us have been through many of these together, good and bad. I just wanted this one to be the best for you. Thank you so much for coming." Standing, the rest of them sitting, Rachel lifted her glass.

Stefan stood up, interrupting her. "Rachel, may I?"

"Yes, of course." She sat.

"It has been an honor to meet all of you at last, Rachel speaks fondly of you quite often. I find that the diversification of your dear friends, Rachel, is incredible. We have Amanda, the clothing designer; her Richard, the cattleman; Janet, real estate mogul; her Robert, architect; Shellie, jazz singer; her Adrian, artist; Della, writer-publisher; Valentin, restaurateur; Allegra, screenwriter; Connie, entrepreneur. I find it amazing for all of you to have come together this New Year's Eve, far from your homes and children, to be with our wonderful host of the year who at this time in her life needs you more than ever."

They all clapped and some blew kisses to her.

"I want to add that ... that I am falling in love with this woman," he grinned mischievously at Rachel, "and ... and I hope you will encourage her to return that love. Tell her what a great guy I am, and remind her that live in Cornwall too, her favorite spot on earth. Will you do that for me? A toast?"

They lifted their glasses in unison, adding their own comments, "hear, hear" "absolutely" "yes, Rachel" and so on. Laughter all around, Rachel included. The fun began.

At nine, after three hours of dining, the group left to see Jessica and the girls in the best show of its type in Vegas, topped off with a firework show they would watch from the roof of the hotel at midnight.

The stage show started at nine-thirty so they had just enough time to pick up the tickets at will-call and be ushered to their table stage-side.

As before, even after seeing the spectacular performance the first night, still it didn't disappoint Rachel. Everyone raved about it, the beautiful and talented dancers, the singers, the costumes and staging, top-notch.

Jessica even gave them a wave when she saw them, and grinned even wider than before. Rachel hoped she would come visit her, come stay with her in England. She felt she could help the girl get on track with a better career, something Jessica could be proud of. Not that she shouldn't be proud of her dancing, but she could do better, if she wanted. The day would come when dancing would no longer be an option. Rachel wanted more for her now.

Right before midnight they all were led to a spot on the rooftop of the hotel. The arrangements had been made before hand, by Jessica. A private area was reserved, where only the owners and higher echelon were allowed, a table had been set up for Rachel's group with food and beverage. It felt like a dream, like being in a fairyland with glittery lights and the dazzling marquees and lights that lit up the city. Rooftop celebrations were once in a lifetime for most, and here it was a third time for Rachel – a New Year's Eve in Moscow, in Malibu, and now another incredible midnight, this one in Las Vegas.

When the countdown began, everyone stood near the see-through shielded railings, toasting glasses poised, all were ready to shout out Happy New Year. At the shout, the firework display from the tops of most of the hotels began. Glasses were tossed and kisses were given.

All the couples exuded happiness and joy, including Rachel and Stefan who were locked in a romantic embrace and kiss.

Again, he told her he could fall in love with her.

He didn't require a reply, just held her closely as they watched the light show in the skies over Las Vegas.

That night they slept together. Literally. Slept. After the festivities they both were exhausted, Rachel more than Stefan. He could've made love to Rachel all night, but he sensed her mood and reluctance. The mere fact she booked separate rooms for them, made him wonder. So, it had been a good idea to have his own room that night.

And now she fell asleep almost immediately after cuddling together for a few minutes. With her body backed snuggly into his, he reveled in the warmth and feminine softness against him, his arm draped lightly over her. While she slept, he wondered. Wondered what she must be truly thinking of him these days.

It had been three months since they were in the explosive incident in Malibu. Explosive in the romance department as well as the house implode. They had spoken on the phone a few times since then, while she was at the Montana cabin, and he was back in England, but their phone conversations weren't of any consequence. He might not have been on her mind at all, contrary to his incessant thoughts of her. Maybe he had done something to put her off. He wondered what Margaret had told Rachel about his engagement two years past. Even Margaret couldn't know the specifics. Someday he needed to have a sit-down with her and clear the air. Maybe Rachel's mourning her son … of course it took precedence, how could he think otherwise. The past three months had been very full for her, in Montana and now in Vegas. He must quit ruminating. Must go to sleep. He had an 11 a.m. flight to catch.

52

The following week, after New Year's Eve, at home in North Carolina, Jessica took a deep breath and spoke succinctly, "So what I'd like to do, Uncle Sawyer, is go on over to England now, and stay with the woman we met in Vegas, she was there speaking at a writers' conference last week."

"What is her name, my child?" Uncle Sawyer asked, frowning.

"Rachel O'Neill. I looked her up on the Internet, she writes mysteries and romances. Movies have been made of some of her books. And it's her, there were pictures of her, so she's not a phony. She lives in Cornwall, has a big house there, and says she'll show me around that part of England, as well as take me to Oxford to get acquainted with it."

"You're sure you want to go to Oxford?"

"Yes, I am, in the Fall, Uncle Sawyer. I've made up my mind."

"Then I don't see why you can't go now. That means you're not going back to Vegas, right?"

"That's right. I'm not going back."

Evangeline entered the room and sat next to Uncle Sawyer.

"What are you two so serious about?"

"Jessica's going to England to go to school. She's not going back to Vegas."

"Oh, that's wonderful, Jessica." Evangeline jumped up and hugged her daughter where she sat. "That makes me so happy."

"She's going right away, Vangie, will be staying with a writer in Cornwall who will show her around," Uncle Sawyer said. "Of course, I'll do some checking on the woman before you go, Jessica."

"Is that the one you met in Vegas?" Evangeline asked.

"Yes, Mama. She's nice. I know I'll be safe."

PART FIVE
England

53

Good to be back home in Cornwall; Rachel had missed Newlyn. She loved her house on the hill, loved the ocean view, the cold British weather, even in winter with the average January temperature of 44 degrees Fahrenheit. Fireplace blazing and blanket-wrapped in an overstuffed chair, that's what it meant to Rachel.

Always the first week of her return to the UK, after traveling abroad, she reacquainted with her surroundings. Straightening and fluffing the house, opening windows to let in fresh air, regardless of the weather. She would check on her flowers that the gardener tended when she left town, noting what needed to be planted or removed. Loved her English gardens. The rest of the time, she'd read and listen to music, sometimes paint, sometimes write. Then after the first week, she'd get down to business, start planning her days, getting back into the routine of writing mostly, her mainstay.

The end of her second week home she began writing a new novel, a murder mystery. She had some of the characters, had blocked them out, had the murder victim, but not the plot or the murderer, not the why or wherefore.

She had just sat at her computer, after making a cup of coffee, when the phone rang.

"Hello?" she said.

"Rachel," Paul Newland said.

"Paul, where are you? Thank you for the beautiful roses. Did you get my messages, I wanted you to join us in Vegas for New Year's Eve?"

"Yes, I got them, but too late to follow through. So I sent the roses instead. How did it go?" he said.

"The best. I missed you."

"My father passed away, Rachel. In Canada. So I went to take care of things, my mother couldn't. You know they were estranged and he had only me. Evidently, he spent the past few years in an assisted living facility. I didn't even know it. He would call but never said where he called from. So, you can imagine the total shock when the call came about his death. I had to telephone mother, she didn't know. Anyway, I just got back from Canada."

"When did he pass?"

"In November. I stayed there two months. Decided to get in some skiing."

Rachel poured a cup of coffee. "Did you go alone?"

"Yes, who would I take? There's no one in my life now. My luck with women is in the tank. And the boys are too independent to be trekking with their dad. They are holy terrors, Rachel. You should see them." He laughed. "All grown up now, or thinking they're grown up."

"Why don't you bring them down sometime? Tell them I want to see my God-sons."

"I'll try. You could always come to London, you know," Paul said.

"Yes, but not yet. I just got home and I'm not going anywhere for quite some time. I'm going to be home-bound, and I need to do some writing."

"Same with me, I need to paint. I'm in demand, you see." He chuckled.

"Well, if you feel like getting away for a weekend, do come to Cornwall, Paul. Okay?"

He hesitated then said, "I will, Rachel. I will. So how are you … after Devin …?"

"It's still hard. You know all about that."

"Yes, sorry to say I do. But I would imagine it's different to lose a son. I don't know what I'd do if I lost Jake or Pauli. I'm so sorry, Rachel. I'll come down as soon as I can."

"Please do. You always make me happy."

He smiled as tears began to form. "Yes, well it's been nice talking to you, luv. Cheerio." He hung up

Rachel didn't feel right. She felt there was something left unsaid.

The phone rang again.

"Paul, is that you?" she said quickly.

"Uh, no. It's Jessica. You know, we met in Vegas? The dancer?"

"Jessica! Where are you?"

"I'm in North Carolina, and I'm genuinely wanting to come to England now. Will that work out for you? You don't have to spend a lot of time with me, just point me in the right direction. I would love to get to know Cornwall first, though." She sounded excited and eager.

"Of course. When do you want to come?"

"How about February First. I can be ready by then, if it's okay with you?" Jessica crossed her fingers and squeezed her eyes shut. Wishing.

"That will be perfect. I'll have time to get some things out of the way, and I'll have everything prepared for you. Send me your email so I can give you traveling information and directions. It's sort of tricky getting to Cornwall. My email is Rachel O'Neill at AOL dot com. Easy to remember. Send me an email today and I'll get to work on it."

"Oh, what a relief! I'm so excited, I can't wait. This will be my first time out of the States. What should I bring clothing-wise?"

"Well, if you don't have to, don't bring much. Wait till you get here to buy clothing that you'll need. Just bring a couple pairs of jeans and a couple pull overs, and a warm jacket. It's cold here. You can always get more later. Travel light, one carry on."

Jessica squealed, "Ohhh ... I can't stand it, I'm so ready to come over there." She giggled.

"I am looking forward to it too, dear."

"Okay, bye," Jessica said, and hung up.

Rachel hadn't spoken to Stefan since the second day she returned to Cornwall. She thought about him now, wondering if she should call and let him know in two weeks Jessica would be there. No, she'd call him later. Right now, she needed to write. Interruptions, and then there are interruptions, the plight of the writer.

54

Where did the two weeks go? Rachel nervously waited at the Newquay Airport for Jessica to arrive. She still hadn't seen Stefan since she'd been back, they talked on the phone, but Rachel had been engulfed in heavy-duty writing, and Stefan said this time of year he buried himself in government business. She decided to call Stefan while waiting for Jessica to land, to let him know her plans.

Her call reached him while he drove on the road to London to attend a Parliament meeting the following day. They chatted for a few minutes about what they'd been doing since they saw each other.

"… so, next week I'll be taking her to Port Isaac for a few days, she wants to look around, get familiar with the place so she can rent a house for the months of May and June. She's hoping the girls will come over and stay a couple weeks while the Doc Martin filming is going on."

Stefan laughed. "Sounds like they're going to have a fun holiday. Port Isaac won't know what hit it."

"I know," Rachel chuckled. "So, when do you plan to come down? You mentioned something about it when we spoke last."

"Things are pretty much up in the air right now, what with

Parliament, my mother's condition, and the wind fields. I want to get it all under control, if I can, before I come. Later this month, I suspect."

"Just give me a call. Oh, got to go, her plane just landed. Talk to you later, bye." She hung up the phone.

The plane hadn't landed. Rachel questioned in her mind whether or not Stefan was just putting her off. Not that she wanted him to visit just now. It just seemed odd to her that given the proximity of his mother's estate and everywhere else in England, all a reasonably short distance from wherever, she knew if she really wanted to see somebody she'd make at least a quick day trip to visit, easily enough. But then, that's the way she had always been. *Expectations of others will always cause you grief,* her mother would say.

She went to the refreshment counter and poured another cup of coffee.

Twenty minutes later the plane landed. Jessica bounded across the tarmac with gusto. A vision of energy in motion. The heads were turning in admiration watching a young woman who had the world on a string tied around her finger, just like the song said.

"Over here, Jessica," Rachel called from the ramp.

"Oh, I am so glad to finally be here," Jessica said, and hugged Rachel.

"I see you didn't have any trouble with the change of flights and all, you're on time."

"Your instructions were perfection. I loved every minute of the trip. It feels like I've been traveling for days, but I feel wonderful. I'm ready to get on with my new life. I've left everything behind. Thank you so much, Rachel, for making this possible and so easy." Jessica hugged her again, and they left the terminal for the parking lot.

On the road heading back to Newlyn, Rachel pointed out the way to Port Isaac. "It's only around forty minutes north. Newlyn is fifty minutes south from here. So, the airport is basically halfway between the two. And when your friends come to join you in Port Isaac, they can take a cab from the airport, it's the easiest way to travel, buses are rather tricky and uncomfortable, must change midstream, etc." Rachel knew she could probably pick up the girls when they came, but it wouldn't hurt for them to learn the ropes and do it for themselves. Independence is best.

"I love all this green ... is it this way all over England? I've

212

heard it is."

"Pretty much," Rachel said as she pulled onto the A30 going to Newlyn and all points on the most southwestern part of England.

"Tell me about Newlyn. I read all I could find on the Internet, and the photos are what made me want to come right away. You live right on the bay?"

"It's a seaside town, as you know. My hillside house has an expansive view of the sea across Mount's Bay, it's an easy walk to the ocean. There's St Michael's Mount in Marazion, I'll take you to that tomorrow while I'm giving you a tour of the area. So, you can get your bearings."

"When can I check out Port Isaac?" Jessica asked, full of excitement.

"Whenever you want. How about this next weekend? We can drive up and spend a couple days."

"That will be perfect. I can't believe I'm here, can't believe it. I never want to leave."

Rachel laughed. "That's what I said when I first came. And here I am. Eleven years later. I never want to leave either. Oh, it's nice to have other places to go, I have the cabin in Montana, and a house in Paris—"

"You have a house in Paris, France? No way."

"Yes, I do. Part interest with Janet. You remember Janet and Robert."

"Do they live in the house?" Jessica's eyes opened wide.

"No, it's there for the three of us to use when we want. Janet, Shellie, and me. And whoever we lend it to." I plan to spend some time there this summer, maybe. It's my second writing haven, Paris is full of inspiration."

"You are so lucky, Rachel. You can go anywhere you want to, all over the world. You have friends all over the world to visit. I want that too. I do. It's my dream. But I want to accomplish something too, not be a free-loader. I want to do it on my dollar. Uncle Sawyer would give me anything I wanted, if I'd let him, but I want to do it myself. He's the most wonderful, generous man I know. And guess what? He and my mama are getting married in August, so I'll be going home for the wedding before I go to Oxford in the Fall. Isn't life exciting? I don't think I can stand it!"

55

The weekend rolled around quickly for Rachel and Jessica. They left the house early on Saturday morning and drove to Port Isaac. Rachel had made reservations for them at the Courtenay House, a large Georgian holiday house, right in the center of the old village of Port Isaac.

After Rachel obtained the key from the rental agent she drove up the narrow alleyway from the tiny bay to the house, stopping in front of the stoop.

"Here, take the key and go ahead and unlock the door, I'll get the bags. Can't park here for very long. As you can see there is absolutely no parking. I'll leave the car running, then I'll park it across the way, up the hill."

Jessica did as Rachel said, and couldn't believe the size of the house when she walked in. "This is wonderful, the rooms are big, aren't they? I'd heard that the rooms were small in England."

Rachel followed behind and dropped the two bags on the floor. "I thought this might be a good place for you and the girls to rent this summer. If you like it, you can reserve it now for the two months, if it's available. Okay, I'm off to the car park. Go ahead and look around.

There are four bedrooms, two baths. Pick a bedroom. See you in a few. By the way there's a bus stop above the village, you can take buses in either direction to neighboring sites and villages, we'll do that while we're here so you can get the hang of it. And you can always call cabs. Okay, be back in a minute."

Jessica roamed through the house, loving the hominess and Englishness of it. Lots of floral and plaid fabrics on the chairs and sofas, as well as the bedspreads. She liked the fluffy duvets instead of blankets and quilts on the beds. She'd seen the lush style in magazines and on the Internet, the style the British favored. She preferred it too. It gave her a warm and cozy feeling.

The delicate lamps of crystal and china were reminiscent of an age gone by, an added comfort to the ambiance of English living. Heavenly. The pictures on the walls were prints of old masters, landscapes and portraits. Yes, she could live with this. Not much different to the way her grandmother Carter had lived.

"Where are you," Rachel called as she entered the front door ten minutes later.

"I'm up here, still looking around," Jessica said. "I love this place. I hope it's not rented out in May and June. Do you think it is?"

Rachel joined her on the first floor above ground floor. In the U.S., it would be called the second floor, but in England and other countries, the first floor.

"We can call them right away, don't want to waste any time. You may have to rent the weeks they have available, if there are any. Shall we call them?"

"Yes. I'll do it." Jessica dug her phone from her oversize leather bag. "You have the number on you?"

"I have the card in my pocket. Here it is. I need to take some Aleve. Got a headache."

Jessica punched in the number and waited. "Hello? Yes, we're staying in the Courtenay House for a few days and I am wondering if it's available this summer for two months. Yes, preferable May, June, or July. Two months. June and July?" She grinned at Rachel and raised her eyebrows. "I would, yes. Shall I come and fill out the papers? Tomorrow? Yes, that will be fine. Jessica Sanford. I'm staying with Rachel O'Neill. Yes, in Newlyn. Okay, hold on. She wants to talk with you, Rachel."

Rachel came from the kitchen, drinking water. She took the phone. "Hello, yes, we just got here. The house is marvelous. Good. We can come by tomorrow morning and fill out the paperwork. Yes, of course. Thank you. Bye."

"Two months!" Jessica jumped up and down. "I'm so happy. I can't wait to tell the girls. They'll be so jealous that I'm in Port Isaac right now. I'm going to text them, do you mind?"

"No, go ahead. I'll unpack my bag in my bedroom, and make some tea. Take your time, no rush. I'll be down in the living room. Then we'll head out and see the village."

The village of Port Isaac looked busier than Rachel expected, although Cornwall and other west counties were fast becoming International destinations. She'd noticed it in Newlyn and Penzance, there seemed to be more travelers than in years past. Could be all the television series being filmed in Cornwall. In all of England, for that matter.

"Oh, look. Music here tomorrow night." Jessica exclaimed as they walked down towards the heart of the village. "It's a quaint little restaurant, two stories. Shall we look?"

"Absolutely! Are you hungry?" Rachel asked, impressed by Jessica's exuberance and youthfulness.

No one would ever guess Jessica could be a Las Vegas showgirl - a movie star maybe, or a model because of her perfect skin, thick wild hair, and the longest legs this side of heaven. The girl glowed inside and out.

"Sure, how about a Diet Pepsi and a sandwich, sound good?"

Rachel melted at her child-like facial expression, "Works for me. Let's do it."

Forty-five minutes later they finished the last bites of their egg sandwiches and the last drops of their drinks.

"So, is Stefan coming here to see you?"

Rachel, didn't expect the sudden question. "Oh. Well, I thought about calling him. We're so near his estate. Maybe he could pop over for lunch or dinner while we're here, would you mind?"

"Hey, don't bother 'bout me, I can entertain myself roaming around the village ... I can't wait to see what's here. You don't have to escort me. Call him. Absolutely. Call him. You can go to his house, if you want. He's such a nice man. A Lord. Royalty, right?"

Rachel laughed. "Well it used to be a general title for a prince or sovereign, but now is mostly a peer, which is a feudal superior. Back in the day, Kings & Queens deemed certain heads of families as Lords and gave them estates & lands. Their lineage inherited the titles … hence, the feudal system. A peer of the realm carries the title of Lord, whether he is a member of the Royal Family or sits in Parliament as a member of the House of Lords."

"I just love all of that. Can't wait to get into the history of England. Love history."

Rachel's cell phone rang. "Oh my, it's Stefan."

"Go ahead and talk to him, I'll just walk around through the shops. Can't get lost here." Jessica stood, took her wallet from her bag and left money on the table. "I've got this, see you in a few." She turned and took off.

"Hello, Stefan. How are you?" She stood and gathered her bag and left the café, not wanting to disturb other diners with her personal phone call.

"I am in London, will be heading back to Cornwall later today. Are you up for dinner at the estate tomorrow night? I've invited a few friends and thought that you might join me."

Rachel hesitated and frowned, not sure if she wanted to. "Well, I have a house guest, you know. In fact, we're spending the next few days in Port Isaac. That's where we are now, arrived this morning."

"Bring her with you. That's perfect. Yes, that would be grand. Will you do that? Do you remember how to get to the estate?"

"Yes, I believe so. Tell you what, I'll run it by Jessica and then give you a call in the morning. Will that be alright?" She took in a deep breath.

"Brilliant! I must attend to mother tonight or I'd come join you in Port Isaac, since it's so close. So, I'll talk to you tomorrow. Do come, though. I miss you. Bye for now."

"Bye." Rachel let out a deep breath with a sigh, and put her cell phone in her shoulder bag. "I don't want to go," she murmured to herself as she rubbed her aching temples and neck.

56

"Are you ready, Jessica?" Rachel stood at the foot of the stairs of the cottage rental in Port Isaac, adjusting her jacket. She was unsure of what to wear to the dinner party at Stefan's. She guessed it might be just shy of formal. If formal, Stefan surely would have told her.

"Coming. I hope this will work," Jessica said as she loped down the stairs. "What do you think?" She turned, holding her paisley long skirt out, swirling it back and forth. "It's fun. Found it in a shop down the lane. It's Batik, Eastern Indian. Perfect with my boots, don't you think?" She pointed her booted toe towards Rachel.

"Yes, black boots, rust and black Batik. And I love your black lacy top and the orange cummerbund. Perfect! The gold hoop earrings are perfect too. So, we're safe with what you're wearing, since we don't know what kind of dinner party it is. What about me, I feel I'm too sporty in this jacket and pants."

"Wait, I've got something to dress it up. Hold on." She ran back upstairs and brought down a black satin camisole with cutouts around the neckline and a wide leather scrunched belt with an oversized rhinestone belt buckle. "Take that blouse off and try this under the jacket, tuck it in and use this belt."

Rachel hesitated, not sure, but she did as her fashionista ward told her.

"Now, turn up your cuffs and collar. Yes, that's it. Now the collar. Lookin' cool, big Mama!" She grinned from ear to ear. "Now we're cooking!"

They grabbed their winter coats and bags and off they went to see the 'Wizard'. In fact, they sang the 'Wizard of Oz' song as they strolled up the lane to the parking lot. Not caring who heard them.

Jessica couldn't believe her eyes as they approached the manor house that was lit up like a Christmas Tree, all four-floor rows across the front and extended back on two sides, forming a U, with dozens of tall narrow windows on each floor.

"This is where we're having dinner? Stefan lives here with his mama? Oh, my! I need to find me a Lord or something like that. Jiminy Crickets! Can you imagine living in a place like that?"

The valet took the car and they climbed the entry steps to the gigantic doors to the foyer.

Stefan came down the grand staircase to greet them. "My lovely ladies have arrived at last. Everyone is upstairs already, having drinks and hors d'oeuvres, you're just in time. Let me take your wraps."

A butler came to the rescue, taking the ladies' coats from Stefan.

"You both look divine. I'm proud to walk into the parlor with two beautiful women." He kissed Rachel's hand and reached for Jessica's.

Jessica blushed as he kissed hers, glancing quickly and raising her eyebrows at Rachel.

"Come, come, follow me."

They entered a large multi-chandeliered room where twenty or so people were gathered, mostly standing, sipping drinks and talking, while being served canapes on silver trays.

"Oh dear," Rachel whispered to Jessica. "I'm glad you dressed me up." The other women in the room were in long skirts and dresses, velvet or silk pants.

"Mother, here are my guests," Stefan said as he led the newcomers to a grand-dame-looking woman standing in a group.

Jessica thought she looked right out of a period film or a Downton Abby segment. She whispered to Rachel, "That's his mother? Oh dear."

The evening went smoothly for Rachel and Jessica, there were no mishaps, no social blunders, both fared very well. And both enjoyed themselves.

There were two young gentry at the dinner who were single, and who swarmed Jessica every chance they could. She held a knowledgeable conversation with them easily enough, having been a student of Uncle Sawyer and having studied and read everything she could get her hands on about England, and about the education system. That turned out quite advantageous for her. One of the young men was an Oxford College student.

Later when they were leaving, she asked Stefan, "Did you invite those guys here to talk to me?"

He just grinned. "Well, did you enjoy them?"

"Yes, I did. I can't tell you how exciting it is to be here in England, where culture is everywhere. I've been preparing all my life for this. I wish Uncle Sawyer were here to see it."

"Well, maybe that can be worked out, sometime in the future."

"You mean it?"

"Rachel tells me your mother and he are getting married in August. Maybe they would like to honeymoon in England, do you think they would?"

Jessica's excitement crested, "Oh I'm sure they would, but you know I have eight brothers and sisters. That would be next to impossible. But, it's a kind thought. I had a very nice evening, thank you so much!" She leaned and kissed his cheek.

"We enjoyed having you, Jessica." He took Rachel's arm and they followed Jessica to the car.

"She seemed to love it, didn't she?" Rachel said as she held onto Stefan, and leaned her head on his arm as they walked. "Thank you for giving her that. She'll always remember this evening, I'm sure."

"Well, I don't think it's over for her, yet. Charles Forsythe, the young blond man, the one who is at Oxford, asked me if it would possible to see Jessica again. He liked her. His parents were sitting next to my mother. Baron Chauncey Forsythe and Baroness Lydia. Charles is next in line for the hereditary title. The Forsyth's holdings are lumber mills and wind power fields, and Charles is studying renewable resources. A fine young man. What do you think? Would she be interested?"

"Oh, I don't know. I don't think she's thinking of men just now, she's interested in a career."

"Well, mention it to her and let me know. He lives near here, maybe while you're in Port Isaac they can have lunch one day. Up to you. Now, as for us … when can I see you again?" He put his arms around her, leaned back and looked her square in the eyes. "Any time soon?"

She closed her eyes, thinking as he held her. Finally, "Well, when do you want to get together?"

"How about I bring Charles with me and we have lunch tomorrow in Port Isaac?" He grinned at his brilliant idea.

Rachel laughed. "Okay, but I won't tell Jessica who or what Charles is. Let's let them discover each other on their own, shall we?"

"Perfect. Yes. Two o'clock tomorrow, at the Mote?"

"Good choice," she said.

They kissed and she got into the driver's seat.

"Good night, Stefan," Jessica called out.

"Good night, Ladies."

57

Rachel awoke at six a.m. Her head throbbed, the pain was sickening. She took four Aleve with a glass of water, then made coffee. She had heard that sometimes coffee would knock a headache. Anything would be worth trying. She had quite a few annoying headaches lately and decided to go see her doctor when she returned to Newlyn.

Reaching for the ice cube tray, she grabbed the OJ too. Before the coffee, she drank some orange juice. Might be good for her. She thought maybe she had been drinking too much champagne lately. Too many parties, everybody drinking Champagne. Time to cool it.

After she downed the orange juice, she made a French Press of strong coffee and took a cup back to bed with her. Jessica usually slept in, a habit from the night life in Vegas. Entertainers slept till noon.

So, Rachel went back to bed. Drank about a half cup of coffee and fell asleep.

Jessica finally awakened at Noon. She jumped up and ran downstairs.

"Rachel, Rachel?" She peeked into her room and saw her still in bed asleep. "Now that's a first, I bet. She says she always gets up early." She looked at her watch, nearly quarter to One. Figured she better get dressed, they were meeting Stefan at Two. "Rachel, time to get up. It's almost One."

Up the stairs she ran, two steps at a time, and jumped into the shower. After she dried off, she put on a pair of designer jeans she brought with her, a purchase in Vegas, with glitz and glam all over them. Then she put on a plain black turtle-neck sweater, and knee-high black boots. She brushed her hair, put on a thin glaze of makeup. Now she could face the world.

Ten minutes till Two.

"Rachel, I'm ready. Where are you?" she said as she came down the stairs. "Rachel?" She looked in the kitchen. The living room, then went back to Rachel's bedroom.

"Rachel?" She went over to the bed and touched Rachel's shoulder. "We're going to be late, Rachel. It's almost Two."

Rachel didn't stir.

"Rachel?" She shook her shoulder. Still no reaction. "Rachel, you got to talk to me now. Come on, wake up." She shook her harder. Took both her shoulders in her hands and lifted her from the pillow. "Open your eyes, Rachel! Right now! Open your eyes!" She dropped her back on the pillows, spun around a couple times, wringing her hands. "Stefan, got to get Stefan!"

She ran out the door and ran the short distance down the lane to The Mote. As she rounded the corner she saw him sitting at one of the two tables in front with Charles from the party the previous night.

"Stefan! Stefan! She screamed. Help, something's wrong with Rachel. She won't wake up. Help!"

He stood up and started for her before she reached him. Charles followed. They all ran back to the cottage.

Stefan made a phone call and within five minutes an ambulance arrived. Before it got there, he held Rachel, dabbing a cold cloth on her head, pushing her hair back from her face, her eyes still closed. In his own terrified state, he tried to console Jessica, who couldn't stop crying.

Charles took over the task of consoling both. He held Jessica while she buried her face into his chest. Placed one hand on Stefan's shoulder. And that's how the paramedics found them. Three distraught people and still no sound or movement from Rachel.

58

Jessica and Charles sat in the corridor, holding hands as Stefan paced up and down, intermittently watching the Emergency Room doors. They had been asked to wait in the hallway until the doctors had answers.

There was a steady stream of equipment and medical personnel in and out the doors, some for Rachel, some not.

After a few minutes of horrifying wait, Stefan sat on the other side of Jessica and put his arm across the chairs behind the two worried-looking young people.

"What could it be, Stefan?" Jessica asked. "Does she have something wrong with her that would have caused this?" Jessica's eyes were red-rimmed and a frown furrowed her brow.

"Not that I know of. She's never said anything about her health. It never came up. We must be positive that it's just something temporary and the doctors can fix it." He didn't feel as positive as his words, however. He worried more than the three of them put together.

"Lord Blackbourne?" A doctor called from down the hallway.

All three of them turned at the same time, and stood up almost in unison, the tension obvious.

"Is she awake?" Stefan blurted.

"She's still unconscious. But the tests are positive. It appears she's had an ischemic stroke, which occurs when a clot clogs a blood vessel, cutting off the blood flow to brain cells. We've administered an Alteplase IV to dissolve the clot." The doctor addressed each one of them as he spoke. "Atherosclerosis could be part of the problem. So, we're running more tests to see if that's the case. There doesn't seem to be any evidence of a brain injury, which is good. If it's a result of atherosclerosis, that can be remedied with medication and change of diet. The only serious concern we have now is if the lack of blood flow caused any brain cell damage. We'll know that very soon when she awakens. Any questions?"

Jessica spoke up quickly, "So she'll be alright, then? We can take her home soon?"

Stefan put his arm around Jessica. "We will, as soon as she's back to normal, yes, we will, Jessica. Is that right, Latham? As soon as we know if there's any damage or not?" He knew the doctor from the many visits to the hospital with his mother.

"That's right, Lord Blackbourne. Yes. So, I'll get back to my patient, and we'll let you know very soon."

"Can I look in on her?" Stefan asked.

"Not yet. I'll let you know when you can." He headed back down the corridor.

"Charles, why don't you take Jessica down to the cafeteria and have a bite to eat. Both of you. You can bring me back a sandwich, if you would, please. Do you mind?"

Charles took Jessica's hand, "Shall we, Jessica? I could do with a sandwich, I'm sure you could too. Cheese and pickle, Lord Blackbourne?"

"Yes, that will be adequate. Thank you. Go on, now. Take your time. Looks like we might be here for a while."

59

The successful Alteplase treatment in dissolving the blood clot produced a very good prognosis. Although no one knew when the clog had happened, it must have been within the four-and-a-half-hour time range that is required for Alteplase to work. If administered in time it would improve the blood flow to the part of the brain effected, full recovery imminent.

Rachel woke up and all signs were excellent.

For the first time since she awakened, Stefan entered the private room, carrying a bouquet of pink roses. "How is my favorite Lady this morning?" he said as he bent to give her a kiss.

"Much better now that you're here. I'm ready to go home now."

"A couple more days, Luv. Must be sure no more clotting occurs," Stefan said.

"How is Jessica, how is she doing? I feel guilty leaving her alone like this. She comes to stay and I end up in the hospital.Not good."

"She is at the manor house, and loving it. Charles goes back and forth to take her where she wants to go. We moved some of your belongings from Port Isaac to the manor house too, and your car. I would like you to come stay there for a few days after you leave here, so we can keep a close watch on you. The doctor suggested it. And that way you don't have to feel you need to entertain Jessica. You need the tending for now."

A nurse put the flowers in a vase.

Stefan held on to Rachel's hand and sat by the bed.

"I don't want you to go to all that trouble. We'll be okay in Newlyn, in my house. I can have my housekeeper come in and look after us. My friends—"

He interrupted her, "It's all arranged. You'll have a suite of rooms next to Jessica. She's already settled in. She and Charles will be returning with me this evening to visit you. I had to promise them an arm and a leg to let me come alone this afternoon." He laughed. "Rachel, I have a question for you."

"Yes, what is it?"

"Will you promise me you'll remain at the manor where there are people to look after you? Or shall I come spend time at your home in Newlyn, until we are absolutely positive that there will not be a reoccurrence of clotting?"

She laughed. "But how can there ever be a guarantee of no more clotting? We don't even know what caused the clot. We only know it clogged an artery. That's what I'll be treated for, with meds and diet. I don't see any reason for you to uproot your life for me. Of course, you can come spend time, if that's what you want, yes. But not because of the clots, because you need to get-away, need a place to hide-out." She laughed again. "I'm perfectly okay with that."

He beamed. "I do need a hide-away from time to time, yes."

"As you wish, I'll stay at the manor for a week after I leave here, if that will make you feel better. And that way I'll have more time to gain my strength back so Jessica and I can get on with plans for her future. Is that alright?"

"Yes, quite alright." He squeezed her hand and grinned lovingly. "You understand, I just want you to be well, yes? Now that I've found you, I don't want to lose you." He kissed her hand.

Rachel's eyes teared up, "I'm not ready to leave this world yet, you can be assured of that. The doctors say I'll fully recover and if I follow their instructions, I'll be around for a long time." She patted his hand holding hers. "And you'll have your own bedroom suite when you come to visit, same rooms you had last time."

But when she left the hospital four days later, she called Jessica to pick her up, and went directly to her own home in Newlyn. She couldn't bear to be away from it any longer. Her haven, her solace, she needed to be in her own surroundings. Besides, she would be a fish out of water at the Blackbourne's manor house. Stefan would be away most of the time anyway, and she didn't want to stay in a house of strangers, especially with Stefan's mother. She needed to get on with her own life and make plans for her lovely guest, Jessica Sanford.

60

On a sunshiny day at the end of March in Cornwall, winter sunrays saturated the biosphere over England's southern region.

The gardens surrounding Rachel's house on the hill thrived since Rachel had time on her hands during her convalescence. She spent every spare minute outdoors tending flowers, digging, planting, cutting, trimming.

"Those are beautiful, Rachel," Jessica said, rounding the corner of the house looking for her benefactress. "You have such a green thumb, love your roses. How many different kinds do you have?"

"Oh, honey, I don't know. Quite a few. Climbers, tree roses, bushes, all sorts. I don't like to plant anything that doesn't flower. Except ferns, I place ferns where they thrive the best, as fillers." She stood up and stretched. "I think that's it for today. How about some tea? We can go over the plans for next week, okay?"

"Yes, I'm so excited about going to Oxford and checking out which schools I'll be going to. Charles texted me and said he'd meet us there for lunch on Monday. At Brown's, he said. Do you know Brown's?"

Collecting her gardening tools, Rachel said, "Oh yes. It's right in the middle of town. Great lunches and dinners. I've been there several times. Years ago, when I first came to England, my dear friend Ethan, who is no longer with us, I told you about him, he first took me to see Oxford. He had professor friends there and I met one of them over lunch at Brown's. It's where everybody goes. And through the years, when I go to Oxford or pass through, I always stop at Brown's." She walked towards a shed on the other side of the driveway. "I'll meet you inside, luv."

Jessica carried the tea tray to the living room and set it on the inlaid wood, glass-top coffee table in front of the overstuffed sofa. To sit in most of Rachel's chairs and sofas, was like sinking into fluffy pillows.

"Here we are," she said to Rachel and poured the tea.

"Thank you, sweetie." Rachel sighed heavily. "Gardening is so invigorating. I promised the doctors I'd keep active, wouldn't sit ten hours a day at the computer like I tend to do. Need to keep my circulation circulating." She laughed.

"But you look so healthy, Rachel. You don't look sick. I think you had a wakeup call. Just a little nudge. And me too, not just you. It made me start thinking about my own health. I want to make sure I take care of myself now, not wait till later when out of the blue, sickness strikes."

"Honey, you are so right. And the way you've been reading up on proper eating and exercise, and listening to what my doctors say, if you take care, you'll be fine when you reach my age, and beyond. I hope it's not too late for me." Her voice became a whisper on the last few words.

"No, no, no! You heard the doctor, he said you'd be fine if you take supplements and the cholesterol-busting medicine, exercise, and don't sit long periods at the computer … keeping your circulation going … and that's probably what caused the blood clot, if the truth were to be known. I read that long periods of immobility are one of the main causes of blood clots forming. When the muscles don't contract." She stood up and began jogging in-place. "See, do this several times a day, take a break from writing and do this. Or just march in-place. Come on, do it with me."

"I'm okay right now," Rachel laughed. "Have been exercising

231

all morning, gardening. But we can go for a walk later, if you want? I love walking to Penzance along the seafront. Want to do that and have dinner at my favorite pub in Penzance? We haven't done that yet." She took a cup of tea to the picture window, gazing out at the flower bed she'd been working on.

"Yes, yes." Jessica said as she plopped down in the overstuffed chair next to the sofa. "A walk along the seafront is good."

"Yes. Now, let's talk about something else I've been wanting to ask you."

"Take it away." Jessica grinned widely, looking like an adorable, inquisitive ten-year-old.

Still standing by the window she turned and said, "So, tell me about Charles. What do you think about him?"

"He is fabulous! So good looking and he's taller than me. That's hard to find." She laughed. "He told me all about his family, his parents, ancestors … he's going to be a baron, did you know that? He's next in line."

"How does that make you feel? Any change in your plans?" Rachel didn't want to be too obvious with her questions. Concerned, yes. Needed to clear the air. She looked down into the shrubbery.

"My plans? You mean Oxford? No, no. I'm eager to start school. I can't wait. It has nothing to do with Charles, by the way. Absolutely nothing. I came over here to go to Oxford. Whether I would have met him, and whether he just happens to be going to Oxford, has nothing to do with my plans. Nothing's changed. Nothing. Well, except, he is to die for, isn't he? And I do like him." Her eyes were sparkling as she grinned at Rachel. But I don't want a serious boyfriend. Can't."

Rachel gave a sign of relief. "Smart girl, and yes, he is to die for. I just hope you don't lose your focus."

"I won't, I promise."

"That's good to hear." Rachel remained standing, looking out the picture window, sipping tea. She loved her house and the ocean view. She loved her garden and Cornwall. She wanted to stay put, now. Travel less. She had accumulated enough research around the world to write a dozen more books without stepping out of her house for years. Something about having Jessica around made her feel very comfy and satisfied. Rachel could feel her needs shifting.

232

Suddenly, the hydrangea bush below the window rustled. It moved quite wildly.

"What the hell?" she said and set her cup on a nearby table. She hurried out the front door to see what caused all the movement. Jessica followed her.

"Omigod! Here baby, take it easy. I'll help you ... hold on there, little one ... ohhhhhh, what a sweetie you are." Rachel lifted a beautiful long haired gray and white kitten from the crook of the trunk of the shrubbery. He was stuck and making quite a ruckus, trying to get out. Rachel lifted him and held him close to her face, petting his soft fur. He couldn't be much over four months old, still had the kitten mew. "Who do you belong to, sweetie ... no tag? You're too little to be out on this hill and street. Yes, you are. Let's go inside and I'll fix you a warm place to rest." She held him tightly under her chin and went back into the house.

Jessica quickly poured milk into a saucer for the helpless kitten nesting on the kitchen table in the sweater that Rachel had been wearing, made into a very nicely formed bed.

"Oh, isn't he cute?" Jessica said as she stroked his fur and caressed his tiny body. "Are you keeping him?"

"Yes, I am. Decision made. He's a sign from above. Now I'll have to settle down and travel less, I'll have him to take of. You think I'm nuts?"

Jessica laughed, then smiled at the way Rachel picked up the adorable ball of fur and kissed him before she set him in front of the saucer of milk.

"Do we have some tuna?" Jessica asked. "I'll mash it up for him." She looked in the cupboard and found a can of salmon. "Salmon works. Shall I open it?"

"Of course, it'll have to do till we go get cat food and litter and all the trimmings." Rachel laughed at herself. "I can't believe I want this cat. I think I am crazy. Too many changes lately, I'm losing my mind."

"No, you're not. To me it's like you're finding yourself, maybe. This little fella is making you happy, that's all that matters. My Mama always said it's the simple things in life that are most important. They are what make us happy. Growing up all I wanted were books, and to read read read. And learn. And I did, and still do. It's what I love doing. Simple things. Maybe it's your time to take a little fella under your wing, to have something to nurture and love. I can see it in your eyes and on your face. This is doing something to you, isn't it?"

"There you go again, where do you get those smarts, young lady? You scare me, and are so right. I have been thinking about my life all morning, thinking about a few changes I might make, like stay home more, sort out my so-called love life, and then this little guy turns up in the Hydrangeas. Trapped, couldn't climb out. Like I feel sometimes. It's meant to be." Rachel picked him up and held him again. "You, little fella, are a sign from the Universe, you are."

61

Early Thursday morning Rachel lounged on the sofa reading chapters she'd written the night before. She petted the new kitten while it slept in her lap. Her normal routine had been of late: gardening mornings, writing afternoons, editing nights. But she didn't feel like gardening this morning. Had tossed all night in her sleep.

Her houseguest, Jessica, remained upstairs listening to music that could faintly be heard by Rachel. She put down her manuscript and smiled at Jessica's choice of music – classical. With every day that passed, the young lady in her care became more and more astonishing and intriguing.

She thought of Jessica, remembered when Jessica had told her the whole story of what had happened to her when at sixteen, and how she'd been through therapy but was still working her way through the remnants of the vivid memory. Being the researcher she'd always been, Jessica had done extensive reading online and in books that dealt with rape and sexual abuse. And when Rachel told her about her own rape experience back in the states, and how she and her dear departed friend Belinda (who had been raped horridly in London) had been part of an organization who helped female victims of violent crimes,

235

Jessica talked even more. Rachel loved Jessica as a mother would a daughter, or as an aunt would a niece.

She placed the manuscript on the cocktail table, placed the sleeping kitten where she'd been sitting and took her coffee cup and French Press into the kitchen for a refill. She set the electric kettle to heat the water.

The house phone rang.

"Hello?" she said into the wall phone receiver.

"Hello, Rachel."

"Stefan! How are you?" she leaned against the counter.

"I think I'll drive down this weekend, is that alright?"

She thought for an instant, hesitated, "Of course, it's alright. We're going to Oxford Monday morning, but the weekend is open. Terrific. When will you get here?"

"Around three tomorrow afternoon, if you don't mind. I'll take you both out to dinner. How's that?"

"Sounds good to me. Do you have clients here you'll be seeing?" She asked.

"No, I just want to be with you. Will I be interrupting your work?"

"Not at all," she reached for the kettle and poured boiling water over the coffee grounds in the French Press. "I'll take a break while you're here. How's that?"

"Are you sure?"

"Yes, of course."

"See you tomorrow afternoon then, I'm driving from London now, stopping overnight in Bournemouth."

After the call, Rachel stood in the kitchen looking out the French doors at the glistening sea. A cool wind created a few whitecaps, she noticed, and sailboats were already out taking advantage of the perfect weather.

She reached for her cup and continued to sip coffee, thinking about Stefan and the part he played in her life. A sincere, kind, and loving person, she knew that about him, and a good guy, but still, should she let it go any further than it already had? Maybe she should back up while she could, and then again, why? She did like being with him. She remembered Sam's words, in Montana. "Stay in the moment, don't make it more than it is …"

"Okay, Sam, I'll stay in the moment and not stress over it. Again." But her thoughts continued. She didn't want a live-in permanent relationship or marriage with any man, ever again. "So, tell me, Sherlock, how do I stop thinking about it?"

"Who are you talking to, Rachel?" Jessica asked as she came into the kitchen and poured herself a cup of coffee.

"Myself, for all it's worth," Rachel said as she turned.

"Why is that?" Jessica leaned back against the counter, her brow furrowed at Rachel.

"Oh, it's nothing, just one of my mind games. Quit that frowning, pretty one! Don't want your brow all wrinkled before it's time for it."

Jessica deliberately smoothed her brow with her fingers. "But what did you mean when you said, 'How do I stop thinking about it?' Is it about me? Have I done something wrong?" Jessica's brow furrowed again.

"Oh, for goodness sakes. No. Not at all, Sweetheart. In fact, I'll tell you what it's about so you won't worry. May as well. Two heads better than one? Right? Let's sit at the table and have a heart to heart, shall we? And not to worry, it isn't about you. It's all about me, isn't that the way it goes?" Rachel laughed and sat with Jessica at the table. "Now, it's true, it's all about me, want you to know that. My problems are all about me. You are not one of my problems. You could never be. In fact, you lift me up, inspire me, I enjoy you being here. I need you here. So, get that out of your mind. Never think it. So, here's my dilemma … my intuition plagues me incessantly and is doing a job on me today. The problem is, I don't know what it's telling me."

"So, what is it saying?"

"Okay, I'll start at the beginning. You know, I've learned as I've grown older that our soul or spirit or heart or being, whatever you want to call it, knows what is best for us. And if we pay attention we'll not make mistakes. Are you a religious person, honey?"

Jessica reached for coffee, "Religious? Well, I had Southern Baptist upbringing, is that what you mean?"

"Yes, that's part of what I mean. So, you've had some experience with the teachings of the Bible. About spirituality and guidance."

"Yes, but I don't practice what I've been taught, my beliefs

237

changed a few years ago." Jessica frowned. "The Bible is the basis of my mama's belief, though."

"That's okay, honey. As we get older we sometimes broaden our truths, they're still connected though, we just learn new approaches, new principles. I was raised Baptist too, by my dear stepmother Lee, so I have the basic Bible upbringing. My father, a total alcoholic all my young life, quit drinking when he married dear Lee. I'll tell you about all that sometime. I'll have another pour, Jessica dear." She scooted the cup towards Jessica. "You see, after I got out into the world and on my own, I changed my young beliefs to no belief, which sounds like maybe that's what you are doing. But when my birth mother came back into my life, after years of believing she'd died, a whole new world opened for me. Unknown to me before then, my mother Lily was a spiritual leader and teacher, gave seminars and wrote books about the higher power within us. My own curiosity had started me on a spiritual path by then, had been reading about other religions, Zen, Buddhism, and so on … and then when I read my mother's teachings and experienced them first hand, with her, I learned that instead of looking for guidance from outside of you, from other people and gurus of all sorts, the best answers come from within, they are there, if we listen. Our spirit and soul know what is best for us, and that's what I'm doing, asking myself … 'so tell me, Sherlock.' My new nickname for my inner-self … Sherlock."

"That's funny. But what is it you were asking yourself," Jessica said.

"About Stefan."

"What about Stefan?"

"I'm afraid I'm too involved. I know I live better alone, it's less complicated, less disappointment." She looked at Jessica, "And less of everything else. Besides they all die."

"What do you mean, they all die? Are you one of those black widow women I hear about?" Jessica giggled.

"No, honey. I just happen to have the worst damn luck on the planet when it comes to men. I mean, most are good men, some even wonderful. At least the last two were. But they didn't live long after I committed. I need to quit committing. That's what I need to do. Need to break that habit. And need to quit falling for wonderful, handsome, loving men. Sounds silly, I know. Here I've just recovered from

Maxim's death and I'm already embarking upon another damn relationship. Why is that? Why do I do that?"

"But it's been over three years, right?"

"Yes, but still ..."

Thoughtfully, Jessica tapped the table with her beautifully manicured long fingernail, and while staring at it she said, "Well, back to spirituality, I have been studying too. I've always been the curious type, have been since a little girl, read everything I could get my hands on. Uncle Sawyer supplied me with all kinds of books from his library. And the way I see it," she took a deep breath, "and what I've learned, we should allow ourselves to receive that inner guidance, like you say. Allow the creative flow, the intelligent consciousness to work through us. Not overthink it to death. Ask and then let go, right? You said it yourself ... the best answers come from within. Live in the moment. Don't fight it." She stood up, "And that's what I'm doing today. I'm going to Penzance for lunch with some friends I just met."

Rachel laughed. "I think you were sent to me by both my son and my mother. They're ganging up on me." She grinned as she took Jessica's hand and squeezed it. "I love you, honey. And you are so right. These things I already know, I just need to listen and not over-think. Thank you for reminding me. Let it flow, let it happen. The universe rules! Have a good time in town."

62

Later that afternoon, Rachel's front doorbell rang.

Jessica was still Penzance with some young Americans she'd met earlier in the week down by the Newlyn docks. The two of them always came in the side door from the carport, through the kitchen, so Jessica wouldn't be ringing the front doorbell.

Rachel went through the living room to the foyer and mud room, then to the front door. A circular drive curved in front of the hillside home where guests parked and came to the doors on the front sea-facing side of the house.

The doorbell rang again.

"I'm coming, I'm coming …" she called out as she opened the door without looking through the peephole.

"Paul Newland! For goodness sakes. Hello." She reached for her dear friend and they gave each other a healthy bear hug.

"I hope I haven't disturbed you," Paul said. He leaned back to look at Rachel as if it had been years since seeing her.

"I am so glad to see you, Paul. My gosh, how long has it been? Come in, come in!" She led him to the chairs in the living room. "What would you like to drink? Coffee, tea, beer? Champagne?"

"If you'll have one with me, I'll have a glass of Champagne, if you don't mind," he said as he sank into one of the chintz chairs. "I love this room, always have. And I love what you've done to it. Only you could make it so warm and inviting."

"Hold that thought, I'll be right back. I've got some in the wine fridge in the kitchen. Just relax." She hurried, smiling and excited, to the kitchen.

Her heart had skipped a few beats when she saw Paul at the door. More handsome than ever. Pale blue V-neck sweater to match his eyes, navy blue collared shirt, tan gabardine pants, tan leather loafers … always the smart dresser. His sun-blonde tresses still shoulder length. Still looking like a romance novel cover model.

She returned carrying an ice bucket with ice and bottle of champagne stuffed in it. "I can't believe you're here. And I must say, I'm glad you are. There we go," she said, and set the silver bucket on the glass table in front of them. "If you'll open, I'll get the glasses."

"I thought you might not be here, or you were too busy to see me." He watched her go to the glass cabinet in the dining room.

"I'm never too busy to see you. Get that out of your head, my dear fellow." She returned with two crystal champagne flutes. "You pour, if you will, please. Sorry the glasses aren't chilled. They'll have to do as is."

"As-is works for me." He popped the cork. "So, tell me, how are you? What have you been doing with yourself?" He handed her a glass of bubbly.

"Oh, well, I have a lovely visitor from the States. I met her in Las Vegas, New Year's week. Shall we make a toast?"

"Yes, we must. Here's to a pleasant meeting once again, for I've truly missed our friendship," he clinked her glass.

"And here's to seeing you much, much more." She startled herself with the blatant response and quickly continued with what she had been saying before, trying to cover her sudden embarrassment. "Anyway, Jessica's a young girl from North Carolina I met in Vegas, and she's entering Oxford University in the Fall. We're going there Monday to check it out, she hasn't seen it yet, but she's done all the research. You'll love her, Paul. She's so bright." She looked at her watch. "Right now, she's in Penzance with some friends she met …"

Paul stared at Rachel's facial expressions as she talked which always mesmerized him. She talked with her face, her eyes lit up when excited about what she said, or what she saw. He loved that about her from the beginning. Although his first sight of her was when she got into a cab at the London Ritz on a New Year's Eve, exposing her lovely breasts in a low-cut evening dress. So many years ago, so many lifetimes ago, so many tragedies ago.

"… and so, she showed up here after I returned and there we are. I'm going to do all I can for her."

"And another cause to pursue, another person in need of assistance. You are good about that." He poured more champagne in both glasses. "You are truly a blessing, Rachel. Truly."

"Enough about me, what about you? Bring me up to speed. How are the boys?" She looked at the second glass of Champagne, knowing she shouldn't drink it.

"Well, the boys are young men, now. No need of a nanny anymore, since they're both enrolled at UCLA, my Alma Mater, and that leaves me alone in London." He tipped his glass at Rachel before looking out the bay window at the sea. "I'm feeling the pull back to Cornwall, Rachel."

"You are?"

"Yes, I'm going back to Mousehole to open up a studio again. The same building is for sale where Belinda and I were. Talked to the estate agent this morning, then we had lunch together, worked out a deal. I'm good to go. So I wanted to tell you the good news." He still hadn't looked at Rachel, afraid of her facial expression if she didn't like his plan.

"I … I …don't know what to say. I never would have thought you'd come back here to live and work. Do you want your house back? I can always—"

He turned quickly. "No no." He saw the tears in her eyes. "I don't want my house back. This is your home now, you bought it. I don't need a big house any more. The boys are gone, and I just want to get back to basics. I want out of the city. London isn't me anymore, but I do love Cornwall, Belinda taught me that." He put his glass down and reached for Rachel's hand. "And I need to be close to our dear friend again, I've missed that."

The kitchen door opened and the screen door slammed shut. "Rachel, I'm back." Jessica called out. "Whose car is in the driveway?"

Jessica stopped suddenly as she entered the living room. "Whoa! I'm sorry. I shouldn't have barged in like that."

Rachel laughed, "It's okay, honey. This is one of my old friends, Paul Newland. Remember I told you about Paul and Belinda, this house being theirs, before I bought it?"

Jessica's incredible good looks stunned Paul for a moment. He stood and reached to shake her hand. "Hello, young lady. I've heard some wonderful things about you. I hear you're going to enroll in Oxford?"

Equally as stunned at Paul's good looks, Jessica blurted, "Yes, yes. Uh … Rachel is letting me stay here till I get settled. Find my way. I guess that's what we're doing? Right? Rachel?"

"So how was the visit with your friends in Penzance, Jessica? Where are they now?" Rachel chuckled.

Jessica stood near a table at the window. "There they go now … they're going to the bus stop in Newlyn to go to Mousehole on the bus. Staying at the Ship's Inn tonight. Then they'll be going back to London tomorrow."

"Wonderful, then you can have dinner with Paul and me. Where shall we go? Anybody have a suggestion?"

Paul spoke up, "How about the Godolphin Inn in Marazion? Before the tide goes out and the sun sets?"

"Oh yes," Jessica said. "Perfect view of Saint Michael's Mount. Is that okay with you, Rachel?"

"Absolutely!"

63

Being at the Godolphin Inn that evening caused a myriad of memories to crowd Rachel's mind. All the way back to Ethan when she first came to Cornwall nearly twenty-five years ago on a visit, long before she moved to England.

Then there was Pete, who she met and fell in love with, in Newlyn. He knew Margaret at the Godolphin Inn and they frequented it often.

"Rachel, are you all right?" Paul interrupted her thoughts.

"Oh, I am just figuring out how long I had been coming to Cornwall before moving here. Okay, I'm back. Sorry." She laughed. "Did you enjoy your fish, Jessica?"

"Yes. Lovely. See, I'm picking up the British lingo." She laughed. "Just lovely."

"And yours, Paul?"

"Superb, as usual. Do you feel like another drink?"

"No, that's enough for me," Rachel replied.

"Were you thinking of Pete?" Paul asked.

"Yes, you know me too well. This place always reminds me of him. He also took me to Charlestown where we found ancestors of mine. You know that story."

"Yes, I do."

"Tell me. I haven't heard that one yet." Jessica said eagerly, eyes wide open.

"Oh, we'll save that for a quiet afternoon recollection, Jessica. Remind me and I'll tell all." Rachel smiled. "So, Paul, I have a guest coming tomorrow afternoon. But that's okay, you are more than welcome to stay, if you want. I don't have a problem with that. I've plenty of room."

"Stefan's coming tomorrow?" Jessica asked.

"Yes, he is."

Paul raised his eyebrows as he lifted his glass. "Oh, well ... no problem, my business is finished here in the morning. I must go back to London and take of things before escrow closes. I'll leave around ten. Is that alright?"

"I don't want you to think you have to leave, Paul. Stefan is from northern Cornwall, has an estate above Port Isaac. He called yesterday and asked to come for the weekend, is on his way home from business in London. I've been seeing him since last summer, not very much mind you, but from time to time. Nothing serious."

Jessica heard the fluster in Rachel's words and saw it on her reddened face. *Uh oh, nothing serious? Who is this Paul?*

"I legitimately need to get back to London in the morning," Paul said. "So, shall we have a nightcap at The Ship's Inn, since I'm leaving tomorrow?"

Jessica's eyes brightened, "And I can see my friends one more time before they leave in the morning. Yes!"

The Ship's Inn in Mousehole was busy. As soon as Paul pushed open the heavy timber door and ushered Rachel and Jessica into the entryway, the noise of the packed throng hit them full on.

"Well, another party night at the Ship's Inn. Just like old times," Rachel said loudly to Paul over the deafening clamor before them.

"Yes, brings back some good memories," he said close to her ear as he placed his arm across her back, hand to her waist, and moved

245

forward, directing her to seats at the bar. "Grab those bar stools, Jessica. At the far end."

Jessica didn't miss Paul's bending down and whispering into Rachel's ear, and the reactionary grins on both their faces. It spread a smile across her own face, as a matter of fact. She grabbed the two end stools, placed her large bag on them, and then sat on the adjacent stool, which placed Paul and Rachel seated side by side at the bar.

"I'll have a coke," Jessica said to the barkeep, as her eyes searched the crowd for her new friends, to no avail.

"Glasses of Champagne for us," Paul added.

"So, when will you be moving back here?" Rachel asked Paul.

Jessica leaned and listened intently.

"As soon as escrow closes. I'll live upstairs over the gallery for now. And I've made an offer on a house up the lane from it. A change has been needed for a long time, been wanting to get back to basics. And of course, I love Cornwall."

"Me too," Jessica replied.

"That makes three of us," Rachel said.

Paul lifted the glass of Champagne the barkeep set in front of him. "So, let's drink a toast to living in Cornwall forever."

"Forever," all three chimed. "Forever!"

To be a spectator watching the three beautiful, cheerful people sitting at the bar toasting to 'forever', one would think they were a very loving family, and very happy.

Rachel wished Stefan would call and cancel the weekend, so Paul would stay longer. Maybe she could call Stefan and cancel. Why not? Nothing lost. *Do it!* she told herself.

"Excuse me for a moment," she said. "I'll be right back." She grabbed her bag and went to the toilet. Once inside she pulled her cell phone from her purse. Pushed Stefan's number. The answer message came on. "Good. Don't have to talk to him ... Hello, Stefan. This is Rachel. Just a quick call to let you know unexpected guests showed up for the weekend, they arrived tonight. So we'll have to put off your stay. Let's talk in a couple weeks and schedule something. So sorry. Hope all is well. Bye." She ended the call with a smile. "There. That's better. Why should I do something I don't want to do?"

A gal came out of one of the toilet stalls. "That's right! We should never do what we don't want to do."

They both laughed.

She knew she needed to reevaluate her relationship with Stefan, and she would. Right now, she wanted to hurry and tell Paul he could spend the weekend,

Back at home, Rachel served tea and cake in the kitchen. Milk for Jessica. Their faces shone with gaiety and pleasure as the first bites of Rachel's famous lemon cake with lemon butter frosting were consumed.

"Ohhhh, I've always loved this cake of yours," Paul said and reached for another bite. "I've missed it."

"So tell me how you two first met," Jessica asked Paul as she gobbled the cake and went for another slice.

"Shall I tell her, or do you want to?" Paul asked.

"You tell her, I want to hear your version." She laughed and sat back, sipping her tea.

"Well, New Year's Eve in London ... I'm telling this from my perspective at the time, not knowing names and players, okay?"

"This is getting more interesting by the minute." Jessica said.

"I hosted a group of Japanese businessmen for the ad agency where I was creative director, had the company limo and we'd just finished dinner at the Ritz. As I ushered them into the limo, holding open the door, making sure all of them were there, I saw this beautiful, buxom woman leaning to get into a cab, with dress so low, she almost popped out of it," his face grew red.

"Paul!"

"Well, that's what caught my eye. I couldn't help it."

"So, I'd splurged and gone out of character for a low-cut evening gown and definitely had a miserable night trying to control my boobs. Not intentional, believe me," Rachel said.

They laughed.

"Go on," Rachel said. "This is fun. Good memories."

"My eyes were glued to her. I wanted to say something, hello, anything. But a very stately, imposing man hurried up the get-away. Must be her husband, I figured. In those days, it wouldn't have mattered to me, I must say. Sorry."

"You still are a rascal," Rachel said.

"I hope so," Paul said. "So we left in the Limo, they left in the cab. I took my guests to Trafalgar Square, something they wanted to experience for the count-down to Midnight. We pushed our way to the front row roped off area with a clear view of Lord Nelson atop his tower, the fountain, and the reclining Trafalgar lions. The square filled up very fast, and suddenly a surge of people behind me literally lifted us off our feet, moving everybody forward. One was pushed smack dab into my backside. I turned and the same woman I saw getting into the cab at the Ritz looked up at me."

"No way," Jessica said. "Too much of a coincidence. You are telling the truth?"

"I am." Paul said.

"Yes, and how do you think I felt? I couldn't believe it. I'd literally pulled Ethan, you know about Ethan, I told you about him, the Englishman I almost married ... forced him to go to Trafalgar Square for the Midnight count-down, against his will. He didn't want to. In fact, he ended up several rows behind me in the crowd at the square. The throng had separated us and shoved me into Paul's back. I hadn't even seen him standing there." She stood up, "I'm going to open a bottle of champagne. Go on, tell her, Paul." She went after the bottle with a giddiness in her step.

"I'll have a glass too, please." His eyes sparkled. "Okay. I turned my head to see who had literally jammed into my back, and looked down on Rachel's exposed boobs."

"Paul!"

"Okay, but it's true. I said 'hello.' Said 'you were the one at the Ritz.' She said 'yes.' Then the crowd did another shift and separated us by three or four people to the side. I'd glance towards her every few seconds to see where she'd gone. When the countdown started, I pushed through the people and at the stroke of Midnight I reached for her. She looked up at me, and we kissed. A very tender, loving kiss, I might add." He blushed again.

"I liked it too. And that's how we met, luv. Enough on that story for now though," Rachel said, red-faced, wanting to change the subject. Embarrassed at her own memories of the kiss, it had been more than a simple kiss.

"One more thing," Paul said. "I just want to add, we ran into each other two more times that weekend in London. At the Odeon on

Sunday, and when she rode by a sidewalk café where I sat, later. That took the cake."

"Destiny, one might say," grinning Jessica added.

"Yes, I agree. Destiny. And fast forward a few months later to running into each other here in Newlyn on the boardwalk when Belinda and I were strolling along the beach our first weekend here."

"That blew my mind." Rachel guzzled her champagne, poured another glass.

"And here we are, years later, a lot of water over the damn, and we've become very good friends. Best friends as far as I'm concerned. Rachel's been there for me, through thick and thin, and I am always available when she needs me." He lifted his glass. "Here's to a very special, everlasting friendship, and may it become even stronger now that I'm returning to Cornwall."

Jessica raised her eyebrows, a habit of hers, darted glances back and forth between Rachel and Paul, lifting her glass of milk and joining the sentiment. *Uh huh, something extra special going on here maybe?*

64

With unpredictable weather on the Cornwall coast, one day the sun would appear in full force, the next would be stormy, but Saturday brought the sun. Gorgeous blue skies, gentle waves rippling the seas, colorful flowers blooming, birds chirping and singing, and mama seagulls searching for food for their babies nesting in rooftop crannies. Bicyclists and sailors were already out in full force along the sea front below Rachel's hill – cyclists on the boardwalk that ran between Newlyn and Penzance, a sailing club visible in their sail boats beyond the waves that rolled up on the pebbled beach.

Rachel stepped out on the patio carrying a fresh cup of coffee and inhaled the prized sea air. She wore black tights with sandals, and a black tank top under a light yellow oversized man's shirt, collar up, sleeves rolled. Her auburn hair, piled on the top of her head, had a tortoise-colored clamp holding it in place, tendrils loose and hanging.

She craved the coolness and the aromas. Mornings like this were what kept her in Cornwall; what drew her there in the first place. She loved the stormy weather too, like on her first introduction to Mount's Bay those many years ago.

"Good morning," Paul called out through the French doors

leading from the kitchen. He poured coffee into a mug. "Another beautiful day. Did you order it up?"

Rachel turned. *My god, he is too handsome to be alive!* "Yes, I did." She laughed.

Paul, wore a light blue, jersey jogging suit, same color as his eyes, with blond shoulder-length hair still damp from an obvious shower. "You look so fresh and beautiful this morning," he said, giving her the once over as he joined her. "You never age, how do you do that? As striking as the first day I saw you."

"Well, I'll accept that compliment, although I know it isn't true. Thank you. I could say the same about you, you know."

"Ha! You could. Are you?" He sat at the patio table.

"Yes, I am." She sat across from him, not wanting to sit too close, her face began to flush. "So what should we do today? Want to do anything special? I would like to see the place in Mousehole, do you have the key yet?"

"Yes, I told him I'd like to take some measurements before I left for London. But now I don't have to rush, do I? Your man friend isn't coming."

Rachel squinted at Paul, wondering if she had detected a slight jealousy in his voice, sure sounded like it.

"I mean, you are having a relationship with him, right? Has been going on a while? Yes? So, it must be more than casual. Am I correct?"

"Why do you want to know? Huh?" She waited for an answer not fast in coming.

"I'm up." Jessica exclaimed as she bounded through the kitchen to the patio table. "Did I miss breakfast?"

"No, you didn't, we're having our first cup of coffee," Paul said, relieved Jessica appeared in the nick of time. "So, shall we eat here, or go to Penzance for breakfast? I'm feeling like a traditional English breakfast ... beans, sausages, bacon, blood pudding, eggs, tomatoes, hash browns, toast ... the works! and that one café in the mall is perfect. We can sit outside and watch the vendors put up the market booths to sell their wares. People watch. What do you say, Rachel?"

"I love that place. When I first came here, before I met Pete, I used to go there all the time to have coffee and watch people. Sounds great to me."

"Who's Pete?" Jessica asked.

"I'll tell you on our walk to Penzance," Rachel replied. "Come on … grab a sweater."

65

The day went well, enjoyed by all. A clear day throughout the afternoon, sweaters nor jackets were needed on the walk to and from Penzance, a perfect day one might say. The calm ocean rippling up onto the shore. On their return walk, they stopped and watched the lawn bowlers for a while

Families with children were picnicking on the beach. Sailboat school fleets were bobbing just past the shoreline, waiting to catch a rare gust of wind. Sometimes the wind would pick up in the afternoon, so they were ready and waiting.

It reminded Rachel of the times she took Paul's young boys to the beach, when Belinda became gravely ill. A very sad time for all. Belinda's death. Rachel pushed the thoughts from her mind.

"Do you sail, Jessica?" Paul asked as they continued strolling back to Newlyn.

"No, not yet. But I want to learn, I want to experience everything I can while I'm in England."

"When I move down, we'll go … do you mind, Rachel? I have a boat now, and will bring it here. In fact, we could take the train to London after I'm all settled into Mousehole, and sail it back. My sons

Jake and Paul Junior should be home from University around that time to give us a hand. Would you like to do that?"

"Oh yes, yes, yes." Jessica said. "Can we, Rachel?"

"Depends on when it is, but sounds like fun to me."

"Good! That's settled. I'll teach you how to sail, Jessica. Every young girl should know how to sail. Might come in handy one day." He winked at Rachel. "Plan to do the trip in about three weeks. Like I said, we'll take a train to London together after I make the move, and then sail the boat back here to Newlyn Harbor." He exuded happiness at the idea, so did Jessica.

Rachel didn't want to show her excitement. She turned away. She thought she had learned to be open and truthful, but here she did it again. Not truthful with Stefan and not truthful with Paul. *But what is the truth? I don't know.*

The afternoon sped by, between Jessica questioning Paul about his life and sons and talking about her education, and Rachel in her office taking care of business with her agent on the phone catching up on budget entries ... three hours passed and now the sun lowered towards the horizon and the sea, shooting shades of orange, purple and red across the clear blue sky.

"What does everybody want for dinner tonight?" Rachel said as she came down the stairs.

"Fire up the pit and I'll go get some steaks and play like a chef. Craving a good fillet. Is that alright with you?" Paul said, as he stood up.

"Sure is. You, Jessica?"

"I love steaks, and I make a killer potato salad," Jessica said, getting excited.

"Okay, menu is steak, potato salad, and broccoli or asparagus, or both ... with garlic bread. I think I have everything but the meat, let's check."

Rachel and Jessica went into the kitchen to forage.

Paul followed and grabbed his jacket from the hook by the back door on his way out. "Are we okay with ingredients? You have A-1 sauce?"

"Yes, just need the steaks. I have charcoal and oak-wood chips, whatever you want to use on the barbeque. And we have wine and

Pepsi. We'll get everything ready while you're gone, but there's no real hurry for dinner."

"Be back in 15 minutes." Paul left.

Rachel and Jessica stared at each other, grinning, eyes wide. Jessica broke the silence. "Wow! He's a mover and a shaker, isn't he? Easy to be around. Comfortable. And so American."

"That's because he is American," Rachel laughed.

"I mean, there's a big difference between him and Stefan. But they're both good guys."

Rachel frowned as she removed things from the pantry.

During dinner, Jessica told Rachel that she had checked her messages upstairs, and the girls had sent her a text saying they wouldn't be coming to Port Isaac in the summer. Disappointed beyond words, she asked if it would be a problem to cancel the reservation she'd made. Rachel told her not to worry, she'd handle it. But Jessica was depressed.

66

Later that evening, Rachel and Paul relaxed on the sofa in the living room facing the bay window.

"I love this view," she said.

"I always did too," Paul replied.

They sipped champagne after a delicious, satisfying meal.

In one way, Rachel felt uneasy, alone with Paul, feeling nostalgic, loving, grateful. A mixture of confusing feelings.

Paul broke the silence, "Jessica didn't have to leave us, she knows that, right?"

"That girl has a mind of her own, and would have stayed if she wanted to," she laughed. "I think she wanted to Facetime her friends in Vegas, she's depressed about the cancelation of their trip. And she wanted to Facetime her family in North Carolina too. Evidently her mother is getting married very soon and Jessica will be going for that. She wants to put off looking at schools, she said. Lots on her plate right now."

"Well, I hope she'll still be able to do the boat trip from London." Paul stood up and walked to the window, glass in hand.

"Are you okay?" Rachel asked.

256

He turned and looked at her for a moment, radiant in her gold and teal silk caftan, her auburn hair glowing, her sparkling eyes, questioning.

Paul's height and stature overwhelmed Rachel, as did his perfect features and handsomeness. She often thought of when they first met.

"I remember when Belinda and I were living here, how we loved this view. The memory has faded though, hard to recreate in my mind. I feel guilty about that. I feel guilty for remarrying, so foolish."

Rachel stood, setting her glass on the table. "No, Paul," she reached for his hand. "You mustn't feel that way. Please."

He set his glass on the lamp table and wrapped his arms around her. "I know, I know. Everything happens for a reason. Your favorite advice. But I still don't know the reason. Now the boys are grown, they'll soon be living their own lives wherever they want. And I'm glad of that. They should carve out their own niche. But part of me feels very alone in anticipation of it. It's like an entire segment of my life is being erased. Gone. Not to be reclaimed." He held her tightly. "I'm so fortunate to have you."

Rachel closed her eyes, half wanting to meld further into his thoughts and life, half wanting to pull away … *Stefan*. She leaned back and said, "Shall we go for a walk, it's a beautiful night?"

"If you want."

Rachel quickly changed into jeans and sweater, they donned their jackets and scarves and down the hill they went to the promenade to walk along the granite beach towards Penzance.

"I remember when you and Belinda were strolling this walk that day, coming from Penzance towards me, and how surprised and shocked I was that you both were here, right in front of me … after first seeing you at the Ritz, and first seeing her at the Odeon on New Year's Day. Couldn't miss Belinda sitting a few rows away, in that colorful jacket, with her mother. And then there you were, again, at the theatre too. Amazing! And *then* … weeks later, you both were *here* on this promenade walking towards me. That, in the real world, seems impossible. Of course, you know how I feel about past lives. How groups travel together from one life to the next. It was obvious, you and Belinda are in my group."

"Or you are in mine," he laughed.

"Yes. So, we are bound together in this lifetime and in the next. Different configurations, yes, but still bound. That's why it's so comfortable and familiar. And confusing at the same time." Rachel squeezed his arm.

"Why do you say confusing?"

"Well, I can only speak for myself. Let's sit on that bench over there. I get out of breath when I walk and talk." Rachel led him to the bench. "You know I'm seeing someone, right?"

"Yes." He frowned.

"And you know how much I adore you, have since the first time I saw you, before I knew your name. Soulmates, traveling together through lifetimes."

"Go on."

"And at times, I have difficulty in separating my feelings from the 'past familiar' to the present life." She took his hands from his lap. "I love you, Paul. I do know that. I do. But I do believe in this life it is a sisterly love, although I am certainly attracted to your good looks, who isn't?" She laughed.

"And I feel an attraction to you too. Have from the beginning."

"But we both went our separate ways, married others, and our paths continued to criss-cross since we met. There is a closeness, yes. An immediate attraction, because we knew each other before. In a past life. And I'm having to continually remind myself of that. But we are forever friends in this life. I'm your sons' Godmother. I became a very close friend to you and Belinda. Look what happened in California, when that evil scumbag tried to murder me! You came to the rescue, you saved me. We are connected."

"And you came to the rescue when Belinda died. Yes." He hugged her.

She leaned back and looked up at him, "And you came to my rescue when Pete died."

"I love you, Rachel. My forever friend and soulmate."

They hugged hard, wiped tears from their eyes. Then they stood up and continued their walk.

"So, when am I going to meet this new man in your life?"

They both burst out laughing.

67

Paul decided not to move the boat to Cornwall after all, he sold it to a friend in London who had been wanting it. Figured it a waste of money to hang on to, just to dock and never use. That phase of his life had ended. Now he had entered a new chapter and by all appearances a boat wouldn't fit in it. His sons didn't want to help him sail it to Mousehole while they were in London visiting, they wanted to get back to the States where they attended UCLA and had girlfriends, and lived in their grandmother's upscale Wilshire apartment. Paul accepted the fact they were not boys anymore, they were young men and had minds and plans of their own. The daddy era, done.

But Paul loved living in Cornwall again. He hadn't realized how much he'd missed it. Seeing Rachel several times a week made him happy too. They took long walks together along the sea front between Newlyn and Penzance, they frequented the pubs in Mousehole and Newlyn, lunched in Penzance and Marazion ... visited each other's houses for meals and conversation. Almost perfect for Paul. Thank goodness, Rachel filled a void for him. He realized he could never have more than she could give, and accepted it. The house he bought and renovated in Mousehole, up the lane a few doors from his studio, he adored. He rented out the upstairs apartment to Claire, his gallery assistant. She'd been recommended by his London agent, and accepted his offer almost immediately.

So now he had a lifestyle he'd always wanted, in a small village doing what he loved most – painting. He'd loved living there when Belinda was alive and they worked together. Since then his art had become popular, accepted and purchased all over the world. In the studio, he had devoted a glassed-in section for all his deceased wife Belinda's metal sculptures, what was left of them after she died. He wouldn't sell any of them, kept them on display in his gallery. They were sculpted in copper, tin, and bronze – animals and birds, with beautiful eyes of colorful, radiant ammonite. He looked at them and remembered his lovely Belinda every day even though it had been years since she tragically died of Lymphoma that had spread to her brain. If it hadn't been for Rachel and Belinda's mother taking care of two small boys losing their mother, he wouldn't have survived the death of his young, talented wife. A very difficult time for him. But the boys were grown young men now.

He took a few steps backward, viewing the painting in progress. "Yep, almost there," he said aloud.

The string of Swiss cowbells sounded, as someone opened the gallery's front door. He reached for the hand wipes kept on a table nearby. wiped his hands and pushed through the swinging doors to the studio.

"It's just me, Paul," Rachel said walking toward him. "Wanna have lunch?"

"Sounds good. I started early this morning, and haven't noticed the time. You're the first person to come in. They're beating down my door these days." He laughed.

"Where's Claire?"

"She took an early lunch, had some errands to run."

"So how is she doing, glad you hired her?" Rachel asked.

"As a matter of fact, she's perfect. We think alike. No problems, whatsoever."

"Well, come on, let's take a ride to Marazion and have lunch at the Godolphin, shall we?"

"Great," he said. "I'll grab a sweater and lock up."

"Good, my car is idling in front."

Rachel had been thinking of Paul all morning. Every time she took a break from writing, thoughts of him came into her mind – wondering where and what he was doing on this perfectly sunshiny day. So, she hopped in her car and drove the five minutes around the bay to Mousehole.

When he appeared through the swinging doors, her heart skipped a beat. He still affected her the same as when she first saw him. She didn't think that feeling would ever fade.

As they drove to Godolphin Inn she listened as Paul told her about the new series of paintings he'd been commissioned to paint.

"They've paid me $500,000 up front, the rest when delivered. Can you believe that?"

"How many for that price? My gosh!"

"Ten. I've painted five already. Six with the one I'm close to finishing."

"Subjects?" Rachel asked becoming more excited by the second.

"My usual. Giant size nudes, with checkerboard smaller nudes in the background. But on these I'm painting palm fronds and foliage bordering the perimeter of the canvas. I'm excited about it."

"Who commissioned them?"

"The casino in Monte Carlo. Unbelievable."

Rachel squealed, "Wowww ... that's fantastic! How much time have they given you?"

"End of the year. They want them hung by New Year's Eve. It's a tough call. But I think I can do it."

"Sure, you can. Anything I can do to help?"

"Just take me to lunch occasionally, and a few dinners, breakfasts too."

"You got it," Rachel said as she pulled into a parking space in Marazion.

Margaret lived part-time in Spain with her husband, which is where she was this particular day. So they had another host at the Godolphin restaurant, but were able to sit at Rachel's favorite table with the view of St Michael's Mount.

"This never gets old, does it?" she said while sipping a Prosecco.

Paul drank iced tea and watched Rachel's every move. "Lovely. Just lovely. Every view. Where is Jessica today?" he asked.

"Oh, I haven't told you what happened. Sorry. She left for the States yesterday. Sort of sudden, her mother is sick and needs Jessica at home to help with the kids. Eight kids, you know. We booked her on the earliest flight out. You know, I'm wondering about her, because she is so young in many ways, adult in others, but I wonder if she's ready for this great big world yet, even though she says she is."

"You think she might be having second thoughts on Oxford?" Paul reached over and picked up Rachel's Prosecco. "May I?"

"Of course. We've a bottle of it, have all you want. I'll get another glass."

"No no no, I just want a sip."

To the host, Rachel motioned for another glass. "I overheard a phone conversation she had with her sisters last week, about being homesick."

"We're ready to order," Paul said to the waiter. "We'll both have the salmon salad, please. And bread. Thank you."

"How did you know what I wanted?" Rachel asked.

"Oh, I'm sorry. Did you not want that? You always order it when we're here."

Rachel laughed. "Yes, I would have ordered it as always. Just ribbing you."

"I apologize. Won't do that again." He tipped his glass at her. "Kids are funny, speaking of Jessica. Think they know what they want early on and then life gets in the way. I remember me at that age. I wanted to be an artist even then, but got caught up in the corporate world of advertising, which I'd never given a thought to before. I went that direction because of the money. But I can't complain, it eventually afforded me my original dream. And here I am. Exactly where I wanted to be. My whole life a detour to here."

Rachel smiled at his telling, radiant face. She sensed his happiness. "I'm happiest here too. In fact, I don't want to do any more traveling for a while. I love where I am in this time and place. Gardening, playing with my Baby Boo Boo ... he's so cute ..."

"He is. Fluffy long hair and all," Paul chuckled. He's majestic, with his attitude and demeanor. So regal!"

"Do you like cats?"

"Yes, I do," Paul said. "But I've had both, dogs and cats."

"Me too."

Paul thought of the first time he saw Rachel, and how they'd been through good and bad times together since then. He had suffered with her, laughed with her, cried with her.

"What are you thinking, staring at me like that?" Rachel laughed self-consciously.

"Oh! I'm sorry. I'm in a world of my own. Remembering the past few years and all that has happened to both of us. But here we are, able to laugh despite it all."

"What else can we do? May as well laugh, right?" Rachel said.

"Right."

On the way back to Newlyn after lunch, Paul asked, "What do you hear from Stefan? You see him lately?"

"Well, it seems to have become less and less. I don't know if it's me or him. Or both of us. I think the honeymoon has worn off." She chuckled.

"Honeymoon?"

"Yes, you know the high you have when you first meet and it carries you through the first few weeks or months. Usually three months is tops for me. If they last past three months that is a good sign."

"But you've dated him much longer than three months."

Rachel pulled into her driveway. "Yes ... Oh. What am I doing?" She laughed. "I need to take you back to Mousehole. Sorry. I'm so sorry." She backed out of the driveway. "Yes, it's been more than three months, but much less if we counted the actual time we've spent together."

"Have you talked to him about how you feel?"

"Last time we were together I didn't encourage him to stay over after we had dinner. Felt awkward. Not in the mood then, had too many things on my mind. Whatever and all the above. Haven't heard from him since. Three weeks ago. So, no. I don't know how I feel about him. Our lives are so different, Stefan and me. I love my life as it is. He is from a totally different world. With Maxim, it took me forever to commit because of our differences, and talk about some huge changes, if he would have lived, I would be living part time in Russia. Can you imagine? So, no, it's just as well that Stefan and I don't go any further. I'm just letting it take care of itself, I think that's best."

Paul's heart beat a little faster upon hearing the good news about Stefan. "Yes, that's the best way. If you feel it's waning, it probably is, and it usually will fizzle out all by itself. I've had a few of those."

"You have, no doubt. A man like you? Good Lord, probably by the dozens!"

They both began laughing.

Rachel's cell phone rang. "Oh, it's Jessica. I'm going to pull over and take the call."

She parked on the shoulder of the narrow lane leading to Mousehole from Newlyn.

"Hello, Jessica. Everything okay?" Rachel asked.

"Oh, Rachel. My mama is so sick, and Uncle is beside himself. The kids are so scared and upset."

Rachel could hear the panic in Jessica's voice. "What is the doctor saying?"

"They don't know yet. All the tests aren't back yet. But Rachel, she's so weak." Jessica whimpered. "I have to stay here, Rachel. I have to stay and take care of my mama." She muffled a sob that escaped. "I'll call you as soon as we know for sure. It doesn't look good. I'm scared."

"Oh sweetie, be strong. Hang in there, honey. Please let me know if I can do anything. Please."

"Uncle Skylar is the strong one, and is taking care of everything, but I need to be here for mama and the kids. They need me so much, and I've positively missed them. Didn't realize how much till I got here." She sounded like a frightened little girl, sick with worry about her mother.

"Yes, I knew you were missing them. You keep in touch and I'll send your things to you when you want me to, if you decide not to return. Don't worry about anything. I love you, and I'm here if you need me. Paul is with me, we had lunch in Marazion, and he just

264

pointed to himself and indicated he's here for you, too."

"Okay, got to go. Just wanted you to know. Oh, wait. Forgot. Uncle Sawyer is going to press charges against Wylie and the other two boys who raped me. No one knows where Wylie is, but I sort of know he won't be back. Regardless, we're going after them, Rachel. If for no other reason than to protect the other young girls in this town."

"That is wonderful, Jessica. And that will help your healing and give you more strength and wisdom going forward in this world. It's the best thing you can do for you and your sisters. I'm proud of you, honey." Rachel's heart hurt for Jessica, she visualized the day Jessica would return to Cornwall, for she truly believed she would. Unfinished business.

"Oh! Almost forgot. Charles has been texting. He wants to come visit. I love you, Rachel. Gotta go. Bye-bye," Jessica said.

Rachel held the cell phone for a few seconds, tears in her eyes. "That poor baby, so much on her plate."

Paul reached over and hugged Rachel. "She'll be alright. She has her uncle there and eight siblings to keep her busy. Sometimes the universe knows best for us. We both know that, no matter how hard it is to accept. She'll be okay."

68

Autumn came and went on the Cornwall coastline. The first winter storm created giant waves that crashed over the promenade from Penzance to Newlyn and filled the bay of bobbing fishing boats in Mousehole Harbor.

On a cold rainy morning, Paul drove from his Mousehole house and gallery to Rachel's hillside home to tell her the news.

"What brings you out in this weather? Come in, come in. Here let me take your coat. You're soaking." She took Paul's coat and scarf and hung them on the coat rack in the wet room before they entered the kitchen. "Where's your umbrella?"

"I forgot it in the excitement."

"Excitement? Tell me, tell me." She ushered him to a seat at the table flanked with four chairs. "I'll make some tea for you, or would you rather have coffee?"

"Coffee, please." He rubbed his hands together trying to warm up.

"Here, wrap this around you." She handed him a fleece throw hanging over one of the dining chairs.

"Thank you. They've set a date for the reveal cocktail party

266

two days before New Year's Eve. Will you go with me? Say you will, please! A week in Monte Carlo? All expenses paid?"

"Wha--?

"We'll be there a week, at the Metropole. We can celebrate New Year's Eve, can stay till after. What do you think?" He wanted her to go with him in the worst way, knew the chance to be slim to none, but he had to try. No pain, no gain. It certainly pained him as he watched her face for clues.

"I don't know, Paul. There's Baby Boo Boo now. He depends on me so much, and I've totally spoiled him. What would I do with him? A whole week?"

"We can leave him with Claire. She'll be minding the gallery, and she loves animals. She can stay here if you want, house sit and cat sit. Or Baby can stay in the gallery with her, in her apartment upstairs. Either way. Your call." He pled his case to the extreme.

"Paul ... I don't know what to say. I mean, I'd love to go with you. I know how important this is for you. I ... I ..."

He stood up and gripped Rachel's shoulders, facing her. "You must say you will go. Say yes. Please."

They were looking into each other's' eyes for what seemed like forever.

Rachel placed her hands on Paul's arms at one point and sighed. "I suppose I could. I could use a few days away. May as well be Monte Carlo. Wow! Monte Carlo?" She grinned up at Paul. "Okay, I'll go with you."

He lifted her off the floor and swung her around and around. "Oh Rachel, you make me so happy. You do, you do."

"Hey, put me down, you're making me dizzy. Put me down, you silly brute." She laughed heartily and so did he. Contagion.

They sat all morning in the living room with the stormy sea view, drinking coffee, making their plans.

In North Carolina, Jessica Sanford wept when Uncle Sawyer married her mama in a small intimate ceremony in the hospital room. Not only did he love and adore Evangeline, they had agreed the marriage would allow him to protect and always provide for the family. He would be Jessica's step father and adoption papers for the rest of the children were already drawn up and signed. Jessica and her mama were relieved to know that the kids would always be safe and secure. Evangeline passed a few weeks later of congested heart failure.

Soon after, Jessica opened a dance studio - she'd promised her mama, and she fast became the go-to dance instructor for children and teen-agers in the County. She and Uncle Sawyer, she still called him uncle, still had their nightly discussions of books and talk about his travels around the world. They would talk about the education of all the kids. Jessica had set her own dreams aside for the time being, but knew one day she would reclaim them. She and her family were happy. But they missed their mama, and talked about her every day.

The day after Christmas, Paul and Rachel drove to the airport in Cornwall and flew to Nice where a car was waiting to take them to the Metropole hotel in Monte Carlo.

Paul's million-dollar painting collection had already been hung and represented an incredible display of his unparalleled talent – unique subject, style, and use of color. The larger two main walls held two glorious 10' by 8' canvases. People congregated in front of them constantly, day and night. The detailed checkerboard of miniature nudes painted as background to the primary nude subject made him famous. Already known around the world, it had all begun when he and his sweet Belinda married and combined efforts in the Mousehole gallery and studios they had created years before – she and her sculptures, he and his paintings. Now years later, at the pinnacle of his art career, a dream come true, and with Rachel standing by his side, he couldn't ask for anything more perfect. Well, he could, but knew he wouldn't. He didn't want Rachel to bolt. He had to curb and hide his desire, especially now that they were in Monte Carlo, staying in the same hotel.

Two nights before New Year's Eve, at the art unveiling celebration, they stood in the foyer of the casino where the festivities had begun. Paul entered GQ handsome, attracting the attention of every female in the room, in his tails and white tie, standing his full 6'5". Rachel wore a long black lace dress, a satin choker adorned by tiny satin rosebuds with diamond studs in the center of each bud, and an oversize satin rose fitted in the small of her back where the backless dress dipped to a point at her waist. They were certainly a beautiful couple to behold.

"Oh, look at those, Paul." Rachel pointed to the series of smaller six canvases bordering an archway of one entrance to the casino. "I love what they did over there."

"Yes, they did an excellent job of displaying my art. I'm so impressed and flabbergasted at the same time. I don't know whether to cheer, or blush, be embarrassed at the ostentatiousness of if all, or what."

"Never be embarrassed. Never! Your paintings are unsurpassed. I'm so proud of you." She reached around his waist, her head resting on his chest, and squeezed as he put his arms around her. "You are wonderful, Paul!"

He tipped her face up and said, "You're not so bad yourself." And he quickly planted a kiss lightly on her lips.

"Rachel ..."

"What?"

"I think you know ..." he said.

"What?" She leaned back, saw the tears glazing his crystal blue eyes. "You're crying?"

"Yes. Because I'm happy."

"I am too, Paul. Very happy. And I just adore you. Always have. From the second our eyes first met. You are adorable!"

He lifted her off the floor and swung around and around while shouting, "I love you, I love you, I love you!" Then he gently lowered Rachel till her feet touched the marble floor, while the applause and cheers of the surrounding patrons made their presence known.

"You are nuts, Paul." she said gleefully.

"Of course! Oh, Claire's on her way here. She called a few minutes ago. I'm a little excited about her coming."

Rachel stepped back. "That's terrific news, Paul! I'm glad. She should be a part of this. Yes. Good. But what about Baby Boo Boo?"

"Her sister is there till she gets back. She already loves Baby Boo Boo, she said. Don't worry. You've got a built-in cat-sitter anytime you need one."

"What I need right now is some water, be right back." Relieved that Baby Boo Boo would be well-tended, and relieved that Claire would join Paul, she needed a few minutes to think. Paul needed a woman, and she hoped Claire would be the one. *Oh yes. Please let her be the one.*

The rest of the evening spelled great success for Paul. He worked the room and commissions for paintings piled in. His agent would pull him aside periodically to let him know the numbers.

Rachel disappeared at one point to go to her room. She saw him surrounded by beautiful attentive women, and smiled knowing he would be alright as soon as his protector Claire arrived. She told his agent she had a headache, and to please tell Paul she'd see him for breakfast in the morning. Then she texted Paul the same, and left him a message on his room phone, covering all the bases. All the falderal had gotten to her.

Although happy for Paul, she was sad at the same time. Sad because of Stefan. In fact, all evening thoughts of Stefan crept into her mind. She wondered where he would be celebrating New Year's Eve. With another woman? She wished she would have called him before the trip to Monte Carlo. Last year they celebrated New Year's Eve together in Vegas.

She undressed and got into bed. The cream-colored silk duvet felt dreamy. The entire room had been decorated in shades of white and cream. Five minutes later, she got up to make tea. She couldn't sleep. Wrapped in a faux fur throw the hotel furnished, she grabbed her phone and tea and sat at the glass table on the balcony, with a view to die for, the star-studded sky and the twinkling lights on yachts and other luxury boats in the harbor. Hesitating for a few moments, questioning her motives, she finally punched in a call to Stefan. Eleven p.m. He should be up.

Stefan answered on the second ring. "Hello, Rachel."

"Hi, hope I didn't wake you."

"Not at all. I'm sitting here strumming my guitar. Thinking about you. Wondering where you are, what you're doing for New Year's."

"I'm in Monte Carlo," she said.

"Monte Carlo?"

"Yes, came with Paul to an exhibition of his art at a Hotel Casino. He didn't want to go alone."

Stefan's spirit took a dive. "Oh. You're with your friend."

"Well, for the exhibition, yes. Quite the unveiling party tonight, but I skipped out after the main event, and am in my own suite now." There, he knew. No one with her.

"So, you're staying for New Year's Eve?"

"Well, that's the plan, but I don't know what I'm going to do. If I go home, I'm sure it'll disappoint Paul, he didn't want to be here alone. And he's such a dear friend, we've known each other for years. Been through a lot together."

Stefan didn't say a word.

Rachel listened.

Finally, "Are you in love with Paul?" Stefan asked. "May as well get it out there. Question asked."

Clear the air.

Rachel hesitated. "I have feelings for Paul, but I'm not in love with him. I wouldn't want to be more than a dear friend to him, Stefan. I loved his wife Belinda, and I love their boys. And he is a part of that love. But I could never go beyond that. And I haven't."

"Well, then … why don't I come to Monte Carlo and celebrate New Year's Eve with you? Would you want that?" he asked, standing and holding his breath, waiting for an answer.

"Yes, yes! Oh yes! Come tomorrow, please. I'll let Paul know in the morning at coffee. You promise to come? You're not kidding?" Her heart beat off the charts.

"I'll be there by noon. Which hotel?" He sounded excited.

"The Metropole."

"See you at noon, after I check in."

"Don't check in, you can bunk with me." She laughed heartily.

"Oh? Well, I can do that. This will be the best New Year's Eve!" he shouted. "The best, ever!"

Euphoria all around.

"It will be for me too, my love. Oh, by the way, bring your guitar." Just thinking of him next to her made her warm and tingly all over. She needed him. She wanted him. Could it be, she loved him? Sure felt like it.

♥

Coming Next!
Seventh Novel in the Rachel O'Neill Series
MIDNIGHT IN MONTE CARLO